Praise for previous Justice Inc. books

Heart Vs. Humbug

"Leave it to M.J. Rodgers to give readers the gift of incomparable storytelling, and add sparkling, witty dialogue to the mix."

—Debbie Richardson
Romantic Times

"Weaving many levels and sub-plots together, M.J. Rodgers gets better and better. Her books never disappoint." —*Gothic Journal*

Baby Vs. the Bar

"The talented M.J. Rodgers sparkles once again with a wonderful array of characters and thoroughly innovative storytelling."

—Debbie Richardson
Romantic Times

"*Baby Vs. the Bar* is a rewarding experience all around." —*Gothic Journal*

Beauty Vs. the Beast

"Fans of legal thrillers will not want to miss *Beauty Vs. the Beast* for its dynamic portrayal of its heroine, its intense courtroom scenes, and its introduction to the promising Justice Inc. cast."

—*Gothic Journal*

"One of romantic intrigue's best, M.J. Rodgers pens another keeper."

—Debbie Richardson
Romantic Times

"Take my word for it, this one will keep your pulse pounding."

—*Rendezvous*

Dear Reader,

Open the gilded doors and step into the world of M.J. Rodgers's JUSTICE INC. A world where principle courts passion. In this Seattle law firm, legal eagles battle headline-stealing cases...and find heart-stealing romance in the bargain.

M.J. Rodgers has become synonymous with the best in romantic mystery. Having written her very first book for Intrigue seven years ago, she has gone on to become one of the bestselling and most popular Intrigue authors. Her books are perennial Reviewer's Choice Award winners, and last year she received the Career Achievement Award for Romantic Mystery from *Romantic Times*.

So turn the page and enter the world of JUSTICE INC.

Regards,

Debra Matteucci
Senior Editor and Editorial Coordinator
Harlequin Books
300 East 42nd Street, Sixth Floor
New York, NY 10017

M.J. Rodgers

TO HAVE VS. TO HOLD

Harlequin Books

TORONTO • NEW YORK • LONDON
AMSTERDAM • PARIS • SYDNEY • HAMBURG
STOCKHOLM • ATHENS • TOKYO • MILAN
MADRID • WARSAW • BUDAPEST • AUCKLAND

This story is for the best editor in the business, Bonnie Crisalli. If I tried to list all those wonderful qualities that make Bonnie special, I'd need another book. So let me just say here that she possesses that rare combination of professional excellence, boundless energy, unmatched dedication, sweet disposition, ceaseless support and an infectious enthusiasm for which every writer prays.

Thank heavens this writer's prayers were answered.

ISBN 0-373-22392-7

TO HAVE VS. TO HOLD

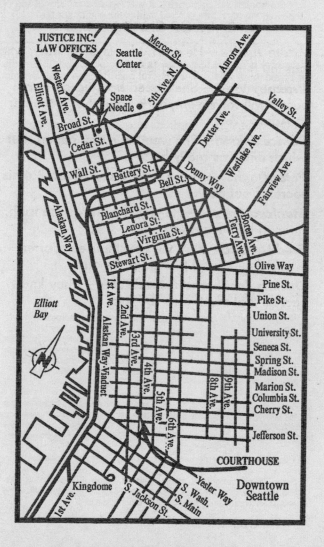

CAST OF CHARACTERS

Adam Justice—He married a mystery lady, who has left him a haunting legal legacy.

Whitney West—She's been holding on to a secret will for seven years...one that leads her to Adam West.

Patrice Feldon—She went by many names. But which one was really hers?

Peter Danner—He was the secret lover. But his secret is out now.

Stanford Carver—He says he knows the truth. But can he be trusted?

Fred Dykstra—He's the courthouse reporter who's determined to dig up the dirt.

Doctors Jacob and Esther Rubin—They know secrets that must never be told.

ABOUT THE AUTHOR

To Have Vs. To Hold is the fifth book in the JUSTICE INC. courtroom series by bestselling author M.J. Rodgers. In the months to come she will continue to bring you the stories of these dedicated attorneys, known as Seattle's legal sleuths.

M.J. is the winner of the *Romantic Times* Career Achievement Award for Romantic Mystery, twice winner of their Best Intrigue Award, and is also winner of B. Dalton Bookseller's top-selling Intrigue award. She lives with her family in Seabeck, Washington.

Books by M.J. Rodgers

Don't miss any of our special offers. Write to us at the following address for information on our newest releases.

Harlequin Reader Service
U.S.: 3010 Walden Ave., P.O. Box 1325, Buffalo, NY 14269
Canadian: P.O. Box 609, Fort Erie, Ont. L2A 5X3

Chapter One

"You Adam Justice?" the gray-faced man with the suspicious look and sour tone asked.

Adam knew this disagreeable man had to be a plainclothes policeman. The only other people in suits who rang doorbells on a Sunday were proselytizers, and they tried to look and sound pleasant when they came calling.

"Yes, I'm Justice."

The man eyed Adam steadily as he slid a hand inside the jacket of his gray summer suit and pulled out his badge for a quick, perfunctory flash.

"Detective-Sergeant Ryson. King County Sheriff's office."

Ryson jabbed a thumb over his shoulder toward his companion. The hefty, red-nosed man standing behind him flashed his identification after sneezing into a handkerchief.

"Detective Ferkel," he managed to say. His voice was unexpectedly high for someone with his hefty bulk. His eyes watered. "I'm not contagious, just allergic."

Adam stepped back. "Come in."

As the two men passed into his entry hall, Adam mentally reviewed his law firm's cases. He wasn't representing any clients charged with criminal acts. Several Justice Inc. associates did have court-assigned criminal defenses. However, Adam was confident these policemen would be knocking on one of his associates' doors if this matter involved one of their defendants. So it had to be one of his.

Litigants in civil suits were known to let their emotions get the better of them. He was curious to find out which one of his clients had lost it seriously enough to occasion this visit.

Adam led the way into the kitchen, set two extra mugs on the white tile counter and automatically filled them. He'd never known a member of law enforcement to turn down a cup of coffee.

Ryson left his coffee black. Ferkel immediately dumped half the contents of the sugar bowl into his mug and then filled it to the brim with cream. His sneezes seemed to have subsided for the moment. He tucked his well-used handkerchief into the inside coat pocket of his well-creased suit.

The two detectives drew bar stools up to the center island and picked up their mugs. Adam sat on the other side of the island facing them.

For a full minute Ryson and Ferkel said nothing, just gulped coffee and glanced around at the neat black-and-white kitchen—Ryson with almost a sneer bearing down on his lips, Ferkel slurping his coffee while wearing an innocuous expression on his fleshy face.

Adam wondered whether the large detective's glowing red nose was seasonal or if the allergy was a permanent condition. If it was a year-round affliction, Rudolph was going to have competition for the front of the sleigh this Christmas.

"This is a nice cluster of homes," Ferkel said. He smiled at Adam pleasantly. "Well patrolled. Guard at the gate checked our badges before letting us in. That's good security."

"For which they no doubt soak you suckers every month in ridiculous maintenance fees," Ryson added in his disagreeable tone. "You wouldn't catch me in one of these money pits."

Adam sat back, took a sip of his coffee and began to wonder about these two. It was unusual for detectives to waste time with small talk—unless they were doing it deliberately to make a suspect uncomfortable, of course.

Were these two detectives just prolonging their business to give themselves a chance to enjoy the air-conditioning after the uncomfortable heat outside? Seattle was normally blessed with beautifully cool summers, but this past week had set some record-high temperatures.

When another long minute of silence ensued, Adam knew it was time to press the matter. These detectives might not have a full day ahead, but he certainly did.

"How may I help you?" he asked.

Ryson took one last gulp of his coffee and set his empty mug on the counter. His cadaverous cheeks and unpleasant facial expression lent a natural somberness to his demeanor. But there was a new intensity in his dark eyes, which warned Adam that whatever this man was about to say wasn't going to be good.

"We found your wife's body."

Adam had been anticipating something unpleasant. But these words had been hurled at him from out of nowhere, like a sucker punch to the stomach.

For an instant Patrice's incredibly lovely face emerged soft and glowing before his mind's eye. Then her image vanished, and all that remained was the stunning aftershock of the words, covering him like the August sun streaming down from the kitchen skylight.

For years he had imagined receiving such news. He thought he would be ready. He was not.

"Mr. Justice, did you hear what I said?" Ryson asked.

Adam's hands circled his coffee mug, feeling its warmth in sharp contrast to the cold that now swirled inside him. His voice sounded strange and detached, even to his own ears.

"Yes."

"She's been dead a long time," Ferkel said after Adam offered nothing else. "From what we can tell so far, she and her companion were the victims of a fatal automobile crash."

Adam said nothing, just stared into his coffee cup.

"It occurred in a remote area," Ryson said. Adam could feel the man's eyes scouring his face as he supplied the rest of the details.

"The car went off a mountain road and landed in a deep ravine. Some hikers came across the wreckage last Friday. A newspaper found behind the seat shows the date of July 22, seven years ago. That's when we figure it happened.''

Adam took a deep breath and concentrated on keeping his tone even. "Was it . . . quick?"

"The front of the car was totally demolished on impact," Ferkel said. "I doubt they knew what hit them."

Adam continued to stare into the blackness of his coffee. But what he was seeing was a midnight blue Porsche speeding off the edge of a mountain road and then falling. And falling. Forever falling.

"Since you obviously haven't heard from your wife in seven years, I'm curious why you didn't report her missing," Ryson said, his harsh voice interrupting Adam's disturbing mental images.

Adam looked up at the detective sergeant. The unpleasant expression on his face perfectly matched the suspicious light beading in his eyes.

Adam now understood why a detective sergeant had been sent to deliver this news to him. He also understood why Ferkel was pleasant and Ryson antagonistic—and why they had taken their time in coming to the point.

They didn't think Patrice's death was an accident. They suspected him.

Since the moment they rang his doorbell, they had been playing their roles. Good cop, bad cop.

"Mr. Justice, I asked you a question," Ryson pressed.

Adam kept his voice perfectly even, perfectly controlled. "My wife wasn't missing. She left me."

Ryson was trying to look surprised. He was failing. Adam was well aware the policeman already had the answers to the questions he was about to ask.

"She left you?" he challenged. "Why did your wife leave you?"

Even after seven years the words didn't come easily.

"She told me she was going away with someone else."

A long moment of silence passed. Throughout it Ryson's eyes stayed aimed at Adam like two black bullets. "Who?"

"My sister's fiancé, Peter Danner."

"Now, that's what I call a shot below the belt," Ferkel said, obviously trying to sound understanding. Adam knew his concern wasn't genuine, of course. The hefty detective was just playing his role of the good cop, trying to give Adam the impression that he was his buddy and would be on Adam's side, no matter what he had done.

Ryson's disagreeable demeanor typecast him perfectly for his bad-cop role.

"Where did they go?" he demanded.

"Canada."

"You didn't try to stop her?"

"She had already left when I came home and found her note on the kitchen counter."

"She left you a note on *this* kitchen counter?" Ryson asked, pointing at the top of the island as though it had been tainted.

"I've had the tile changed since," Adam said, straight-faced.

"Where is her note, Mr. Justice?" Ferkel asked.

Adam leaned slightly toward the hefty policeman and lowered his voice, just as he did when asking a witness on the stand a personal question that begged the obvious answer.

"Would you have kept such a note?"

Ferkel responded with a quick shake of his head, just as Adam's witnesses usually did. Adam leaned back on his bar stool.

"Exactly what did this kiss-off note say?" Ryson's grating voice demanded.

Adam willed the words to come out calmly. "That she was going to Canada with Peter Danner. Nothing more, Sergeant."

"And this Peter Danner was your sister's fiancé?" he repeated, as though he hadn't heard the first time.

"Yes."

"And that was that?" Ryson said. "You just let this Peter Danner steal your wife from you?"

Ryson's combative tone sounded like what a drunk would use if he were itching for a barroom brawl. Adam understood Ryson was trying to goad him into a reaction. What Ryson didn't understand was that Adam was not a man who could be goaded into a brawl—physical or otherwise.

"Patrice made her choice, Sergeant."

"You're telling me you didn't try to stop her from running away with this guy?"

Adam coolly returned Ryson's stare, leaned forward slightly and lowered his voice once again. "Are you one of those men who believes forcibly dragging a woman back is the way to get her to change her mind?"

Ryson's forehead furrowed in immediate irritation. His voice grated even more than usual. "Come on, Justice. You must have suspected something was going on between them long before you found her kiss-off note. Only a fool wouldn't know his wife was making it with another guy."

It was another deliberately provoking comment. Adam once again refused to be bullied. He said nothing, just continued to eye Ryson calmly.

Tension filled the long moment that passed between the two men.

"Did you ever hear from her again?" Ferkel finally asked.

"No."

"You never wondered where she was?"

"No."

"Not in seven years?"

"No."

"So why haven't you asked me who it was who died with your wife?" Ryson challenged.

"I know it was Peter Danner."

A very smug look descended on Ryson's face. "How do you know?"

"The day my wife left me was July 22, seven years ago, the same date on the newspaper you found in the back seat of the wrecked car. It's only logical she would have been traveling with Peter Danner on that day."

Ryson's smug look collapsed into one of annoyance.

"How did your sister feel when her fiancé ran off with your wife?"

"You'll have to ask her," Adam said.

"You don't know?" Ryson pressed.

"No one can ever really know how someone else feels," Adam said simply.

"Why didn't you file for divorce?" Ryson demanded.

Adam inhaled deeply, then slowly and quietly let the air out of his lungs. "I never gave it any thought."

Ryson's face wore a look as openly sarcastic as his accompanying tone. "You, *a lawyer,* never gave it any thought? Ferkel, did you hear that? His wife could have returned and claimed half of all the money he'd earned while she was shacking up with this Danner guy, and he never once thought of divorcing her!"

Ryson's punctuating bark of a laugh crossed way over the line into insult territory.

Adam wondered if Ryson knew how transparent he was being with these taunts.

"Aw, give the guy a break," Ferkel said in his best good-cop tone. "Maybe he still loved her. Maybe he hoped she'd come back to him."

Ferkel's "sympathetic" statement and inquisitive look in Adam's direction clearly invited a response. Adam made no comment.

A long quiet moment passed, during which Ryson's gray complexion blackened with irritation. "What's inside you, Justice? You not made of blood and bone like the rest of us? The bitch who betrayed you and the bastard who came on to your sister while he was getting it on with your wife are dead, man. You should be breaking out the booze and celebrating. Hell, if you have some cold beer, we'll even join you."

Adam set his nearly full cup of coffee on the counter and slipped off the bar stool. "Sergeant Ryson, Detective Ferkel, I won't keep you from your other duties."

Ryson loped off his bar stool and landed in front of Adam, a deep, angry flush suffusing his face. "We'll be conducting a thorough investigation into this matter, Justice."

"What matter would that be?" Adam asked, purposely sounding unconcerned.

"It was probably just an accident, of course," Ferkel added quickly, too quickly as he slid off his bar stool and came to stand beside Ryson, dwarfing the shorter, far leaner sergeant with his hefty bulk. "But I'm sure you understand, Mr. Justice. Two people have died. Naturally we must check these things out."

Ryson crossed his arms over his chest. "We're going to get to the bottom of everything that happened seven years ago, Justice. Everything. I want to see what your wife left behind when she took off with Danner. Now."

"If you can convince a judge that you have a right to search my home to find something my wife may have left behind, I will not stand in your way," Adam said calmly.

Ryson's lips tightened unhappily—very unhappily.

And that told Adam what he needed to know. There was no evidence that Patrice's and Peter's deaths were anything but accidental. If there had been any real sign of foul play, Ryson would have further insisted on searching for anything that might have belonged to Patrice and confiscating it.

He had no warrant to do that. Not yet, anyway. So despite these detectives' obvious suspicions, they were still just suspicions.

"Has my sister been told about Peter Danner's death?" Adam asked as he started out of the kitchen, confident the policemen would have to follow.

Out of the corner of his eye, he saw Ryson glancing at the watch on his wrist. "She has by now."

Adam knew the fact that the police had chosen to tell A.J. personally wasn't a good sign. It meant that she, too, was being sized up as a possible suspect, should the deaths be determined to be other than accidental.

Adam wasn't surprised. He and A.J. were the ones with motives. The betrayed husband. The betrayed fiancée. Yes, to a policeman's mind it would seem a little too convenient that the betrayers had met with such swift deaths following their betrayal.

Adam headed for the entry with a crisp step. He had no desire to prolong this interview. He opened the front door and stepped aside, clearly inviting the officers to leave.

"Neither my wife nor Peter Danner had any family," Adam said as Ryson and Ferkel filed past. "I will be responsible for the burial arrangements."

Ryson stopped and turned to face Adam. "You're even going to foot the bill to bury that bastard who was sticking it to your wife behind your back?"

Ryson's parting shot was a good one. Still, Adam did not respond with the reaction Ryson was trying so hard to elicit.

"I'll have a funeral home contact you," Adam said. "Should you have any more questions, you know where to find me."

And with that he closed the door on Ryson and Ferkel.

Adam took a long, deep, steadying breath and slowly let it out. He knew he should fight the impulse that already had him turning toward the study. He knew he wouldn't.

He made his way directly to his desk and opened the bottom drawer.

It was in the very back, beneath the family album, beneath the stack of his law-review honors, on the very bottom, exactly where he had wrapped and placed it seven years before.

Carefully he removed and unwrapped the eight-by-ten-inch crystal picture frame. It was delicate and exquisite, but paled into insignificance next to the picture it contained.

For *she* was incomparable. Large, velvety, violet eyes set in a heart-shaped face. Porcelain skin surrounded by thick golden curls cascading over the gentle swell of her breasts to a tiny waist. And that angelic smile, just made to melt a man's mind. Her flowery handwriting covered the right corner:

> To my Adam,
> Love always,
> Patrice.

Adam set the picture facedown on the top of his desk. Still, her image stayed in his mind—clear, never changing—just as it had stayed for seven years.

Just as he feared it would always stay.

He rested his forehead in his hands as the familiar sear of pain shot down his neck . . . and into his heart.

DETECTIVE-SERGEANT Ryson stomped across the manicured lawn in front of Adam's house to the unmarked green Ford parked at the curb, ignoring the Please Use The Sidewalk signs. If Justice was watching from inside that pricey place of his, he'd see that Ryson was a man who didn't hesitate to cut a corner when he wanted to.

Ryson reached the car, pulled open the driver's door, plopped onto the seat and slammed the door closed. He frowned down at his shoes, covered in moist grass clippings. Ferkel piled into the passenger seat a few seconds later and sprayed the inside of the car with an enormous sneeze.

Ryson glared at his partner with all the irritation that had been growing inside his gut throughout that far from satisfactory interview with Justice. "I thought you were getting a stronger antihistamine medication."

"Sorry, Sarge. It's all the freshly mown grass around this place. Hell on my sinuses. Justice must have one great cleaning woman. Or else he's never home. No bachelor I know lives that neat. Did you notice everything was in black and white? This guy's definitely not normal."

"You can say that again. He's a proud rich bastard who cares about nothing but himself," Ryson said, nearly spitting out the words. "You saw. He reacted to nothing. Not the news that we found her body and Danner's. Not even the jabs about their betrayal."

"You think he didn't care that she left him?"

"Oh, he cared, all right. But only because it was a slap at his pride. There's no way that man would have just rolled over when his wife took off with someone else. No, a guy like

Justice would have had to teach her a lesson for his ego's sake.''

"His never filing for divorce is what has me convinced,'' Ferkel said. "Lawyers are about money. There's no way he wouldn't have protected his legal butt if he had thought she was still alive.''

Ryson glanced back at the large expanse of manicured lawn and the lush, perfectly pruned bushes, plants and trees around the well-tended home. Adam Justice was just like his surroundings, too perfect. Ryson had never come face-to-face with a man he couldn't get to react. Until now. No matter what hot button he'd pushed, Justice had remained in complete control.

That burned Ryson more than anything.

"Didn't I tell you there was something wrong about this so-called accident from the moment I heard who the victims were?'' he said.

"Yeah, Sarge, that you did.''

"Was it quick?'' Ryson repeated, deliberately mimicking Adam's somber tone. "Like we're supposed to believe that he really gave a damn if the wife, who cheated on him and took off with his sister's fiancé, suffered before she died.''

"Yeah. I don't think Justice had to ask us anything.''

"Damn straight, he didn't. Justice knows exactly what happened to his runaway wife and her lover. He's known it for seven years. I'd bet my badge on it. We can forget the sister. This is the one who did it. All we need is for forensics to prove it wasn't an accident and we can move in. Maybe a double charge of murder will rip that damn impassive mask off Adam Justice's face.''

Chapter Two

"Funerals should always take place under gloomy skies, preferably with pouring rain," Octavia Osborne said to Adam as she stepped beside him at the grave site. "It's a waste to have to attend to death on a day blessed with such a brilliant sun."

Adam looked over at Octavia, the only one of his partners at the Justice Inc. law firm who refused to speak to him with sympathetic platitudes this morning. Octavia was as unfettered by conventional restraint as the resplendent red hair that draped across her shoulders.

She was outspoken and impossibly impulsive—as opposite to Adam as opposites could be. And yet, despite their personality differences and their frequent disagreements over the way she "interpreted" legal ethics, Adam was proud to call Octavia a friend. For when it came to loyalty, Adam knew Octavia's was not open to interpretation.

"I appreciate your coming," he said, simply, meaning every word.

He felt her eyes draw to his face, then switch to his hand. Her voice was concerned and thoughtful, not unkind. "Are you going to be able to bury her now?"

Adam realized then that his hand had been unconsciously stroking the scar that extended from his neck to beneath his collar line. He dropped his hand to his side. Octavia was the only Justice Inc. partner who had known Patrice and had understood how Adam had felt about his wife.

"I don't know."

Octavia rested her hand briefly on his arm. It was a gesture of both understanding and sympathy, the genuine kind, the only kind Octavia knew how to give.

The clergyman stepped up to say the appropriate words over the caskets containing the remains of Patrice Justice and Peter Danner.

But Adam knew "ashes to ashes and dust to dust" were not the right words. He hated the idea that he was standing here just going through the motions. He was a man who needed to find meaning in everything he did.

And in this most of all.

Adam's eyes roamed over the faces of the Justice Inc. partners who were present here today for his sake. Kay Kellogg stood beside her fiancé, Damian Steele. Marc Truesdale was holding his adopted son, Nicholas, with his new wife, Remy, by his side. Next to Octavia stood Brett Merlin, her intended.

Despite the solemnity of the occasion, Adam could see that there was a new air of contentment about his partners that he hadn't taken the time to notice before today.

This past year at Justice Inc. had challenged each of them with an unusual case. Still, it wasn't the professional success from those legal battles he was reading on their faces. It was another kind of fulfillment. All of his partners had now found someone to be with through all their battles, successful or otherwise.

Adam's eyes moved to his sister's face. A.J. stood alone, watching as the caskets were lowered into the earth. Her expression was calm.

Still, as adept as A.J. was at hiding her feelings, Adam knew she had loved Peter. He had seen that much seven years before. Peter had been A.J.'s world then—just as Patrice had been his.

While Adam watched, Zane Coltrane stepped up behind A.J. and rested a hand on her shoulder. Without turning around, she raised her hand to cover his. And that was when Adam knew that A.J., too, had found someone.

He was glad for her. And yet, at the same time, he suddenly had never felt so alone.

His eyes caught the form of an old woman, hunched over, leaning on a cane, dressed in black and heavily veiled. She was standing by herself about forty feet away. Since Patrice and Peter were the only burials this morning, Adam surmised she was at the cemetery to visit a grave.

How many times had she come to visit that grave, he wondered? Was she living in the past? Or was she still trying to make her peace with it?

Adam suddenly felt cold, bone cold, despite the sun beating down on his head and shoulders.

The formality of the solemn ceremony finally drew to a close. Everyone drifted away as the workmen moved in to cover the caskets.

Everyone but Adam.

After the workmen had left, he was still staring down at the newly packed earth.

He did not want to return to this place. He wanted to find the right words to make his peace with his past.

But the seconds stretched into minutes, and the minutes into an empty void. He found no words. Or peace.

Seven years, and nothing had changed.

Adam turned to go, but halted immediately when he found himself suddenly face-to-face with a woman.

She had been standing directly behind him—for how long he had no idea. He noticed her eyes first. They were large and liquid and full of changing lights, like looking into the depths of a fine, warm brandy.

"Are you Adam Justice?" she asked.

Her voice stirred through the hot, still air like a cool breeze. She stood tall, only a few inches shorter than his six-three. Her hair was a deeper brandy than her eyes and fell in thick, soft waves around her suited shoulders. Her skin had a golden flush beneath the full rays of the sun.

"Yes, I'm Justice."

She held out her hand. "Whitney West."

Adam took her hand in his. Her skin was smooth and warm, her handshake firm. Her eyes stayed focused on his.

"I have something for you from your wife."

Adam immediately dropped Whitney's hand. He shifted on his feet, feeling a sudden need to readjust his sense of balance.

"I've just buried my wife, Ms. West."

"I realize that. I'm sorry to intrude on this private time. But your wife's instructions to me were specific."

Adam's curiosity rose as Whitney paused to slip an eight-by-ten-inch faded manila envelope out of the enormous shoulder bag hanging at her side. She held the envelope out to him.

"She told me to give this to you on the day of her burial. Not a moment sooner or later."

Adam held his eagerness in check as he resisted the impulse to grab that envelope.

"How did you know my wife was dead?"

"The story of her and Mr. Danner's bodies being found in that seven-year-old car wreck has been featured prominently in the news."

Yes, it had. The legitimate press had found the truth sensational enough. The tabloid embellishments had set a new record for the ridiculous. Such extensive coverage had already resulted in more than a few crank calls and letters.

Adam studied Whitney West, her dark brandy hair and light brandy eyes and golden skin glistening in the sun. It would be very hard to believe she could be a crank.

Still, Adam wasn't one to take a stranger at face value—not even when that stranger had a face as lovely as Whitney West's.

"No news story carried either the time or location of the funeral services," he said. "How did you know it was here and this morning?"

He watched as the smile that drew back her lips caught the sun in tiny lines at the corners of her eyes. "I'm resourceful."

She would certainly have to be to find out what every reporter had failed to do. A.J.'s security arrangements were extremely thorough. Who was this woman?

"Why did my wife give this envelope to *you?*" Adam asked.

"I'm an attorney, Mr. Justice. Your wife asked me to hold it for safekeeping."

An attorney? Adam said nothing for a moment as he digested that surprising bit of news.

"Do you know what's in the envelope?" he asked.

"I believe it's her will."

"If my wife wanted her will prepared, she would have come to me."

"Many people feel more comfortable dealing with strangers for sensitive personal arrangements. Haven't you found that to be true?"

Yes, he had. Still, if Patrice hadn't wanted to involve him in the preparation of her will for some reason, she could have used one of the dozen or so attorneys she had come to know through her association with him. And if she had used one of them, surely they would have come to him by now and told him so.

"Did you prepare my wife's will, Ms. West?"

"No. I don't even know for certain that her will is inside this envelope. All I can tell you is that when she placed it in my hands seven and a half years ago, I had the impression that it contained such a document."

"How could my wife have known she was going to die?"

"I doubt she did. I remember her saying something about this just being a precaution in the event of an accident."

In the event of an accident. The words beat uncomfortably against Adam's ears.

He took the envelope and turned it over. The back was sealed. As eager as he was to unseal it, he still wanted a few more answers first.

"You say you're an attorney, Ms. West. For whom do you work?"

"I'm in private practice in Seattle."

"I'm not familiar—"

"With my name?" Whitney interrupted. "I'm not surprised. My partner and I don't handle the big corporate clients you do, Mr. Justice. We share a floor with a baby photographer, a P.I. firm and a pet groomer. This last year the only one who could afford new drapes was the baby photographer."

Adam watched the very nice smile that drew back her lips and once again crinkled the skin around her eyes. It contained a ready amusement and not a whit of apology. She liked what she did, and *she* knew she was successful. It didn't matter to her that anyone else thought so.

He recognized the self-confidence and personal satisfaction that such a rare smile represented. He was surprised to find it on this thirtyish face. In his experience such smiles didn't begin to materialize until after the fifth decade, if indeed they materialized at all. This was a very interesting woman.

"Where did my wife find you?"

"In my office. She walked in one day and asked me if I would agree to hold this sealed envelope for safekeeping. She also asked me to be present when you opened it. I have her letter here with that instruction."

Whitney slipped the letter out of her shoulder bag, and Adam took a look at it. It was a short note in Patrice's distinctive handwriting. He wondered why Patrice would make such a stipulation. He was getting more and more curious about the contents of this manila envelope.

"I would like to attend to this matter now," he said. "Would you mind following me back to the Justice Inc. offices?"

"I don't think we need do this inside a stuffy office, if it's all the same to you. Across the street is a small park with a bench beneath an obliging fir tree. It's such a lovely day. Why don't we take advantage of it?"

Adam had never attended to business on a park bench. Clearly this attorney was used to practicing a more informal type of law. But as he thought it over, he could see no logical reason to reject Whitney's suggestion.

He nodded his agreement, and they made their way out of the cemetery grounds. Adam automatically slowed his normally quick pace, but soon resumed it when Whitney proved to possess a long, easy stride, fully equal to his own.

She marched to the edge of the sidewalk and leaned over the curb, looking right and left at the streaming traffic. She clearly was getting ready to dash across to the other side as soon as a space opened up.

Adam firmly took her arm and steered her down the sidewalk toward the crosswalk.

She flashed him a surprised look. "It's two blocks away."

"Which is still a lot closer than the emergency room."

"We would have made it."

"*We* wouldn't have tried."

"You don't jaywalk?"

"It's against the law."

"You're not serious."

"On the contrary, Ms. West. I'm perfectly serious."

He could feel her staring at his profile as he whisked her down the sidewalk. His hand grasped the lean muscles in her slim arm beneath the thin fabric of her dark suit. It was a lawyer's suit, loose, skirt to the knee, acceptably shapeless.

But his male eye had already assessed the frame beneath it as feminine and far from shapeless. He also noticed she was wearing a light fragrance that smelled fresh and sweet like this summer day.

"I do believe you are serious," she said after a moment. "You never do anything against the law, do you?"

"That's a strange question coming from an attorney."

"Even attorneys—correction, particularly attorneys—inch a few miles over the speed limit, take that questionable deduction on their income tax and tell Aunt Agnes that her blue hair looks just fine."

"I don't remember a law on the books prohibiting a lie to Aunt Agnes."

"No, but I bet you wouldn't even do that. Would you?"

"Since I don't have an Aunt Agnes, the question is moot."

"But the point it illustrates isn't. Confess, Adam Justice. Even if you had an Aunt Agnes, you wouldn't tell her a white lie, not even to make her feel good—isn't that right?"

Whitney's question annoyed Adam. Being honest was a commendable trait, not a despicable one simply because such honesty might fail to bring happiness to a nonexistent aunt with blue hair.

"That's a very fast psychological assessment for someone you've just met, Ms. West. Did you train as a therapist, as well as a lawyer?"

She laughed. Her laugh was deeply mellow and even warmer than her smile.

"I'm impressed that you managed to ask that with perfect equability, Mr. Justice. No sarcastic inflection in your tone. No evidence at all that you're annoyed at my observation. How is it you manage to maintain such politeness in the face of such provocation?"

She was asking another one of those annoying—and to her, obviously amusing—personal questions. He hadn't known her five minutes and she already had him noticing that she was attractive, interesting, self-confident and possessed a natural ability to irritate him. This woman could prove to be trouble.

"No response to that question, Mr. Justice? No, of course not. That would be descending to my level of impropriety, and we can't have that. You remember, of course, that I can walk without assistance?"

Adam saw the slightly amused look on her face and realized he was still holding on to her arm. He quickly released it.

The sun's rays, which had failed to penetrate earlier, suddenly seemed to be working overtime to make him feel warm. He was looking forward to the shade of that tree.

Fortunately they had reached the crosswalk and Adam could legitimately divert his attention to the reluctantly slowing traffic. Once on the other side, he fully intended to take control of this conversation by steering it to the business at hand and keeping it there. No more of this sidetracking into hypothetical aunts with blue hair and other annoying personal questions.

But when they had crossed the street, it was Whitney who spoke up first. "Now I know what your wife meant when she said what she did about you."

It was one of those maddeningly suggestive comments that was obviously meant to hook someone into asking for elaboration. Adam had learned long ago to ignore all such obvious ploys.

"You don't want to know?" Whitney prodded.

"Ms. West, whatever my inclination in the matter, I doubt it will be sufficient to prohibit you from indulging in the pleasure you are so obviously anticipating from the sharing of such information," Adam said in his most polite tone.

Whitney's laugh was even heartier this time. "That's the most elaborate and evasive response I've ever received. What's more, I have no idea if it was a yes or a no. Do you talk like this all the time?"

"Are you trying to annoy me, Ms. West?"

"So it *is* possible. Anyway, I won't keep you in suspense any longer. Your wife said your highly developed sense of right prohibited you from ever doing any wrong. I confess I've been rather interested in meeting the man behind that description."

They stopped in front of the park bench. She was openly staring at him—yet there was nothing flirtatious about her scrutiny.

Adam had never had a woman look at him as Whitney was looking at him, as if she was curious to see if he did indeed represent a new species on the planet. It disturbed him in a way that he couldn't quite define. He felt as though she had just issued him some kind of unspoken challenge, although what exactly it was, he had no idea.

This woman was trouble, all right.

He waited for her to sit down and then established a socially acceptable distance between them before taking his seat. But when he slit open the manila envelope and pulled out the contents, she scooted right next to him and leaned over his shoulder to get a closer look.

Adam suddenly found himself fully aware of her thigh casually pressed against his, of the silky texture and sweet smell of her hair. For a very long moment his body rejoiced in the very unexpected, interesting stimuli sent its way.

"Wouldn't it be easier to read those documents if they were right side up?" she asked.

His eyes drew to her face. She had a light spray of amused golden lights in those brandy eyes that said she was totally oblivious to what she was doing to him.

This woman was definitely crowding him in more ways than one. For just a second he indulged himself with some tempting visions of what she would do if he decided to forget the fact that he was a gentleman and crowd back.

The mental picture of her scurrying off this bench brought about an internal smile. But the other picture—the one of her remaining and continuing to pursue some purposeful crowding of her own—started his pulse racing most alarmingly.

Adam forcibly redirected his attention to the documents in his hands as he turned them right side up.

The first item was a letter addressed to him in Patrice's handwriting. It was dated seven and a half years previously. It caught his complete attention.

Dear Adam,

Enclosed you will find a copy of my will and birth certificate. The originals of both documents are in a safe-deposit box at the Washington Federal Savings on Pike and Fifth in Seattle. The key to the box is inside this envelope I have left with Whitney West. Please take her to the bank with you when you open the safe-deposit box. She will be your witness as to what you find.

The information in these documents will come as a surprise. I hoped I might be able to tell you someday, but the fact that you are reading this letter means I never found the courage. I didn't think I would.

You will have to forgive me, Adam.

I've made you the executor of my estate. You are the only one I trust to carry out my wishes. I am relying on you to see that what I have stipulated goes to my named beneficiaries. They are the ones who deserve it. Represent their rights as you represent mine. I know your honor and expertise will prevail.

Patrice.

Adam refused to deal with the confusion that stirred deep within him as he read Patrice's words. He put the cover letter aside and studied the document directly behind it.

When he realized he held the birth certificate of Patrice Dulcinea Feldon, born August 2, 1964, he began to understand what Patrice meant in her letter when she wrote about surprises . . . and forgiveness.

Chapter Three

Whitney saw no change in Adam's expression as he read the letter from Patrice. But when he glanced at her birth certificate, Whitney felt his thigh muscles instantly flexing against her own.

"What is it?" she asked, ignoring the wave of warmth that had suddenly invaded her body and instead concentrating on the far more important business of finding out what had caused his response.

He said nothing for a moment, his face retaining its impassive mask. When he finally spoke, it was with perfect control, his deep voice holding that deliciously cultured cadence that reminded Whitney of those legendary men in British Sterling ads.

"This is not the birth certificate of the woman I married."

Whitney felt the jolt of his words, wondering if she could have possibly heard him right. "Are you saying she married you using a name other than Patrice Feldon?"

"I knew her as Patrice Anne Waring. And her birth date was February 4, 1964—not August 2, 1964."

"Patrice Waring?" Whitney repeated, trying out the unfamiliar name on her lips. "But surely her driver's license would have shown her real name."

"Her driver's license was in the name of Patrice Waring," Adam said. "After we were married, I was with her when she turned it in and had her last name changed to Justice."

Whitney reached into her shoulder bag and brought out a small pad and a pen. She quickly jotted down the name of Patrice Anne Waring and the birth date of February 4, 1964.

"She was living under an assumed name," Whitney said as she clicked her ballpoint closed, the words exhaled on a long note of disbelief. "Why?"

"I don't know."

His voice was perfectly calm. Whitney wondered what he was thinking and feeling. It occurred to her that Patrice had certainly had a lot of gall to appoint Adam her executor when she'd married him under a false name and then deserted him for another man.

Then Whitney reminded herself that at the time these documents had been given to her, Patrice still loved her husband and the other man had not even been in the picture. No doubt Patrice would have changed the executorship if she had lived.

If she had lived. It was still hard for Whitney to accept that Patrice was dead. She remembered so clearly how full of life Patrice had been that day, seven and a half years before, when she had breezed into Whitney's office.

"Just a little something I want you to take care of," Patrice had said. She had mentioned nothing about going by the name of Waring—or marrying Adam Justice under it.

"Wait a minute," Whitney said excitedly. "I just realized something. If she used a false name, this means that you two were never legally married!"

"Yes," Adam replied simply.

Whitney watched his expression for any change. There was none. He remained so seemingly unaffected. How did he do it? He had just learned that the woman he'd married was...well, wasn't the woman he'd married. And there he sat. Undaunted. Unmoved. Whitney fell back against the park bench. Well, he might be unaffected, but she was feeling absolutely stunned.

What possible reason could there be for Patrice Feldon to take an assumed name and then presume to marry someone under it? And how could the man she did it to be so calm and collected when he learned about it?

She wrote in "Justice" next to the name Patrice Waring on her pad. Only she inadvertently made a space in the middle of the word. When she reread what she wrote, she realized it spelled two words: "Just ice." Pretty accurate description of the man actually.

Out of the corner of her eye, Whitney watched Adam put the birth certificate aside and begin to read "Last Will and Testament of Patrice Feldon," the third and final document in the envelope.

Whitney leaned over Adam's shoulder once again to get a closer look. The introductory paragraph addressed the typical "sound mind" and "not acting under duress" statements. Then began the articles:

Article I

I hereby declare that I am not married and have no children, although I have also gone by the name of Patrice Anne Waring Justice.

Article II

I hereby give, devise and bequeath all the property which I may own at the time of my death, real or personal, tangible or intangible, wherever situated, to be divided as follows:

1. One-third to Beatrice Lynn and Danford Thomas D'Amico of Trectime Place, Tacoma, Washington.
2. One-third to doctors Jacob and Esther Rubin of Seattle, Washington.
3. One-third to Huntley and Brinkley Carmichael of Overton, Nevada.

Whitney jotted the names of the beneficiaries onto her pad. "Do you know who these people are?" she asked.

"No."

"You've never even heard of them?"

"That's correct, Ms. West."

"What do you think of the will?"

"I believe Patrice copied it from a sample will I use in my practice. The wording is identical, except for her specific bequests. She's followed my checklist. She had the will witnessed by two bank tellers and notarized by a third. She also included a self-proving affidavit for the witnesses."

"It's in order, then. When will you take it to probate court?"

"I'm not filing it with the court."

"But you just said it was valid. Why—?"

"Patrice didn't have any money."

"Well then, maybe you can tell me why she prepared a will."

"She might have wanted the will in place for the time when she would have money. It's a prudent move."

That explanation might be acceptable to Adam Justice's prudent mind, but it didn't sit right with Whitney's pragmatic one—particularly not in light of what she remembered Patrice Feldon having said that day in her office.

"I put aside a little something before marrying Adam. I'd like it to go to the right people in case anything were to happen to me. Not that anything will, of course. Being prepared for the worst always prevents it from happening, right?"

Unfortunately, in this instance Patrice had been wrong.

Whitney had no intention of sharing Patrice's "little something" comment with Adam, however. She wanted to know what kind of man he was first. And depending on what she learned, she realized she might never tell him everything she knew.

"Are you certain she had no money?" Whitney prodded.

"When I met her, she was attending classes at UW and working as a cashier in a clothing store. After we mar—got together, she continued attending school. She was still several years away from graduation when she . . . left."

Whitney had been trying to penetrate Adam Justice's armor to learn how he felt about the woman he had called his wife. But his ultraformal manner and deeply calm and even voice gave nothing away.

He was a strikingly handsome man with that black hair and those light blue eyes set in clean, strong, classic features. Everything about him—from his custom-fit dark blue suit to his wonderfully deep, cultured voice—marked a man of distinction, intellect and influence.

An invulnerable man. An impassive man. A cold man.

She had come prepared to find the fault that had driven his wife into the arms of another man. She was certain she had found that fault. Her mother had put it best when she said, *"A man can possess everything in material possessions the world has to offer, Whitney, but if he doesn't possess a loving and loyal heart, he has nothing of value to offer you."*

"Patrice must have told you something about her past," Whitney said.

Adam assessed Whitney for a long moment with those piercingly cold blue eyes that seemed to be iced over in a perpetual winter. She had no doubt that such a focused look from him would probably have half the female population swooning at his feet and the other half scurrying away in fear. She figured the half that ran had the right idea.

"She said she was an orphan who had been raised in foster homes."

"Well, since Washington State does not recognize a common-law marriage, you don't owe her estate any community property," Whitney said. "If she really didn't have any money of her own, it looks like these beneficiaries are out of luck."

"What the state does or doesn't recognize has no bearing on my actions, Ms. West."

"Excuse me?"

"The fact that Patrice lied to me about who she was does not invalidate the pledge I made eight and a half years ago. I will see to it that those she has designated as her beneficiaries receive half of the money I earned while Patrice and I were . . . together."

"Really? You mean that?"

"I don't say things I don't mean, Ms. West."

She wondered if that were true. If Adam Justice really was intending to give those beneficiaries money, he was a most forgiving and unusual man.

She watched him slip the safe-deposit-box key out of the envelope and return the documents to it. He had long, lean, capable-looking hands. She remembered the feel of iron strength in the one that had circled her arm.

Whitney suddenly had the compelling impression that whatever those hands held, they would hold tightly and would only release when they were ready. That observation caused a vague disquiet in her. What had happened seven years before, when he found his wife was leaving him for another man?

"If you are not committed elsewhere for the next hour, Ms. West, I would appreciate your accompanying me to that safe-deposit box."

Whitney rose to her feet, pushing her vague disquiet aside. "My calendar's free."

"Finding parking in the financial district at this time of day will be difficult," Adam said. "Ride with me, and I'll bring you back to your car after our business is concluded."

"That's very thoughtful, Mr. Justice."

"It is for my convenience, Ms. West. Were you to be unable to find a parking space, we would be unable to complete this matter expeditiously. My car is over there."

As she walked beside Adam, Whitney wondered whether he really suggested she ride with him only for his convenience. It was hardly convenient for him to drive another fifteen miles back to the cemetery when their business was concluded.

Adam Justice was not an easy man to understand. She wondered how long it might take to find out who he was behind that impassive, polished exterior.

They approached his car, an immaculate black Jaguar XJR sedan with no personal license plate. Whitney decided it fit him perfectly. It was as highly respectable, formal and impersonal a label as his dress and everything else about him.

He opened the passenger door and held it for her in a very proper kind of courtesy. That fit him, too. She sunk onto the cool leather seat.

As he circled around to the driver's side, she noticed he had a phone, a computer and even a fax machine installed on the front console.

The air-conditioning roared to life along with the engine, and then both obediently retreated into a pleasant purr. Cool air bathed her face as a soft instrumental piece seemed to compose itself all around her. She could hear the drums rolling up behind her, different strings in both ears, the piano notes as clear as if she sat at the keyboard.

What a far cry this was from her thrifty beige Saturn, with the stiff vinyl seats and the nicks in the door. She nestled farther into the butter-soft leather, concentrating fully on the sensuous feast this ride had to offer.

Still, as good as this was, she didn't envy Adam Justice the luxury, convenience or sleek sophistication of his unblemished vehicle. She liked her little Saturn with its vinyl seats and door nicks. Just like people, a car needed a blemish or two to give it heart and make it lovable.

When they pulled into the parking lot adjacent to Washington Federal Savings Bank on Fifth, the attendant handed Adam a ticket and pointed to the first space. Whitney watched the attendant put up a Full sign on the driveway to block any more cars from coming through.

"I don't believe it," she said.

"Believe what?" Adam asked, apparently totally oblivious to his good fortune.

"You not only got the last parking space, you got the best," Whitney answered, pushing open the passenger door before he could come around to open it for her. "Do you part seas, too?" she added under her breath as he led the way to the bank next door.

Washington Federal Savings was one of those well-established institutions that sat on the corner of a busy, prosperous intersection. Yet once inside, Whitney found it was beautifully quiet, with gleaming black marble walls and soft recessed lighting.

Heads rose as they passed. Whitney wasn't surprised. Adam Justice's bearing exuded an air of someone important. He was a man people would always notice.

She wondered if he was as oblivious to that as he seemed to be to all the other fortuitous things in his life.

Adam spoke for several minutes with a very attractive bank vice president. Although Whitney couldn't hear what they were saying, she could see the lady wore an adoring look in her eyes and was close to melting in her chair.

The vice president consulted her computer, secured a set of keys, then led them to a thick glass door at the back of the bank. She opened it and gestured for them to go inside.

The room they stepped into was relatively small and narrow, barely five feet wide by twelve feet long. It was lined on one side by safe-deposit boxes. Adam fitted his key into the lock of number 105, third from the bottom on the far left. The bank vice president fitted her key into the adjoining lock.

Adam removed the safe-deposit box and set it on a small shelf in a free-standing cubicle on the edge of the room that resembled a portable polling booth, only without the privacy veils.

"Can I do anything else for you?" the vice president asked, a clear suggestion in her tone, a hopeful look in her eyes.

"No, thank you," Adam said in his formal, cool tone. It was clear his total attention was on the safe-deposit box.

The vice president left on a disappointed sigh, closing the glass door behind her. Whitney didn't know many men who would have passed up the chance to at least flirt with the very attractive and obviously willing lady.

There were no chairs in the room. Whitney stepped over to Adam's side as he opened the safe-deposit box. The original of Patrice's will and her birth certificate were on top.

When Adam removed these, Whitney saw a yellowed newspaper clipping sitting on top of a thick bunch of stock certificates.

While Adam verified the entries on the original will and birth certificate, Whitney took a closer look at the newspaper clipping.

It was from the Business section of *The Weekend Sun*—a Vancouver British Columbia newspaper. A stock abbreviated as EP had been circled. It was selling for thirty cents a share.

Whitney glanced at the first stock certificate. It didn't look like any stock certificate she had seen before. It represented five hundred shares in a firm called Emery Pharmaceuticals. Both the newspaper clipping and the stock certificate were dated nine years previous.

Whitney couldn't tell exactly how many stock certificates were in the safe-deposit box, but she could tell there were quite a few. She couldn't help wondering whether this stock was that "little something" Patrice had mentioned.

Adam put down the documents he had been checking. He glanced at the newspaper clipping and the stock certificate in Whitney's hands.

"You didn't know she had this, did you?" Whitney asked.

"No. We'll need to find out how much this stock is worth in today's terms."

"I doubt the state insurance commissioner will be able to help. Actually I've found the best place for tracking down the value of old stock certificates is R. M. Smythe & Co. on Broadway in New York. But even they may have difficulty with a foreign company."

Whitney felt Adam's eyes draw to her face. "It sounds as though you've been involved in tracing stock certificates before," he said.

"My partner and I have had several people come in with certificates they've found in the attic that some parent or grandparent purchased and then forgot about. Most of the time the company has gone broke and they prove worthless. It generally takes a few weeks to give the client the bad news."

"We shouldn't have to wait a few weeks to find out about these," Adam said. "Marc Truesdale, one of my partners, is close friends with a highly respected investment counselor by the name of Gavin Yeagher. Yeagher is hooked up to the kind of international financial network that should yield the answer we're seeking."

"Great. Do we go see this Gavin Yeagher or call?"

"Calling will be faster."

Adam pulled a cell phone out of his pocket and punched in a number.

She heard Adam's side of the conversation as he asked Marc to put him in touch with Gavin Yeagher and explained why.

Then he replaced the cell phone in his pocket and turned to her.

"Marc will convey our request to Yeagher and ask him to get back to us. He's paging him on the racquetball courts. While we're waiting, we should count the stock so that we have an accurate number to give to Yeagher."

Whitney lifted the rest of the stock certificates out of the safe-deposit box. She divided the pile between herself and Adam.

It took less than a minute to check and count them. "Each one of my forty-eight certificates represents five hundred shares," Whitney said.

"Each of mine also represents five hundred shares, and I have fifty-two," Adam said. "That adds up to fifty thousand shares."

Whitney reached into her shoulder bag for a hand-held calculator. She entered the numbers and multiplied them.

"Fifty thousand shares at thirty cents a share is fifteen thousand Canadian dollars. What is the exchange rate these days, about seventy-five cents Canadian to one American dollar?"

"In that neighborhood."

Whitney did the calculations. "Then a conservative estimate would place the value of this stock at more than eleven thousand U.S. dollars," she said. "Not a bad chunk of change. I'm surprised Patrice didn't cash these in when she was attending UW and trying to make ends meet. That's what you said she was doing, right?"

"She was living in a very small apartment and working at odd jobs. The money would have certainly made things easier."

"When did you meet Patrice?" Whitney asked.

"Why do you ask?"

"I'm trying to understand the time perspective on this."

"We met eight years and nine months ago."

"Three months after these stock certificates were issued. And you married her three months after you met?"

"Yes."

"I wonder where a struggling college student got eleven thousand dollars to invest in a stock purchase?"

"I doubt she bought it herself."

"You're thinking that maybe someone else bought this stock for her? Who?"

"I don't have a specific someone in mind. Patrice had been keeping company with several men when I met her. One of them might have given it to her as a gift."

"That's unlikely."

"It is customary for a man to show his affection with a gift, Ms. West."

"I met your wi—Patrice Feldon. I'm well aware she was one of those phenomenally beautiful women who turned every male head when she walked into a room. Lavishing gifts upon such an outstandingly beautiful woman is the way men respond, I grant you."

Whitney paused to shake her head. "I suppose coming upon such perfection seems like a religious experience for them. They all feel they have to pay homage at the altar of her beauty or something."

"Is this knowledge you acquired while pursuing your psychological degree, Ms. West?"

Whitney smiled at the beautifully measured, crisp cadence that had delivered that spate of sarcasm.

"I have two older brothers, Mr. Justice. Watching them struggle through adolescence was more informative than any Ph.D."

"Forgive me for having assumed your education was of the inferior, formal kind," he said with a small bow of his head.

Once again he had responded with that elegant, precise diction and not even the barest hint of annoyance.

Whitney's smile got bigger. She was becoming more and more certain that somewhere beneath that smug sophistication and those tranquil tones lurked a far from tranquil irritation. Although why that pleased her she wasn't quite sure.

"Still, as certain as I am that there were guys lining up to offer Patrice gifts—and pretty much anything else she wanted—I doubt that's where she got this stock," Whitney said.

"You seem most certain of that."

"I am. Admirers give gifts like magnums of champagne, boxes of chocolate, dozens of long-stem roses, sexy lingerie, jewelry. A bunch of stock certificates hardly puts a gal into a romantic mood."

"The stock was worth more than eleven thousand dollars," Adam said.

Whitney chuckled. "You must be a delight to date. Romance isn't about money, Mr. Justice. It's about an expression of feeling. When a man gives a woman a gift, it has to be one with some heart in it. How did you ever get Patrice to accept you over those other men? Did you hit her over the head?"

"What a charming image. And such stirring insight."

Whitney chuckled delightedly at the impudence of his words encased in such an ultrapolite tone.

"Has anyone ever made you mad?" she asked after she got herself back in control.

"I beg your pardon?"

She leaned closer to him. God, he smelled good—clean and rich and exotic, like the smoky incense of forest woods with just a hint of combustible clove.

"Let me rephrase that," she said. "Has anyone ever made you so mad that you actually showed your anger?"

He leaned back, reestablishing a socially acceptable space between them. "Indulging anger feeds that anger and ends up making one even more angry. It is a harmful ritual."

"What do you say to all those people who contend you should let out your anger?"

"I would say that those people are probably angry most of the time."

"You just keep it bottled up inside?"

"Ms. West, just because anger is not indulged does not mean it's being bottled up."

"Look, Adam, if we're going to argue about this, I really think you should call me Whitney."

"We are not going to argue about this. I never argue. Why should I call you Whitney?"

"Because calling someone by their first name is more friendly. And the friendlier we become, the less likely you'll be to throw a punch my way."

"I do not throw punches. Not even well-deserved ones."

Whitney chuckled. "Formal delivery notwithstanding, that sentence definitely contained a message that I deserve a punch. I have made you mad, haven't I?"

"No one can make me anything I don't choose to be."

"Yes, I'm beginning to think that must be true. I can see now why Patrice selected you over her other suitors. And it wasn't because you hit her over the head. Shall I tell you?"

"Another character assessment, Ms. West? How could I refuse?"

This refined form of smooth sarcasm was really quite entertaining. Whitney found herself warming to it even more. She leaned closer, deliberately invading his space yet again and inhaling his exciting scent.

"You weren't easy like the rest of them, Adam. You didn't immediately fall at her feet. You remained reserved, cool, aloof, because that's your style. What an irresistible challenge you must have represented to Patrice. You must still be fighting them off. Well, that *certain type* of woman anyway."

"That certain type of woman?" Adam repeated.

"Oh, you know the kind," Whitney said, leaning back and flashing him a deliberately elusive smile.

"Given your powers of acute observation on human nature, I can only conclude that this knowledge I possess is temporarily beyond my recall."

Whitney laughed again. "Despite that cool indifference that you exude out of every one of your cosmopolitan pores, Adam Justice, I'm beginning to suspect that you really are curious, so I'm going to tell you."

Whitney paused for a moment to see if she could detect any change in his calm expression. There wasn't any.

"She's the type of woman who needs the adoration of all men, Adam. Only when she meets you, that adoration isn't immediately forthcoming. So, naturally yours becomes the adoration she needs most of all."

For just an instant Whitney thought she saw some emotion flash behind Adam Justice's cold blue eyes. But then the cell phone in his pocket rang, and by the time he reached for it, whatever emotion it was had vanished—if indeed it had ever been there at all.

Adam's half of the conversation was too sketchy for Whitney to follow. She concentrated instead on piecing together the impressions that had been collecting in her thoughts about Adam Justice.

She kept recalling Patrice's comments about him as she sat across from Whitney in her office those many years before:

"There's no one better looking than Adam. Or smarter. I told you he's a lawyer? Well, he's never lost a case. He never will, either. He does everything the best. He's the best husband, the best lover. He'll be the best father, too. We decided to have kids right away. It would be impossible not to love him."

Six months after those words had been uttered, Patrice had left this man whom it would be impossible not to love.

Whitney's attention returned to the present when Adam closed the cell phone and replaced it in his pocket. His expression gave nothing away about what he might have learned.

"So, is the stock worth anything?" Whitney prompted.

"One hundred and fifty U.S. dollars per share."

Whitney shot forward. "That much?" Whitney punched the numbers into her calculator excitedly. "Dear heavens, that's...that's seven and a half million dollars! I can't believe this stock is worth that much!"

"It isn't," Adam said.

"But you just said—"

"Since these certificates were issued nine years ago, Yeagher tells me this company has split its stock four times. When the reinvested dividends are taken into consideration, the value of this stock is well in excess of thirty million dollars."

Chapter Four

A.J.'s normally deep voice rose several octaves in Adam's ear. "I don't believe it, Adam. I don't mean I don't believe you, it's just... I don't believe *it*. She married you under a false name. She left an estate worth more than thirty million dollars. Who in the hell was Patrice?"

"That's what I need to know, A.J."

Adam had stepped just outside the bank vault room and stood with his back against a wall to be sure no one was in hearing distance when he called his office and then his sister's investigation firm.

"Do you really have to get involved in this matter, Adam?" A.J.'s voice asked.

"Patrice made me executor of her estate."

"She held back so much from you, even her real name. Who knows what we'll find if we delve into this mess? Dump the executorship. Walk away. You certainly don't need the lawyer's fees. Or the heartache."

"But I need to know, A.J."

A.J. exhaled audibly. "Yes, I was afraid of that. Okay. What do you want me to do?"

"If I'm to safeguard this money and see to it that it gets to the beneficiaries stipulated in her will, I'm going to have to find out more about her and how she came to possess this stock that now comprises her estate."

"Fax me a copy of Patrice's real birth certificate, and I'll get right on it. How soon will you have a record of the individual stock-certificate numbers?"

From his position Adam could see through the glass door to the safe-deposit box room. Whitney was bending over the stock certificates. She had begun the task of recording each one. She was obviously used to doing everything herself at her small law practice. And competently, too, he would wager.

"My first call was to the office to request a stenographer be sent over here to record the numbers from the stock certificates," he said to A.J. "When that's finished, I'll have the list faxed to you. For the time being I'm returning the originals to the safe-deposit box."

"When I get your fax, I'll get Piper Lane to work with Gavin Yeagher to trace the stock purchases. Piper's my best investigator when it comes to digging out that kind of stuff. And just so we know who all the players are, I'll run a background check on this Whitney West, too. With luck I should have a preliminary report on your desk late today."

"Thanks, A.J."

"Please don't thank me, Adam. I'm doing what you ask, but I very much doubt I'm doing you a favor."

As soon as Adam disconnected the line to A.J., his cell phone immediately rang. He answered it.

"It's Octavia. I just wanted to call back to let you know that I've sent a security guard along with the stenographer. I figured with that much money at stake, it might be a prudent move."

"Thanks, Octavia. I should have thought of it myself."

"I don't know how you can think at all. This is numbing news. Do the police know yet about Patrice's real name or the extent of the estate she's left?"

"They may suspect something. I was tailed from the cemetery this morning."

"The police are following you? Adam, I don't like this."

"I'm not thrilled with it myself."

"Could that lawyer, Whitney West, have tipped them off about Patrice's real identity and the extent of her estate?"

"It's difficult to suspect her. She looked genuinely shocked to learn Patrice had lied to me about who she was. She was positively floored at the enormous estate Patrice left."

"'Enormous' is right. How are you going to handle it?"

"As soon as the stenographer and the security guard arrive, I'm going over to the courthouse to file the necessary documents and officially start the probate process. I'm taking Ms. West with me as my witness to what I've found in Patrice's safe-deposit box. Afterward I'll fax the details about Patrice and her estate to Sergeant Ryson."

"Adam, you realize Ryson is not going to believe you didn't know Patrice's real name until now. They told you they're investigating. Let them find it out on their own. Legally you don't have to volunteer it."

"But ethically it's the right thing to do."

"You and your lamentable brand of ethics, Adam Justice. I don't know who is worse, you or Brett."

Adam almost smiled. "When are you two getting married?"

"It's still up for debate, quite a bit of debate lately, as a matter of fact. I like the idea of living in sin, as he calls it."

"Probably because it makes Brett uncomfortable."

Octavia laughed. "I can't help it. There is a delectable formality about Brett that just begs to be mussed. You'd best be careful, Adam. You have that quality, too. And one of these days you're going to meet the woman who will not rest until she's mussed it."

"Once is more than enough, Octavia," Adam said, his somberness fully returned.

"For your sake I hope you're wrong. Adam, why don't you let me go to the police as your attorney? That way it will seem more official when I give them the facts you've learned about Patrice and her will."

"I appreciate the strategy, but I must do this myself."

"You realize that during this past week the police have interviewed all Justice Inc. staff at their homes, despite the fact that none of them was even with us seven years ago."

"Yes. The police are wasting their time. You and I are the only two who even knew Patrice."

"If anyone really knew her. I'm beginning to have my doubts about that. I always thought it strange that someone as beautiful as Patrice was so camera shy. You had to browbeat her into having even that one picture taken. Maybe there's something there. You've put A.J. to work on her background?"

"Just got off the line with her."

"Good. She'll come through. Something is making the police think the deaths weren't an accident, Adam. What could it be?"

"You know as much as I do, Octavia."

"And it's not enough. I should be able to find a spy over at the sheriff's office who can let us know what Sergeant Ryson has—or thinks he has. I'll work on it."

"The stenographer and the security guard just entered the bank and are heading this way, Octavia. I'd best go. I'll keep in touch."

"Adam?"

"Yes?"

"It wasn't your fault, Adam."

"Octavia—"

"Adam, please listen to me. Until the day you accept that, this will never be over."

WHITNEY HAD PREPARED lots of wills in her nine years as a practicing attorney, but she had never had to see an estate through probate. Still, she knew the basics and was not surprised when Adam filed the appropriate forms with the office of the clerk of the court on the sixth floor of the King County Courthouse and received a twelve-digit estate number.

But when they arrived in room W285 for the next step of the process, Whitney was surprised at the large number of people waiting to be called. As Whitney stood in line with Adam to turn in their papers, she noticed that those attorneys who had handed in their papers were asked to take a seat on the wooden church-pew-like seats. And wait some more.

Finally it was Whitney and Adam's turn to approach the bored-looking clerk behind the long bench. His name tag said he was Dwight Errent. Adam handed him the forms.

"Estate of Feldon," Adam said. "No bond."

When the clerk's eyes skipped over the "Petition for Probate of Will" to the "Petition for Order of Solvency," his eyes shot off the page to Adam's face. He flew to his feet and bent toward Adam, lowering his voice to an excited whisper. "You're estimating Patrice Feldon's total estate assets at *thirty million dollars?*" he asked, his voice rattling excitedly on every syllable.

"It's a conservative estimate," Adam assured in his ultra-formal tone.

The clerk turned and bolted toward the door behind him with the label of Courtroom B above it, the papers clenched in his hand.

"Wait here," Errent called over his shoulder, almost as an afterthought.

"What's he doing?" Whitney asked.

"I believe he's gone to talk to a court commissioner."

"They don't use judges in the Seattle probate court, do they?"

"I take it this is your first time?"

"Yes. The only client who died after I prepared her will didn't have an estate over the magical thirty-thousand-dollar mark, so it never got probated. How many probates have you handled?"

"I've been the executor in twelve."

"*Twelve?* Adam, are you telling me twelve people made you executor of their estates and then *died?*"

"You say it as though that makes me a serial killer."

"What other explanation could there be?"

For just a moment there Whitney thought he might smile. But the moment passed, and the smile didn't materialize. She was rather disappointed it hadn't. She was beginning to wonder what the stoic Adam Justice would look like in a smile.

"Ten of the twelve were executives in a major corporation, one of my firm's clients," Adam explained. "Preparing their wills was all part of the comprehensive legal service Justice Inc. provides to firms we handle.''

"So what happened? Did they show up to the boardroom one day with six-shooters strapped to their waists and blow each other away?"

"You appear to possess a distinct criminal bent to your mind, Ms. West."

"Thank you."

"It wasn't a compliment."

"I know. Are you going to tell me what happened to those executives?"

"They were killed when their private jet crashed."

"That must have been rough on their families and the firm. You didn't service the plane for them beforehand, by any chance?"

"The FAA attributed the crash to pilot error."

"I guess that lets you off the hook. So you've handled twelve of these probates, with number thirteen coming up. Are you superstitious, Adam? No, of course you're not. Superstition is illogical, and that's not even a word in your vocabulary."

"Thank you."

"It wasn't a compliment, Adam."

"I know."

Whitney was chuckling delightedly when Dwight Errent, the court clerk, reappeared and gestured to them.

"Mr. Justice, Ms. West, the commissioner will see you now. This way, please."

The eyebrows of a half-dozen attorneys rose. All of them had arrived before Whitney and Adam and had been waiting for a while. Whitney felt as though she had just cut into the front of a long line at a supermarket.

"I thought these were handled on a first-come, first-served basis," she whispered to Adam as they followed the clerk.

"That's the normal procedure," Adam said.

"Are we getting the royal treatment?"

"We're not. But a thirty-million-dollar estate is."

The clerk stopped in front of Courtroom B, rapping lightly on the glass. The nameplate just outside said Taylor Snowe, Court Commissioner.

"Come in."

The voice was strong and female. When they stepped inside, the woman behind the high bench in the left corner gestured to the two chairs in front of it without lifting her eyes from the papers in her hands.

"Mr. Justice, Ms. West, make yourselves comfortable while I read over the rest of this filing."

Whitney and Adam took the offered chairs in the very small room while Dwight Errent left, quietly closing the door behind him.

Whitney studied the court commissioner. She was in her middle thirties with silver blond hair drawn back into a tight bun, revealing every bone in her slim face. Her skin was so pale, it looked translucent against her black robe. She wore no makeup. She should have. Were she standing next to a white wall, Whitney imagined everything from her neck up might have faded right into it.

Taylor Snowe looked up suddenly, and Whitney was surprised to find she possessed both warm and intelligent gray eyes.

"Thank you for waiting." She favored Whitney with a quick glance and then addressed her comments to Adam. "Mr. Justice, is this the will of your wife I'm holding?"

"She was not my wife, Your Honor."

"She identifies herself as Patrice Justice in it, as well as Patrice Feldon," Taylor Snowe said in a tone that pulled no punches. "I watch the TV news, Mr. Justice. I know your wife's body and that of her lover were recently found."

Whitney looked at Adam. Commissioner Snowe's bluntness had registered not at all on his cool, collected countenance. Whitney was not surprised. She was coming to realize that nothing and no one ever disturbed Adam Justice's calm demeanor.

Adam proceeded to tell Commissioner Snowe in his deep and even voice about the items in the envelope Whitney had brought to him, and about their subsequent visit to the safe-deposit box. He handed over copies of Patrice's letters and the Feldon birth certificate. He managed the explanation with an admirable economy of words.

The court commissioner studied the documents in her hands for several moments before speaking. When she looked up, her eyes reflected her concern. "Did you know Patrice Feldon had that safe-deposit box, Mr. Justice?"

"No, Your Honor."

"How were the fees for the safe-deposit box paid these last seven years?"

"The bank clerk advised me that Patrice had arranged for the fees to be automatically withdrawn from a small savings account she kept with the institution," Adam said.

"Did you know Patrice Feldon had these stocks?"

"No, Your Honor."

"Is it your intent to find out how she obtained them?"

"I have an investigator already working on it."

"This woman who called herself your wife seems to have suffered from a deplorable lack of honesty and loyalty to you. I realize the attorney's fees for handling an estate this size will be substantial, but do you really think you can put aside your personal feelings in this matter to be a proper advocate for the deceased?"

"I am prepared to do so."

Whitney watched Commissioner Snowe study Adam. Snowe looked concerned that she could read neither his rock-set features nor his equally fixed tone. Snowe tapped the pen in her hand against the documents lying on her desk.

"You've never appeared before me, Mr. Justice. You'd best understand I feel personally responsible for every estate that passes through my hands. I don't care whether it's thirty thousand or thirty million. What I do care about is that the will is properly prepared and executed. That the deceased was not under undue influence during its preparation. That she or he now has a competent and dedicated advocate. That blood relatives are properly represented. That creditors have their say.

In short, that I end up sending the money where it's supposed to go. That's what I care about. What do you care about?''

"Representing the deceased's wishes as she has stated them in her will.''

"That's all? No hidden agenda to circumvent the deceased's wishes because of her treatment of you?''

"None, Your Honor.''

"Do you know these beneficiaries she has listed?''

"No, Your Honor.''

"You've never even heard of them?''

"That's correct.''

Commissioner Snowe tapped her pen some more. "I tell you candidly, Mr. Justice, I'm uncomfortable with this. If it weren't for your reputation of outstanding ethical behavior, I would not grant your petition to serve as the personal representative on this estate. And your reputation notwithstanding, be assured that I will be watching your actions carefully.''

Commissioner Snowe turned to Whitney. "Ms. West, you held Patrice Feldon's will and these other documents for Mr. Justice at Patrice Feldon's request?''

"Yes, Your Honor.''

"Did you prepare this will for Patrice Feldon?''

"No, Your Honor.''

"Do you know who did?''

"Mr. Justice told me earlier that he believes Patrice copied a standard will he had prepared for use in his practice.''

Commissioner Snowe's eyes immediately went to Adam's face. "Is the format the same on this will and the sample you prepared, Mr. Justice?''

"Yes, Your Honor.''

"So you believe Patrice Feldon typed up this will herself?''

"That would be my judgment call,'' Adam said.

"Well, there is no law against that. The will appears valid *on its face*. The language is correct. The witnessing affidavits are all to form.''

Commissioner Snowe turned back to Whitney. "Was anyone with her at the time she gave you these documents?''

"No, Your Honor, and the envelope was sealed. Until Mr. Justice opened it this morning, I did not know what was inside."

"This handwritten note from Patrice Feldon directed you to accompany Mr. Justice to the safe-deposit box in order that you be witness to what he found. Did Patrice Feldon tell you she was going to make this request of Mr. Justice?"

"No, Your Honor."

"Do you know Mr. Justice personally?"

"No."

"Have you had any other business dealings with him before this matter?"

"None. We met this morning for the first time."

"So you are a disinterested party and have come here only to give witness to having received the documents from Patrice Feldon and to having viewed the extent of the estate, is that correct?"

"I'm also here because I'd like to be appointed *guardian ad litem* for the unknown heirs, Your Honor."

Whitney watched Commissioner Snowe's gray eyes widen in surprise. "Ms. West, such an assignment is premature. The paperwork has only just been submitted on this probate."

"I understand that, Your Honor, but if I don't speak up now, you may appoint someone else. Patrice Feldon has stated she had no children, no family—other than Mr. Justice, whom we have learned she married under a false name. I know that the court must therefore appoint a guardian for the unknown heirs. *Nemo est heires viventes*—nobody dies without leaving heirs. I would like to perform the function of representing those heirs."

Whitney watched Commissioner Snowe giving her a considerable once-over. She understood why.

It was unusual for a lawyer to make such a suggestion, particularly since most probate judges, or in Seattle's case, commissioners, had their list of favorites to whom they automatically gave such choice assignments. And this would certainly be such an assignment, since the fees from a thirty-million-dollar estate were bound to be substantial.

But Whitney had the impression that Commissioner Taylor Snowe didn't play that kind of political payback game with her pets at the big law firms. It was one of the reasons that Whitney had decided to take a chance and ask for the assignment.

"Ms. West, were I to appoint you to this position, you would have to make a concerted effort to find Patrice Feldon's heirs, and if you were successful and they wished you to represent them, your job would be to show that this will is invalid or incomplete—otherwise, they wouldn't be able to collect."

"Yes, Your Honor. I know."

"Are you personally acquainted with any of the beneficiaries mentioned in Patrice Feldon's will?" Commissioner Snowe asked.

"No, Your Honor."

"Have you ever held such an appointment before?"

"No, Your Honor."

"Have you been an executor personal representative or administrator personal representative in a probate action?"

"No, Your Honor."

"Have you ever represented an interested party in a probate case?"

"No, Your Honor."

"Ms. West, you're asking me to let you cut your baby teeth on this whale bone of an estate."

"I'm a quick and thorough researcher. And a very hard worker. I can do it."

Once again Whitney felt Commissioner Snowe's eyes on her. This time, though, they seemed to be dwelling unnecessarily long on Whitney's far from new suit. Whitney kept her carriage straight and hoped that the woman sitting across from her wasn't going to be so shallow as to shoot her down for not wearing expensive threads like Adam's.

"Since Mr. Justice will be sworn to uphold the will and the deceased's wishes, you and he would be working closely together. You may also end up in adversarial positions."

"Yes, I know, Your Honor."

"He is an experienced litigator in these matters. Do you think it fair to the blood heirs to be represented by a neophyte?"

"My job will be to locate the blood heirs, Your Honor. Once I do, if those heirs are not convinced I can represent them competently, they can certainly seek other counsel. However, if they recognize that experience can't hold a candle to hard work and enthusiasm, I think they might choose me to be their advocate."

A very slight smile lifted Commissioner Snowe's pale lips. In the next instant it was gone, and her sober countenance was back. "If you make a mistake, Ms. West, I will not be forgiving."

"Does that mean I have the appointment, Your Honor?"

Commissioner Snowe turned her eyes to Adam. "Do you have any reservations about Ms. West becoming *guardian ad litem* for the unnamed heirs, Mr. Justice?"

There was a small—but to Whitney, significant—pause between Commissioner Snowe's question and Adam's answer.

"No," he said simply.

"All right, Ms. West, you have the appointment. But remember. An estate this size is bound to catch the attention of the news media. If you do err, you will not be able to bury your mistakes in obscurity. They will be out there for all to see."

"Yes, Your Honor. Thank you, Your Honor."

"And the same goes for you, Mr. Justice. Don't let your previous experience make you complacent. I've seen veteran litigators wearing egg on their faces because they forgot every estate is different and did not bone up on their statutes."

"Yes, Your Honor."

"May I begin placing advertisements for the heirs in the newspapers?" Whitney asked.

"You won't have to advertise," Snowe said. "Once this story breaks, both blood heirs—if there are any—and bogus heirs—and they'll be plenty of them—will be beating down your door. Before I put the preliminary hearing for this case on the calendar, I want Mr. Justice's investigator to fill in the gaps on Patrice Feldon's background and find out how she obtained these stocks. The last thing we need is for the press to speculate in these areas. Let's keep this case out of their hands until then.''

"That will delay my locating the heirs," Whitney said.

"You'll have plenty of time to perform your G.A.L. function, Ms. West. If the news media is not approached prematurely, you'll also have far fewer bogus claims to wade through. May I count on your cooperation on this?''

"Yes, Your Honor," Adam and Whitney said in unison.

"Good. Keep me completely informed of your progress. I want to know everything as soon as you do. Please leave your phone numbers with my clerk. Good afternoon.''

As soon as they were outside the court commissioner's chambers, Whitney turned to Adam. "I appreciate the fact that you didn't give voice to your objections back there when Commissioner Snowe asked you about my appointment.''

"Whatever reservations I have about your lack of experience in these matters, Whitney, it would be unprofessional of me to allow them to interfere with your earning the fees attendant to the assignment.''

"Thank you, but I didn't apply for the G.A.L. position because of the fees.''

"Are you after the publicity, Ms. West?''

Whitney chuckled. "Have you noticed that you only resort to calling me 'Ms. West' now when you want to be emphatically formal?''

"I asked you a question.''

He certainly had. What was it about that oh-so-deadly-serious tone of his voice that sometimes sent a chill up her spine?

"No, Adam. I didn't ask for the position because I want publicity.''

"Then why did you ask for it?''

Whitney waited until they had exited the room full of people and had gained the relatively deserted hallway before stopping and turning to answer Adam. "When Patrice put that envelope in my hands more than seven years ago, she made me a party to this mystery. I want to see it through to the end. And that means learning who she was and where she got this stock. Being on the inside will help me to get those answers. Just like being on the inside will help you to get those answers. That's why you're agreeing to be her executor, right?''

"Why didn't you tell me you were going to ask for that G.A.L. appointment?"

"Because I didn't know myself until I met Commissioner Snowe. It's the kind of lucrative assignment outsiders like me never get. But she didn't seem to be someone who played favorites, so I thought I'd take a chance. Now, why don't you answer my question?"

Adam looked at his wrist. "What question would that be?"

"Just about any one of the last dozen would do."

"The answer is no, Whitney. I do not part seas."

She chuckled. "But apparently you do listen, Adam. And that I find a miracle in itself. You're looking at your watch again. Are you late for something?"

"I have an appointment on the other side of town in thirty-five minutes. It will take five to return the original copy of Patrice's will to the clerk of the court on the sixth floor. It will take at least thirty minutes to get you back to your car. I must call to cancel my appointment."

"Blonde, brunette or redhead?" Whitney asked irreverently.

"Bald," Adam said with no hesitation.

Whitney stifled a smile. "She probably pulled out all her hair because you've already canceled on her too often. You don't have to waste your time driving me back to my car. I can catch a cab."

"I have no doubt you can. However, I promised to return you to your car."

"Adam, it's really not necessary to—"

"I will return you to your car," he said.

There was no arguing with that commanding, emphatic tone. Whitney was rather fascinated and more than a little surprised to find that she suddenly had absolutely no desire to argue with it, either.

"DAMN!" Ryson exclaimed loudly as he read the faxed message the clerk had just placed in his in-basket.

Ferkel lifted his hefty bulk out of his chair and leaned over their facing desks, bringing with him the odor of onions. "What is it, Sarge?"

Ryson leaned back as his nose twitched. "Can you believe this? Justice's now saying the woman wasn't even his wife! And she's left a fortune he claims he never knew about, too!"

"Let me see."

Ryson flipped the sheet in Ferkel's direction. The hefty detective caught it in midair. Ryson watched Ferkel digest the fax as he licked the grease off his fingers from a just-finished street-stand hot dog. Halfway through he burped loudly.

Ryson winced. He couldn't stand Ferkel's personal habits—precisely the reason why the lieutenant had saddled him with Ferkel. The lieutenant had it in for Ryson ever since he'd heard Ryson joking about the school picture of the lieutenant's fourteen-year-old daughter looking like a shot of Andy Rooney on a bad day. Some guys just didn't have a sense of humor.

"You believe he didn't know this, Sarge?" Ferkel asked as soon as he dropped the now-greasy sheet to his desktop.

"Yeah, like I believe in the tooth fairy. Of course Justice knew. I just don't know whether he knew all the time they were putting on this charade of a marriage, or whether it was something he found out just before he killed her."

"The prosecuting attorney is going to love this, Sarge. Justice had enough reasons to kill this woman seven times over. Damn shame forensics came up with zilch from the wreck."

"Well, just because everything was too rusted and corroded for them to analyze, doesn't mean Justice is going to get away with murder. I got approval to send the wreck to the FBI lab for analysis. With all the Feds' fancy computer stuff, those guys will come through. It will take a little time, but they'll figure out what Justice did to that car.''

''My money says he drove up beside them, slammed into them and whacked them off that road,'' Ferkel said gesturing with his hands and ending in a slap of his palms.

Ryson shook his head. ''Naw, too risky. That's not Justice's style. He'd play it safe and smart. I can just see him fixing Danner's car so it would smash up. Then he followed them and waited until it happened. When they went off that mountain road, Justice got out of his car and made his way down to the wreck to be sure they were dead. He's the type that would be that thorough.''

''Except he screwed up. He didn't know he left his calling card in Danner's car.''

Ryson smiled. ''I can't wait until he finds out. I'm going to be the one to tell him, too—you just wait and see. It'll be right around the time I'm putting the handcuffs on and reading him his rights.''

Chapter Five

"You're finally back," Jack Novak said as Whitney swung open the squeaky-hinged door and entered the modest office suite of Novak and West. "It's been hours."

Jack was standing by their secretary's desk, a brief from the files in his hands, an expectant look on his face.

"Where's Isabel?" Whitney asked as she slipped into the side chair next to the secretary's desk.

"She's down the hall at Checkmate fixing their second-hand copier," Jack said as he dropped the brief in the secretary's in-basket and plopped down on the checkered sofa in the small reception area. "You know our Isabel. If it's broken, she has to get that little screwdriver kit out of her purse and try to fix it."

"Have you warned them over at Checkmate that the score so far is machines twenty and Isabel zilch?" Whitney asked.

"Naw. They're P.I.'s. Let them exercise their surveillance-and-observation techniques. Besides, why spoil Isabel's fun?"

"Jack..."

"Oh, don't worry. I called our local repair shop. Mr. Guru Fix-it will be arriving just about the time Isabel's last screwdriver bites the dust. Happy?"

Whitney smiled. "You're a good guy, Jack."

"Yeah, that's what all the women tell me. It's one of my favorite accolades, ranking right up there with 'I think of you just like a brother.' Now, stop stalling and tell me how it went with Adam Justice."

Whitney chuckled. Jack really possessed a down-to-earth niceness that matched so well with his unruly mop of sandy hair and his smile so full of boyish charm.

"Adam Justice is everything they say about him, Jack. Darkly handsome, erudite, ultraclassy, the epitome of suave sophistication."

"I didn't mean Justice personally," Jack said impatiently. "I meant the papers his wife left for him—the ones we've been madly speculating about for the last week. Come on, give. Her will was in the envelope, right?"

"And a couple of other surprises."

"I recognize that sparkle in your eyes, Whitney West. If you don't start talking soon, I'm strangling you."

Whitney laughed, then quickly related what had happened, enjoying Jack's rapidly changing and readable expressions. What a difference it was being with a man who wasn't afraid to show what was going on inside him.

Jack was really likable. She'd often thought it was a shame there were no sparks between them. The last man who had gotten her passion to pounding had been Skip. And dear old Skip had skipped out three years before.

It always struck her as ironic that Skip—who possessed so much in the way of physical passion—had so totally lacked passion for all the really important things in life.

In the end she was glad to see him go. A man who didn't care about what *really* needed to be cared about was a waste of a woman's time.

Besides, not even Skip had been able to give her the exciting rush she felt in front of a jury, standing up for the rights of her client, knowing what she was doing was important. As long as she had that, she could do without the inferior, transitory physical passion that a man could provide.

"Unbelievable," Jack said, slumping against the back of the couch when Whitney had finished relating the day's events. "You didn't have any idea about this business before Justice opened that envelope?"

"Not an inkling. Like I told you, Patrice never mentioned she had married Justice under a false name. And the 'little something' she said she wanted to go to the right people was at that time, worth around eleven thousand—more in line with the 'little something' description."

"And now it's worth more than thirty million dollars. Wow. What a media circus this probate is going to be."

"And as G.A.L., I'm going to be in on it all the way."

Jack frowned as he rested a knee on the edge of the reception area's checkered couch. "Whitney, this isn't our kind of case, and these aren't our kind of clients."

"What if I find Patrice has a blood heir somewhere, and the guy's a blue-collar worker who's just lost his job, or a single mom just barely making ends meet? Those are our clients, Jack."

"You're reaching, Whitney, and you know it. Besides, there may even be some rule prohibiting you from taking this G.A.L. appointment."

"Like what?"

"Like the fact that you knew Patrice personally."

"Be careful not to say that where it could be overheard."

Jack came forward on the couch. "You're not serious. You can't keep something like that a secret on a case this big."

"Why not? It doesn't matter that I knew Patrice personally. At least not legally. I can still represent her unnamed heirs—as long as I'm not one of them."

Jack looked at her straight and hard. "What's going on? I've never known you to lie in your life."

"I haven't lied. No one asked me whether I knew Patrice before she came to me with that envelope for Adam Justice. If they had asked, I would have admitted I did."

"Then why aren't you volunteering the information?"

"Because I want a chance at this case. I won't get it if Adam Justice or Commissioner Snowe learns of my prior relationship to Patrice. They're both so staid and cautious. I told you, Snowe almost didn't allow Adam to be executor, and Patrice appointed *him* herself."

"Why is it so important for you to be on the case?"

Whitney got up and walked over to the window. She gazed out at the busy, narrow Seattle street outside. The storefronts of a cornucopia of small shops and struggling businesses were crowded into old, worn buildings. It was a respectable area, but lacking the expensive crispness of the big-business section of the city.

Cars whizzed by, horns honked and brakes squealed as people jockeyed for the few available parking spaces. It was a typical scene that passed before her eyes every day. She wasn't really seeing it.

What she was really seeing was the face of a beautiful woman with large violet eyes and long golden hair—still vivid in her memory after all these years.

"Patrice entered my life at a crucial time, Jack. Knowing her changed its direction completely."

"You've told me about it, Whitney. I understand."

"Still, I've never understood why she did what she did."

"Is it important that you do, Whitney?"

"Yes, Jack, it is. I need to understand. I had a chance to find out once before, and I let it slip by. I've regretted it ever since. Now I've been given another chance. I'm taking it."

FRED DYKSTRA was not happy. The deadline on his gossip spot for the seven-o'clock news was late. He'd turned off his cell phone so his producer couldn't bug him. He frowned as he sipped the bitter courthouse-cafeteria coffee.

This summer had really marked a dry spell in terms of human-interest stories. The most exciting thing he had reported in months had been one of the judges going nude beneath her robes because the air-conditioning vent had gotten clogged, and her courtroom had turned into an oven. And even that juicy little tidbit didn't hold much in the way of a titillation factor, considering the judge in question was sixty-two.

Where was a good adulterer when you needed one?

Fred looked up to see Dwight Errent. He knew him as a senior clerk in room W285, the place where a hodgepodge of minor legal issues was resolved—civil dissolution, name-change orders, probate, guardian, adoption, minor settlement and receivership orders. It was the most boring place in the entire King County Courthouse. Fred avoided it.

But lately he was finding that Dwight wasn't so boring. The clerk was standing at the edge of the cafeteria with a full luncheon tray, surveying the tables, just as he had done every day this past week. Fred saw the clerk's eyes come to a dead halt when they spied Tiffany Kurrey, the new court reporter.

She was sitting alone at the table next to Fred's: early twenties, five-six, shaggy hair, extrashort skirt, extralong fingernails. Her lips were large and painted with that new lipstick that stayed intact like shellac, even after a full lunch. She was sipping a diet Coke through a straw.

Every day for the past week Fred had watched while Dwight looked for Tiffany only to then go sit at a table for one.

But today Dwight had a daring look in his eyes. Fred saw the clerk take a deep breath, make sure his hold on his tray was firm and then walk directly toward Tiffany.

"Tiffany, hi. Remember me?"

Fred felt sorry for Dwight. Both the guy's tray and voice were rattling.

"Nope," Tiffany said.

"We were introduced your first day. I'm Dwight Errent. Can I sit down?"

"I guess." Not exactly an enthusiastic invitation.

Dwight set his tray on the table and slipped onto the chair next to Tiffany. "So, how do you like the job so far?" Dwight began. Thankfully the tray had stopped rattling at least.

"It's okay, I guess."

"Something wrong, Tiffany?"

"The cases are so boring here. My sister is a court reporter in L.A. She says it's always full of action down there. She's been telling me I should move in with her."

"There's a really interesting case that will be in our courts soon, Tiffany," Dwight said fast, way too fast.

Fred wondered if Dwight was blowing smoke or if there was something to this.

Tiffany put down her drink. She leaned a little toward Dwight. "What's this interesting case about?"

Obviously Dwight was enjoying the way Tiffany was leaning toward him. Fred could also tell the young man probably realized his chance with his dream girl had come and he was only going to get this one shot.

Fred had anticipated Dwight's nervous scrutiny of the area. He had picked up a discarded newspaper on his luncheon table and had it completely shielding his face at the precise instant that Dwight looked in his direction.

One of the things that Fred had learned in his fifteen years of covering the court beat was that if people didn't see your face, they rather had a tendency to overlook the rest of you.

"All right, Tiffany," Dwight said, "but you have to swear to me that you won't talk about this."

"Come on. You can trust me."

Dwight's voice lowered. "You heard about that attorney's wife and her lover who were found in that old car wreck?"

"Well, yeah. It's been all over the news. It was that real good-looking attorney's wife. Adam Justice, right?"

"Wrong."

"But, Dwight, I'm sure they said it was Justice's wife. They ran his picture and mentioned the Justice Inc. law firm."

"Only it turns out that the woman used a false name when she married Justice, so they never were married at all."

"They weren't? Oh, wow. Did he know?"

"Not until he discovered her real birth certificate and a secret will under the name of Patrice Feldon."

Tiffany's words were expelled in an excited whisper. "A secret will?"

"And it gets even better."

Dwight paused. For effect, Fred realized. He was a far cry from the rattler who had approached the table only a few moments before.

"What?" Tiffany prompted.

"Patrice Feldon, the woman who was never really Adam Justice's wife, has left an estate worth more than thirty million dollars. It's all in stock in some pharmaceutical company."

Fred nearly dropped his newspaper.

"Thirty million dollars. Wow. Who gets it?"

"You'll have to wait until the case gets heard."

"You can't do this to me, Dwight. I have to know. Please?"

Fred kept his newspaper at his nose, listening intently to hear if Tiffany could weasel any more information out of the court clerk. Unfortunately for Fred, Dwight Errent had revealed all he was going to.

Still, Fred knew he had enough for a start. He'd just make a couple of calls to verify a few facts.

His producer was going to be very happy.

Of course, Fred was pretty sure Adam Justice wasn't going to be too thrilled.

"TIME TO UP THE ANTE, Mr. Justice," Mr. Kline said.

Adam turned to his personal trainer—who had the body of a mud wrestler, a face like a frog and a head as bald as a bowling ball—and watched him add another twenty-five pounds to his barbell.

"Why the extra weight?" Adam asked.

"That's the penalty for missing your session this afternoon. When your muscles hurt tomorrow, it will be a reminder not to let anything interfere with the maintenance of your health in the future. Remember, without your health, that fancy law practice of yours will mean nothing. Now give me eight of them. Slowly. Feel the burn."

Adam lifted the barbell without comment. When it came to physical fitness, he and Mr. Kline had an understanding. Mr. Kline spoke and Adam listened.

Adam's parents had first hired Mr. Kline as their personal trainer. When Adam's parents had retired to Hawaii and left him the law firm, they had also left him Mr. Kline.

Most days Adam couldn't decide which of his parents' legacies proved the more demanding.

In all the years that they had been together, he and Mr. Kline had never addressed each other any way but formally. Mr. Kline had insisted on the formality. He told Adam it was because he wanted him and all his clients to understand that maintaining health was a serious business.

Adam was not uncomfortable with Mr. Kline's formality—it fit easily with his own. And he took exercising seriously, just as he took everything seriously. It was another legacy from his parents. They lived by a motto that he had adopted at a very young age: You Do Something Right, Or You Don't Do It At All.

It had been a long time since Adam had missed a midday weight session. The only reason he had today was that he had given Whitney West his word that he would drive her to her car. He knew that he could have paid her taxi fare, and she would undoubtedly have considered his word kept. And handling it that simply would have served his conscience.

But he hadn't done that. He had deliberately prolonged being in her company today. And the reason was simple. He had wanted to be with her.

He was very used to women responding to him in undisguised invitation or distinct discomfort. Whitney West, however, refused to be either impressed or repressed by him. She seemed amused at his restraint and intent on challenging his control at every opportunity.

She was a bright, beautiful, desirable woman and she had ignored everything about him that reflected his masculinity. No woman had ever done that to him before.

He had read A.J.'s preliminary report on her. She and her law partner, Jack Novak, had been on the law review together in school and had been graduated at the top of their class. Both could have had their pick of some excellent associate positions at major Seattle firms. Today they could be commanding enviable salaries and probably even be on the fast track to partner.

Yet they had chosen to go into practice together on a shoestring in what was clearly a less-than-prosperous neighborhood. Their consistent wins in court proved they had what it took. But they handled mostly small cases and poor clients.

Still, Whitney West was satisfied and happy with what she was doing. Adam saw that very clearly today. What's more, he'd liked seeing it.

She wasn't married, and lived alone in a small house with a big mortgage on the east side of town. A.J. had found out that much personal background.

Adam knew the kind of women to avoid—those who were just playing at careers and who considered their real career to be finding a husband. Whitney was not that kind of woman. She had gone out and made her own life and was living it—with confidence and with pride.

That fullness of spirit and personality drew him as strongly as her beauty. But it was her refusal to respond to him that challenged everything about him that was male.

Naturally he had no intention of getting into anything heavy with her. He wasn't a man who repeated his mistakes.

But they would be working together on the Feldon estate. And as long as it didn't interfere with getting the job done, he saw no problem with accepting the challenge she had issued and proving to her that the man in him could not be ignored.

"That's enough, Mr. Justice," Mr. Kline said.

"I thought you said eight?"

"You just did twelve. Something bugging you tonight, Mr. Justice?"

"I'm . . . preoccupied."

"Get your focus back, Mr. Justice. You're too experienced to forget that if an exercise is to have true value, it has to involve both body and mind."

Mr. Kline was right, of course. Adam mustn't let thoughts of Whitney West distract him. He would have to be careful to handle this harmless flirtation with her just right.

Adam's cell phone rang. He laid the barbell down and picked it up, answering with his name.

"Mr. Justice, it's Sarah at the answering service. I just got a call from Fred Dykstra of 'Channel 5 News.' He suggested you watch his court-beat segment coming up in a few minutes. He also mentioned he'd be by the phone for the following half hour should you have any comment you'd like to make."

Adam thanked Sarah and disconnected the phone, trying to keep his sense of foreboding at bay.

"Mr. Kline, may I use the television in your office to watch a news report?"

"It's time for your next eight, Mr. Justice. I suggest you get one of your minions to tape the show for you."

"This is not something that can be delegated."

"Neither can your health."

Adam faced Mr. Kline squarely. He said nothing, but he knew his body English was clear. After a moment Mr. Kline shrugged and stepped back.

"You'll have to use the knobs on the front of the set to turn it on. I don't believe in using remote controls."

"Thank you, Mr. Kline. I will be back."

"And when you get back, Mr. Justice, there will be another fifty pounds on this barbell."

WHITNEY SAT at the kitchen table with her favorite meal in front of her. The carton called it a light and healthy stuffed turkey breast with sliced apples in raisin sauce. She called it a quick and no-hassle way to eat on a hot summer evening.

She took a bite and sighed in appreciation. It was yummy.

Jack always said that the worst part of being single was eating alone. But Whitney disagreed. Here she sat deliciously cool in just a T-shirt and panties, not having to worry if her thighs looked fat, eating exactly what she wanted, getting all the breeze from the fan, in full control of the TV remote.

Ah, pure heaven.

And afterward there was chocolate-cheesecake ice cream—a whole pint of it. All hers.

She could even eat it right out of the container. A fork and a spoon would be the extent of her dinner cleanup.

Yep, when it came to a quiet meal at home after a full day at the office, this single stuff wasn't bad at all.

"And now it's time for the courthouse beat with Fred Dykstra," the anchorman on the TV news said. "What do you have for us tonight, Fred?"

Fred Dykstra's familiar carrot-colored mop flashed on the screen. Whitney had seen the commentator once down at the courthouse while he was attempting to get a quote from a man who had tried to ride a horse into the building to protest a raise in parking fees.

Whitney couldn't remember much about the would-be cowboy, but she remembered how easily Dykstra had positioned himself in just the right spot to get his quote. Even the obnoxious, pushy newspeople hadn't been able to compete.

Of course, Dykstra's courthouse spot was more gossipy than real news. But it was generally entertaining. Whitney leaned back in her chair with her TV dinner on her lap and gave it her attention.

"Tonight I have an exclusive for you. An interesting new development has come to light following the mysterious deaths of Patrice Justice and Peter Danner, the couple whose bodies were discovered last week, apparently the victims of a fatal automobile crash seven years ago."

Whitney shot forward so fast she spilled raisin sauce on her thigh. She quickly dabbed her paper napkin at the spill, not taking her eyes off the TV screen.

"As you may recall from the news accounts of this story, Patrice Justice was the wife of Adam Justice, the senior partner at the small, prestigious Seattle law firm of Justice Inc.

"Or at least Adam Justice thought she was his wife. She wrote her name as Patrice Anne Waring on their marriage license when they wed eight years ago. But now her real birth certificate has been discovered, which proves that Patrice Waring Justice was really Patrice Feldon and she and Justice were never married at all.

"Why did she pretend to marry Justice? That's the mystery, folks. And not the only one that this woman's death has suddenly brought to life. It seems that Patrice Feldon has left an estate worth thirty million dollars. Yes, you heard me right. Thirty million.

"What's more, the estate is made up entirely of stock in a pharmaceutical company. Interesting, isn't it?

"I for one would like to know who this mysterious lady was and where she got all that stock that adds up to so much money. I rather think Adam Justice is probably wondering about that tonight, too.

"Well, that's your juicy tidbit from Fred Dykstra. Tune in tomorrow for more from behind the scenes on the courthouse beat."

Whitney punched the Mute button and sat back in shock as she digested Dykstra's report. How could he have gotten that information?

Her mind was still buzzing when the phone on the counter pealed suddenly. Whitney picked it up and said hello.

"This is Adam Justice," he announced calmly, coldly.

As if that deep, chilling voice could belong to anyone else.

"No, Adam, it wasn't me," Whitney spoke quickly, sitting straight up as though she were coming to attention. "And I'm convinced it wasn't you. God knows not even physical torture would have dragged confidential information out of you about this case, to Dykstra or anyone else. So, who was it?"

Whitney waited through what seemed like a very long pause for Adam Justice.

"Speculation at this point would be nonproductive, Ms. West."

"Which, I suppose, translates to mean you have no idea, either," Whitney said, leaning back in her chair. "And please, Adam, drop the 'Ms. West.' I'm innocent, remember?"

"What's on your calendar tomorrow?"

"Just a few routine items. Jack Novak, my partner, can handle them if necessary. Why? What do you have in mind?"

"I'll pick you up at seven-fifteen."

"To go where?"

"To start seeing these beneficiaries Patrice has named and advise them of her bequest before that, too, appears on the news."

"Do you think it will?"

"If Dykstra had known the beneficiaries, I've no doubt he would have revealed them. Whoever his source is either doesn't know who the beneficiaries are or is holding back on that information. Still, Dykstra won't be the only one on this now. After tonight the regular newspeople will be pursuing everyone and every lead associated with the subject."

Whitney exhaled a long breath. "Yes, you're right, of course. I'm pleased that you trust me enough to include me in these interviews with the beneficiaries, especially knowing that we could end up adversaries on this matter."

"This is not about trust, Ms. West. This is about professional ethics. I intend to conduct this discovery in an above-board manner. I expect you to do the same."

"Yes sir, Mr. Justice," Whitney said with a burst of exaggerated formality.

"You find my words amusing, Ms. West?"

"No, but I find their delivery reminiscent of the Sermon on the Mount," Whitney said smiling from ear to ear.

"Thank you."

"It wasn't a compliment."

"I know."

Whitney chuckled. "Look, Adam, I can understand your concern that we try to reach the beneficiaries first, but seven-fifteen is a little early for me. Can you make it eight?"

"At eight o'clock you and I will be in Commissioner Snowe's chambers, assuring her that Dykstra did not get his information from us."

"Yes, I suppose that would be a prudent move. She's going to be really ticked about this getting out. You must be pretty ticked yourself. By the way, if you ever want to yell or anything, I can lend a sympathetic ear—as long as you're not yelling at me, of course."

"I never yell at anyone," Adam said in his all-too-formal tone.

Whitney was more than tickled at the polished delivery of that disclaimer. "Someday you're going to have to tell me how you do that."

"Do what?"

"Say what you do with such absolute conviction. If you have a pen and paper handy, I'll give you my address."

"That is not necessary. I have it."

"You have it? How could you? It's unlisted."

Whitney came forward suddenly in her chair. "Wait a minute. So is my home telephone number. How did you get it?"

"I'm resourceful. I shall be at your door tomorrow morning at seven-fifteen. Good night, Whitney."

He hung up before Whitney had a chance to respond. Still, she smiled as she replaced the receiver on the base. She recognized the "I'm resourceful" line as the same answer she had given him that morning when he asked her how she knew about the funeral.

Adam Justice did listen, all right. And he definitely had a droll sense of humor, which delighted her. She was beginning to suspect he might even have a whole set of other emotions hiding behind that cool, impassive face and maddeningly proper tone.

And that rather delighted her, too.

"DO YOU THINK Commissioner Snowe believed us, Adam?"

Adam took his eyes off the road momentarily to look over at Whitney. She was wearing a lemon-colored cotton dress today with a long, full skirt, a short fitted jacket and her hair flowing soft around her shoulders. It didn't follow the current styles, but fitted her casual business style and natural warmth.

Adam reluctantly returned his eyes to the road. "What Commissioner Snowe believes is irrelevant, Whitney. We know we were telling the truth. That is what matters."

He could feel her smile and turned to see her eyes dancing suddenly with that ready humor that infused them with golden lights.

"I'm beginning to appreciate that in you, Adam."

"Appreciate what?" he asked, careful to maintain his nonchalant tone despite his rising curiosity.

"That air of unequivocal confidence you exude. It can't be acquired. It's too perfect. You must have been genetically encoded with it while still a sperm."

Adam returned his attention to the road once again, fighting a smile. It occurred to him that he had to fight a lot of smiles since he'd met this woman. He wasn't sure if that was a good or bad sign.

"So what have you learned about the D'Amicos of Tacoma?" Whitney asked.

"Beatrice D'Amico is Danford D'Amico's mother and apparently a homemaker. Danford is an illustrator at his uncle's store, a place called Kirkbin's Road Kill."

"Not exactly an enticing name for a firm."

"My investigator says it's a speciality store with posters and clothes geared to adolescents. Apparently they find the name attractive. The company is small, but it's been growing steadily, particularly over the last five years."

"The investigation firm you use is run by your sister, isn't it?"

"Yes. A.J. is helping out on this case."

"So her name is A.J. What do the initials stand for?"

"Courage."

"Either your spelling is atrocious or you're being deliberately obtuse."

"As you are such an astute observer of human behavior, Ms. West, I'm certain you can decipher which one."

"You're being obtuse."

"Thank you."

"It wasn't a compliment."

"I know."

She smiled. This polished, stylish man definitely had an engaging way about him.

"I assume you called the D'Amicos to make an appointment?" Whitney asked.

"My secretary was unable to reach Beatrice or Danford directly. A Mrs. Kirkbin advised my secretary that Beatrice is going to be at a doctor's appointment all morning and Danford at his uncle's store."

"So we're going to see him there. How old is he?"

"Danford Thomas D'Amico is twenty."

"That means he would have only been thirteen when Patrice died seven years ago. Has A.J. been able to find a link between Patrice and Beatrice or Danford?"

"No. But she has checked on the birth certificate Patrice left with her will. It's a forgery."

Whitney's eyes darted to his face in surprise. "You're not serious. The birth certificate that identified her as Patrice Dulcinea Feldon is a phony?"

"Yes."

"But she said that was her name," Whitney protested.

"She also told me her name was Patrice Anne Waring when we met."

"But in her will she said she had only gone by Waring and that Feldon was her real name. This is crazy. How many names did she have?"

"That's an interesting question," Adam said. "Let's see which one Danford D'Amico recognizes."

One frazzled, thirtyish salesclerk was trying to handle three young customers at Kirkbin's Road Kill when Adam and Whitney walked into the small, crowded shop filled with what looked more like battle armor than clothing. Adam did not approach the clerk immediately, but gave her time to attend to her customers' various demands for spiked helmets and swords.

Adam took the time to study the posters on the walls. Most of them combined the features of the human male with formidable beasts. The resulting hideous mythical beings had dripping fangs and were attired in full battle armor over the parts that remained identifiably human.

"These look like scenes out of bad nightmares," Whitney said as she moved up beside him, lightly brushing his suit-coat sleeve and treating him to a brief whiff of her warm, sweet scent.

"Can I help you?" a voice asked from behind him.

Adam turned to see the salesclerk escorting her last young customer out of the door with arms full of the accoutrements for conducting war and mayhem. The clerk was smiling, probably pleased to talk to an adult for a change.

"We're looking for Danford D'Amico," he said.

Her face went blank. "Danford D'Amico?" she repeated. "Oh, you mean Danny," she said as recognition dawned. "He's in there, where he always is."

She pointed to a door at the back of the small shop. It was nearly hidden behind a barrel filled with shields and swords.

Adam and Whitney skirted the barrel to stand before the closed door. Adam knocked on it. There was no answer.

"Just go on in," the salesclerk called. "He'll never hear you."

Adam opened the door and entered behind Whitney. The room was small, square, windowless, dark. It was crowded with freestanding, bar-on-wheels wardrobes filled with T-shirts. In the far corner, bent over an artist's easel beneath a single bare light bulb dangling from the ceiling, was a young man.

He had his back to them. As they drew near, Adam could see him sketching some hideous part-man, part-dragon figure. Similar figures had been imprinted on several T-shirts hanging off nails hammered into the bare wall behind him. He didn't look up from his work. He didn't even seem to be aware of their presence.

"Danford D'Amico?" Adam asked.

Adam's voice so startled the young man that he spun around, lost his balance and fell off his stool. Adam immediately stepped forward to offer his hand.

"Let me help you."

Danny looked a little uncertainly at him. Adam got the impression that Danny wasn't used to being offered a helping hand.

"Sorry, I . . . sorry."

What Danny was sorry for wasn't clear to Adam. It didn't seem all that clear to Danny, either. If Adam had to guess, he'd say the apology was an automatic reflex. Danny released Adam's hand the moment he was on his feet.

"Are you all right?" Adam asked.

"Yeah, fine. No problem."

Danford Thomas D'Amico was short, pale, gawky and way too thin. He had curly dark brown hair, ill-fitting glasses that were wearing a groove into his fine Roman nose and large brown eyes that had a bruised look to them. He seemed a lot younger than his twenty years, although Adam believed that impression might stem from his obvious lack of confidence.

"You are Danny Thomas D'Amico?" Whitney asked, her voice warm and sunny as she flashed the young man a smile.

Danny looked at her and blinked. "Y-yes."

"I'm Whitney West and this is Adam Justice, Danny. Your aunt told Mr. Justice that you'd be here. If you have a few minutes, we'd like to talk with you."

"Uh, sure, I, uh, I'm sorry but I don't have any chairs back here. You can sit on my stool."

Adam watched Whitney take the young man's stool and smile at him as though she had been given a place of great honor. She seemed to have a knack for knowing that attention from an attractive older woman went a long way toward giving a young man more confidence and putting him at his ease.

And from everything he had seen so far, Adam could tell Danny D'Amico was definitely a young man who needed someone to put him at his ease.

"Mr. D'Amico," Adam began, "Ms. West and I are attorneys. We've come to see you about a confidential legal matter."

Danny's face paled.

"There's nothing to be concerned about," Adam said evenly, recognizing his words had alarmed Danny. "Do you remember Patrice Feldon?"

"Who?" Danny asked.

"Patrice Feldon."

Danny looked at Adam blankly. "Sorry, don't know her."

"Does any other family member share your name, Danny?" Whitney asked.

"Nope."

"What is your father's name?" Adam asked.

"His name was Thomas Desmoni D'Amico."

"*Was?* He's dead?" Whitney asked.

"Yeah," Danny said. "He died when I was a baby."

"I'm sorry," Whitney said. Adam noticed she didn't just say the words. She sounded as though she meant them.

"Do you have a grandfather or uncle who shares your name?" she asked.

"My grandfather died before I was born, and my dad was an only child. I'm the only D'Amico left. On my mom's side they're all Kirkbins."

"Are you certain that the name Patrice Feldon does not sound even vaguely familiar to you?"

"Yep."

"Where were you seven years ago, Mr. D'Amico?"

Danny looked at Adam as though he had to be kidding. When Adam maintained his sober expression, Danny shrugged. "Right here. I've been working for my uncle since I was thirteen."

"In this small, dark room?" Whitney asked, her tone and facial expression displaying obvious dismay at the thought.

Danny shrugged. "I'm used to it."

"How did you get started?" Whitney asked.

"My uncle wanted me to sketch out some of the designs the kids at school were asking me to paint onto their leather jackets. He had my designs imprinted on T-shirts and sold them. When I got out of high school, he hired me to design the posters and T-shirts and stuff at the store."

Whitney squinted at the emerging nightmare on the easel. "Your attention to detail is remarkable," she said after a moment.

"But the subject matter sucks, right?" Danny said, surprising Adam.

"It's just not my taste," Whitney admitted.

"Yeah, it's kids who like this sort of thing," Danny said, trying to sound superior. "I did once, too, before I outgrew it. I've been tired of doing this stuff for a long time now. Only thing is, they sell pretty good so my uncle tells me I got to keep doing them."

"What would you like to draw?" Whitney asked.

Danny shrugged. "Different things."

"May I see some of those different things?"

Danny's eyes darted uncertainly to Whitney's face. Adam imagined he was trying to determine if it were genuine interest in her eyes. When he seemed reassured, he turned toward Adam.

"I would like to see, too," Adam said.

Danny hesitated a moment more before stepping around Whitney to rummage behind several paintings he had stacked up in a corner. Just before pulling one out, he looked uneasily at the open door into the shop.

"Shall I close it?" Adam asked, sensing Danny's disquiet.

Danny nodded, and Adam quickly and silently closed the door.

Danny hesitantly handed the first painting to Whitney. Adam stepped closer to see.

The painting was far different from the man monsters lining the walls. It featured three smiling faces, two adults and one child. As dissimilar as the man and woman's features were on either side, the child's face in the middle linked them together. He reflected the big brown eyes and prominent widow's peak of the mother, and the Roman nose and curly brown-black hair of the father.

"What a beautiful family," Whitney said, the sincere warmth in her voice filling the room.

For the first time a small smile found Danny's mouth.

"That's you as a young boy, isn't it, Danny?" Whitney asked, pointing to the child.

He nodded.

"And your parents?"

"That's my mom. I never saw my dad. But this is what I think he must have looked like."

"He's a handsome man, Danny. Did your mother help you to compose his face?"

"No, my mom's . . . she's never seen this picture."

"Are you saying you painted what you imagined your father would look like based on your mother's features and yours?"

"Yes."

"That's remarkable. He looks so perfect I can't imagine his appearance any other way. How did your dad die?"

"It was a bus accident. It wasn't his fault."

Danny's tone had suddenly become defensive when he added that last, hasty sentence. He looked down at his paint-stained hands, uncertain if he had said the wrong thing.

Adam understood when Whitney's next question smoothly eased away from what was obviously a painful topic. "Have you done anything else like this portrait of your family?"

Danny nodded and rummaged again through the stack of posters coming out with several more composites. Adam noted a light layer of dust on the edge as he handed the first one to Whitney.

"When one of the salesgirls saw my family's painting, she asked me to draw her and her boyfriend and what their future child would look like if they had one."

Like the first drawing of faces, Adam could see that this one included the images of two adults. Only this time there was a little girl between them. Her happy little face picked up subtle features inherent in those of the prospective parents. It was a remarkable projection and very believable. Despite the nightmares that populated his other illustrations, Danny obviously had an eye for beauty when he concentrated on the human face.

"This is great," Whitney said, her natural warmth once again coming through her tone and expression.

Danny's smile was even bigger this time. "This is just an early sketch. The final one was much better. The salesgirl insisted on paying me for it. She showed it to her friends. For a while there I was spending all my spare time doing this kind of stuff."

Danny handed over the rest of the sketches to Whitney. Adam could see each of the fictional children emerged with the best of the features of its prospective parents, yet with a distinctive look and personality of its own.

"Danny, I'm so impressed," Whitney said after she had studied them all. "I've never seen anything like these drawings."

"Ah, stuff like this is done all the time now," Danny said, but his eyes were shining. "They've even programmed computers to do it. They call it the Gene Machine or something like that. The couple goes into this booth and have their pictures taken, and then the photo machine combines their features to project those of their future child."

"Still, I doubt a machine could do anything as beautiful as these," Whitney said. "Are you still painting them?"

Danny looked down at his hands. "Naw, my uncle found out. He got real mad and made me stop."

"Why is that?" Whitney asked.

"He doesn't like me to fool around with stuff that isn't going to make the store money."

"Not even when you do it on your own time?"

"Yeah, well, I guess you could say I owe him all my time."

"Why would you think that, Danny?"

"He took me and my mom in when my dad died. We didn't have any money or anything. We still live with him and my grandfather. We owe them everything."

As Danny said the words, his shoulders slumped as though they were strapped in some kind of tight emotional harness.

Adam watched as irritation passed through Whitney's eyes. "I'm sure you've more than repaid any debt, Danny," she said, the irritation coming out in her tone.

Danny looked at her with a curious expression in his eyes.

"Mr. Justice is the executor of Patrice Feldon's estate," Whitney continued on a lighter note. "Ms. Feldon has named you and your mother as beneficiaries in her will. Would you try to remember her for us? She might have been using another name, Patrice Waring."

"Sorry, but that name doesn't sound familiar, either."

"She was a very beautiful woman with large violet eyes and long blond hair."

"Naw. Someone like that I would've remembered. Besides, it stands to reason there's been a mistake, doesn't it? I mean why would anyone like her leave *me* anything?"

"What's going on in here?" a voice boomed out as the door suddenly swung open. Danny jumped backward, his face freezing in what Adam recognized as pure dread.

Chapter Six

Whitney swiveled in her seat to see a middle-aged man standing in the doorway with too much girth around his waist and too much arrogance around the cigar hanging out of his mouth.

She watched as the man's eyes swept over Danny, Adam and then her, coming to rest on the drawings she held in her hands.

His face twisted in anger. "So that's it. You're at it again."

"No, no," Danny said. "It's not what—"

"Shut up!" the man screamed. "Don't tell me any of your lies, you little bastard. I got eyes."

Whitney put down the drawings and got to her feet, anger rising in her throat. "Now, listen here—"

"No, you listen, lady. I'm Edgar Kirkbin, this is my shop, Danny works for me and he does what I say. And I say he doesn't do that crap anymore. So you can just take your boyfriend here and hit the road."

Whitney's anger rose so fast against this foul-mouthed man and his foul-smelling cigar that she had to fight to get a disclaimer through her lips. "This man is not my boyfriend, and we are not here to—"

"Yeah, yeah, sure. Outside."

Kirkbin lunged forward to grab for Whitney's arm. He never connected. Because suddenly Adam blocked his way.

Whitney was used to fighting her own battles and normally resented any interference. But she felt a very uncharacteristic feminine flutter in her midsection as she saw how Adam stood like an impenetrable wall between her and Kirkbin.

Adam's eyes were ice blue daggers. For the first time Whitney noticed a faint white scar reddening on the side of his neck, snaking down into his white dress-shirt collar. He said not a word. He didn't have to. His considerable height, breadth and menacing expression said it all.

Whitney smiled in satisfaction as she watched the arrogant look on Kirkbin's face disintegrate into one of growing alarm. He stepped quickly back, retreating to the door.

Adam slowly and deliberately turned his back on Edgar Kirkbin. That piercing cold light that had been trained on Kirkbin a mere second before disappeared completely from his eyes as he looked at Danny. His voice was even, formal, respectful.

"Mr. D'Amico, please accept my apologies for coming by at this inconvenient time. Here is my card. If you will let my secretary know when you and your mother are available, we can meet to further discuss the legacy left to you. Ms. West?"

Before taking Adam's formally offered arm, Whitney turned to Danny and extended her hand and offered a smile.

Danny pocketed Adam's card and took her hand, looking a little dazed at the treatment he was receiving from her and Adam.

Whitney gave his hand a warm shake. "It has been a pleasure meeting you, Danny. Thank you again for indulging my curiosity regarding your drawings. Do contact Mr. Justice's secretary at your earliest opportunity. You will not be disappointed to learn the details of your inheritance."

Whitney took Adam's arm then and walked with him out of the small back room, not missing the look of incredulity that had the cigar drooping limply out of Edgar Kirkbin's mouth.

"It was something less than discreet to tell Danny that he would not be disappointed to learn the details of his inheritance in front of his uncle," Adam said as he held open the passenger door of the Jaguar for Whitney a moment later.

Adam's voice was deep and even, his facial expression as calm and unchanging as always. But Whitney understood all too well the reprimand he was sending her. She slipped into the seat and waited for him to circle around to the driver's side before responding.

"I was trying to give Danny a little dignity back after his uncle so rudely tried to snatch it away," she said. "And you can't pretend that you weren't doing the same thing when you made such a point of mentioning 'the legacy left to him.' Why, you positively rode to the rescue of both me and Danny when that foul-mouthed Kirkbin started throwing his weight around."

Adam fitted the key into the ignition but didn't start the car. "You say that accusingly, Whitney. Am I to understand that such gestures offend you?"

"Offend me? They floor me. Mind you, I am perfectly capable of fighting my own cigar-smoking dragons with grabby hands, thank you. And I would appreciate your letting me do so in the future. But the fact that you took it upon yourself to dispatch that one so effectively has left me in awe, Adam Justice. Who would have guessed that inside all the formal armor you wear so well there really was a knight?"

Whitney leaned over to plant an appreciative kiss on his cheek. Her lips lingered on the smooth firm heat of his skin while a warm tingle wiggled down her spine. And then quite suddenly Adam turned his head, and she found her lips on his.

For one mouth-watering moment they stayed motionless—their breaths mingling, his warm and tantalizing on her skin as their lips barely brushed. Her pulse began to pound as his formidable presence invaded her body and that clean, sophisticated, woodsy scent of him filled her senses so fast she felt dizzy.

Then his deep voice strummed in her blood as he murmured against her mouth, "Penetrate any armor, Whitney, and what you will encounter is not the knight, but the man."

Whitney willed her body to heed the serious tone of his warning, but the only response it gave was a soft, beckoning sigh.

His lips answered that sigh as they pressed against hers, spreading a luscious liquid warmth throughout her entire body.

The heat was so sweet and intense that it shot like pain through her. In the space of a heartbeat she was totally lost to the pure ecstasy of it.

She moaned, her lips parting eagerly beneath his on-slaught, wanting, craving the invasion. He moved in deeper, wetter, hotter. Her head swam with the scent and taste of him. Passion, swift and sharp, engulfed her, shooting down her spine, spearing deep in her womb.

She gripped his shoulders, drawing him closer—wanting more of him, so much more. She could feel his muscles tensing hard beneath her fingers. His arm circled her waist, and he drew her tightly against him, breast to breast.

The shock of feeling his rock-hard chest against her breasts sent a wave of high-powered voltage through her. She felt deliciously singed in every cell of her body. Adam Justice kissed with the same devastating perfection with which he did every-thing else.

The sudden, loud beep of a horn behind them caused Whitney to stiffen. Adam released her immediately and pulled back. They both swung around to look out the rear window.

A harried-looking woman in the driver's seat of a van full of eager adolescents was gesturing at them impatiently. She obviously had been waiting for Adam to vacate the only parking space in front of the store.

Adam turned the ignition key and started the engine, oblig-ingly pulling away from the curb.

"My apologies, Whitney," he said, his voice cool and for-mal. "That was extremely poor judgment on my part."

Whitney was still vibrating and breathless and thrilled to the bone. The last thing in the world she wanted to hear was that he was sorry he had made her feel this way. She studied his hard, polished-marble profile. Not even a strand of his hair was out of place. Just as though nothing had happened. And apparently for him nothing had.

It was at that precise moment that Whitney knew it wouldn't be hard at all to hate this man.

She crossed her arms over her chest. "You're right. It was poor judgment," she said, trying to sound as nonchalant as he, but fearing she sounded just disappointed.

"Next time I shall select a time and place that will preclude any interruptions."

Next time? Whitney sighed as her arms relaxed along with her pique. Next time. He was planning on kissing her again.

On second thought she was beginning to think it might be very hard to hate this man.

She stole another look at his profile, a hundred questions crowding into her mind at once. "You seem pretty sure I'm going to want you to kiss me again."

"Are you going to tell me you don't?"

Whitney opened her mouth to say something, then closed it because she had no idea what to say.

She certainly couldn't deny she wanted him to kiss her. Not after her enthusiastic response. She liked kissing him. *Liked*. What an understatement.

They didn't speak for a couple of miles. It was just as well; Whitney doubted she could have managed any coherent conversation. She was shaken.

The logical part of her brain analyzed the situation and told her that she had simply been kissed. No big deal. She had been kissed before.

But another part of her—the part that was still whirling and humming and way out of control—knew it had been a lot more. She had never been kissed *like that* before.

She stole another look at the clean, classic lines of his profile and the beautiful shape of his mouth—that hot, demanding mouth. And her body erupted in a whole new set of tingles.

"Whitney?"

God, she loved how the beautiful cadence of his deep voice vibrated in her ears and melted her bones when he said her name.

"Yes, Adam?"

"Have you filed the proper papers with the court to establish your G.A.L. status?"

Here she was, still all tied up in emotional knots by his kiss, and there he was, right back to business.

She crossed her arms over her chest once more.

There's a lesson to be learned here, she told herself. *Don't let yourself get so damn carried away just because some far too handsome, coldhearted hunk kisses you until your ovaries go into overdrive.*

"Yes," she answered in her best imitation of his formal tone. "Took care of it yesterday afternoon while you were with the bald lady."

What the hell, if he could be so damn detached about this, then so could she.

"I'm reassured to hear that, Whitney. It would be disappointing to lose your company now due to an administrative oversight."

Whitney looked over at his profile and saw the slight rise to the side of his lip.

And that's when she understood. That comment had been Adam Justice's very formal way of saying that he had liked the kiss, too.

"You do that so well," she said after a semblance of thought and speech and breath had returned to her.

"And what is that?"

"Surprise me."

Adam reached over to the stereo control on the dashboard and changed the music from a bold classical selection to a soft instrumental one. "You are rather proficient at rendering surprises yourself."

"Thank you."

"It was not a compliment."

Whitney smiled. "I know. Is it my imagination, or are you moving a bit stiffly today?"

"My muscles are a little sore."

"Well, good for the bald lady."

"There is no bald lady, Whitney."

"Is there any lady?" In light of her current feelings, Whitney realized this was something she had better find out.

"That depends on why you are asking."

Whitney turned in her seat to look at his profile. There was a message in his careful wording—a very clear message. She was beginning to realize that Adam Justice always selected his words very carefully.

"I asked because you kissed me, Adam."

"If you are concerned about what complications might arise from something more than a professional relationship developing between us, the answer is no, there is no lady."

Something more than a professional relationship. His formal phrase in his elegantly formal voice stirred up a whole new set of thrills and chills inside her. This situation was getting serious. Whitney knew that she was showing all the physical and emotional signs of coming down with a bad case of Adam Justice.

She reminded herself that she was smarter than this. These feelings for Adam might have crept upon her unawares, but now that she recognized them for what they were, it was time to put them in perspective. She hardly knew this man.

"Actually I asked because I was concerned that it might be a jealous lady friend who's been following us," she said, proud to hear a touch of nonchalance in her tone.

His pause was short and entirely unreadable.

"What makes you think someone is following us?"

"A brown Chevy pulled out behind us when you picked me up at my place. That same brown Chevy is behind us now. And although it's a little too far back to be certain, it could be a woman in the driver's seat."

"Could it?"

"You tell me. I've seen you checking it out in your rear-view mirror several times on our way to Tacoma and now on our way back."

"You are observant."

"You don't seem too concerned that someone is following us. Aren't you even the least bit curious? I could be dating a very jealous, grim-faced goalie with the Seattle Thunderbirds who is taking exception to my being here with you."

"I would find that very difficult to believe."

"Oh? Why?"

"If you were involved with someone else, I do not believe that you are the kind of woman who would have responded to me the way you did. On the contrary. I doubt you would have kissed me at all."

He was right, of course. But he didn't have to sound so damn sure of it.

"You think you know me that well, do you?"

"That well, yes."

"I see that inborn confidence you exude extends into personal matters."

"Thank you."

"That was not a compliment."

"I know."

The side of his mouth was lifting again. Whitney turned her head so he couldn't see her smiling. This handsome, stylish and sophisticated hunk had his own distinctive and compelling charm—no two ways about it.

"It would be helpful to find out why Patrice left Danny D'Amico so much money when he seems to have no knowledge of her."

And there he was back to business again. Well, maybe she'd best get back to it, too. She gathered her most casual tone and concentrated on looking out of the windshield and ignoring the far too handsome man beside her.

"Maybe Danny's mother is the connection."

"That is the probable explanation," Adam said.

"I wish Danny's mother hadn't had a doctor's appointment this morning. My curiosity is just slightly less than my impatience. Where are we going now?"

"To keep our appointment with Dr. Rubin."

"Won't we be early?"

"No, I gave Dr. Rubin a two-hour span for our arrival, anticipating our meeting time with Mr. D'Amico might run short or long. The Rubin address is on the other side of Seattle. We'll be there within my agreed-upon time frame. Once we get within cell range, I'll call to let Dr. Rubin know we're on our way."

"That's at least twice you've said *Dr.* Rubin. I thought there were two of them—Esther and Jacob?" Whitney said.

"When I called to set up the appointment for this morning, Dr. Esther Rubin said she would be the only one available to meet with us. Her husband, Jacob, has patients he is committed to see."

"What kind of doctors are they?"

"Psychiatrists," Adam answered.

"Do you know if Patrice ever had occasion to see a psychiatrist?"

"Not that I'm aware of."

"Where do the Rubins practice?"

"Downtown Bellevue."

"And they live in Seattle? Well, at least they're driving against all the commuter traffic. Still, I feel for people who have to spend huge chunks of their time getting to and from work. I'm fifteen minutes away from the office—five of which is spent finding a parking space—and I even grump about that. You still living up on Queen Anne Hill?"

"How do you know where I live?"

"Patrice mentioned it that day in the office. She said she was happy with the house but wanted to change the decor—something about getting rid of the busy wallpaper, covering the furniture in white silk and doing the floors in black marble."

"You have a remarkable memory."

It was probably sounding too remarkable. Whitney cautiously added a disclaimer, reminding herself to watch her words in the future. "I don't get too many clients who live on Queen Anne Hill. Or ones with the money to re-cover furniture in silk and redo floors in marble. Those things tend to stick in one's mind."

"COME IN, Mr. Justice, Ms. West," Esther Rubin said as she showed Adam and Whitney into her old, gray, towering Victorian in an older residential section of Seattle.

Esther Rubin was a short, slim, silver-haired woman, with dark, curious eyes and Ben Franklin glasses perched on the end of her nose. Despite her sixty-odd years, she walked down the hallway with the energy of a youngster. She preceded them into a cool, large cavern of a living room, lined with faded wallpaper and filled with lots of furniture odds and ends, none of which matched, but all of which had a homey, lived-in look.

She gestured for them to be seated, then stood before them with her hands folded together at her waist. "How about some hot tea?" Esther coaxed, pointing to the bright yellow ceramic pot with the one yellow and two blue cups sitting on the coffee table.

"I'd love some," Whitney said.

"Not for me, thank you," Adam said.

Esther poured Whitney and herself a cup, then sat down next to Whitney and across from Adam on a worn love seat that had definitely seen better days. For practicing psychiatrists, the Rubins didn't appear too prosperous.

"Dr. Rubin, I appreciate your seeing us on such short notice," Adam began.

"I must admit, you rather piqued my interest, Mr. Justice. I don't get many calls from lawyers telling me they have a confidential matter to discuss. So what's it about?"

"Do you know Patrice Feldon?"

Adam watched as Esther's eyes squinted and a curious tightness gripped her shoulders. She took a small sip of tea and set her cup down on the table.

"Yes, I do," she said very carefully.

"Dr. Rubin, Patrice Feldon has died and named you and your husband as beneficiaries in her will."

Esther's eyes opened, and sadness flowed into them. Her shoulders slumped as the tension left them. "Patrice dead?" she said. "I can't believe it. How did it happen?"

Adam looked at Esther's sad eyes and slumping shoulders and suddenly found himself at a loss for words.

"She died in an automobile accident, Dr. Rubin," Whitney said, filling in the silence of Adam's pause. "It happened seven years ago, but her body was only recently found."

"Seven years ago?" Esther repeated, her head cocking to one side as she chewed on the inside of her cheek. "Why does that sound familiar? Who else was it who...wait, you don't mean hers was the death reported in the news last week?"

"Yes," Adam said.

Esther jolted upright on the love seat as she apparently recalled the particulars.

"Dear heavens, you're *that* Mr. Justice. The news report said Patrice married you and then left with...oh..." Esther's sentence trailed off without completion.

"I'm sorry, Mr. Justice," she said hurriedly, clearly embarrassed. "I didn't know. I mean when I heard the name Patrice Justice, I didn't connect her with the Patrice Feldon I knew. They never ran Patrice's picture, you realize. And when you gave me your name this morning, I didn't think—"

"It's all right," Adam said, eager to end Esther's continuing apology. "Dr. Rubin, did you watch the courthouse-beat segment with Fred Dykstra on last evening's news?"

"No, I have dinner to get in the evenings. We have a big family here at present. I have time for very little else."

"Then I will be the first to tell you that Patrice left an estate in excess of thirty million dollars."

"Thirty million dollars?" Esther repeated, her eyes growing wide as her right hand clutched the frayed arm of the love seat.

"Patrice has stipulated that you and your husband are to receive a third of what remains after taxes, probate costs and whatever debts may arise are addressed," Adam said.

"Where did Patrice get thirty million dollars?" Esther asked no one in particular. She was looking off into space, her eyes glazed and unfocused. Adam had the distinct feeling that the woman had not heard anything he had said from the time he first mentioned the sum.

"Dr. Rubin?" Whitney called after a moment, obviously trying to get the woman's attention. When her first call received no response, Whitney raised her voice. "Dr. Rubin?"

Esther snapped her head in Whitney's direction. "Oh, I'm sorry. It's just so...I'm quite stunned."

"That's perfectly understandable," Whitney said, smiling.

"Dr. Rubin, how did you know Patrice?" Adam asked. Adam watched as Esther Rubin's eyes suddenly squinted again as they turned toward him.

"Why do you ask, Mr. Justice?"

"Because I'd like to know who Patrice was to you and you to her."

Esther said nothing, her shoulders once again tensing.

"It will help Mr. Justice to understand your relationship to Patrice when he goes to court to represent your interests in the estate," Whitney explained.

"Go to court?" Esther repeated in a startled voice as she turned toward Whitney.

"The will is to be probated in court, Dr. Rubin. And with this kind of sum at stake, there are bound to be a lot of questions. The thirty-million-dollar figure was announced on television last night."

Esther Rubin's face paled. "Were our names mentioned?"

"None of the beneficiaries were mentioned," Whitney said. "But it's just a matter of time. The will's been filed. Once the case comes up on the calendar—"

"No," Esther breathed on a long exhale of breath. "Please, no."

"What's wrong, Dr. Rubin?" Whitney asked, alarm in her voice as she set her cup down and leaned toward the woman.

Adam, too, was becoming concerned at the growing pallor and despair on Esther's face.

"I know Patrice meant well by her bequest," Esther began. "But you must stop this. We don't want the money."

"You don't want ten million dollars?" Adam asked.

"I'm throwing myself on your mercy, Mr. Justice. Please, take our names off the will. Please."

"That's not possible," Adam said, more than surprised. It wasn't often he met someone who was so ready to reject a fortune.

"What is the problem, Dr. Rubin?" Whitney asked. "Why are you so determined to turn down this money?"

"I can't tell you. I . . . I'm sorry. Maybe it would be best if you left now. I have to . . . to call my husband."

"Dr. Rubin," Whitney said, "Mr. Justice is sworn to represent your interests in this matter. He's on your side. Please, don't send us away. Let us help you."

Esther Rubin sighed and slumped back against the love seat. "What if Jacob and I just refuse the money?" she asked.

"Your refusal would undoubtedly make even more headlines than your acceptance," Adam said solemnly.

"Mr. Justice is right," Whitney added. "You'd be swamped by reporters wanting to know why. And if you refused to tell them, then that would just mean they would go digging for the answer."

"Then it's . . . hopeless," Esther said on another long sigh.

"Maybe not," Whitney said. "Tell us what's troubling you, Esther."

Whitney's voice had become very soft and gentle as she switched to Dr. Rubin's first name. The look on her face matched her tone. Adam could see Esther reacting to both.

"Do I dare?" she asked, although the question seemed directed mostly to herself.

"Esther, we don't want to invade your privacy," Whitney said. "But we can't help unless we know."

Esther chewed the inside of her cheek. "There is so much at stake."

"I can see that, Esther," Whitney said, resting her hand on the woman's arm.

"Where would I start?" Esther asked no one but herself.

"Where it's comfortable," Whitney answered anyway.

Esther studied Whitney for a moment and nodded, seemingly reassured by what she heard and saw. "At the beginning, then," she said.

The air in the room seemed to still as Esther leaned forward and rested her hands on her knees. Adam watched as the light in her dark eyes focused on images far beyond the confines of those in her viewing range.

"Jacob and I met in medical school. We were married the same day we were graduated. Seven years later we became reconciled to the fact that we weren't going to be blessed with children. Still, we had our professions as psychiatrists. And each other. We were happy. Then one night we came home and there he was, all tangled up in my rosebushes.''

"He? Who?'' Whitney asked.

"Joe,'' Esther said, a small smile circling her lips. "He was nine years old. Thin. Cold. Tired. Hungry. Starving. And so very scared. He'd gotten caught in my rose trellis when he'd climbed up to try to eat the birdseed in a feeder at its top. The trellis had split and he had fallen through, trapping his leg in the lattice.

"Jacob and I untangled him and brought him inside. He was shaking like a little leaf. I bandaged his hurt leg. Gave him some hot food. Poor little tyke ate like he hadn't had any food in days. As it turned out, he hadn't.

"He wouldn't speak. At first we weren't sure he even could. I was determined to find out. I stayed home with him the next week while Jacob went off to take care of our patients.

"Joe followed me around like a puppy, helping me around the house, cutting the lawn, pruning the bushes. He was so eager to please and so grateful for a kind word. It took all seven days before he told me his name. His age came next. And gradually the rest.

"As practicing psychiatrists, Jacob and I had dealt with the painful adult trauma that results from childhood abuse. But we had never met an abused child in the flesh before. It was quite an awful experience to look into Joe's sad eyes while he spoke of the atrocities his parents had committed and pointed to the evidence on his scarred little body. Jacob and I, we...well, we were so angry and sad and...we just knew we had to help.

"We contacted the authorities and reported the abuse. They contacted his parents. They claimed Joe was a discipline problem. He was placed right back in their hands.''

"The authorities didn't believe the boy?'' Whitney asked.

"This was twenty-seven years ago, Ms. West. Joe was just a runaway to them. And their job was to see that runaways were returned home to their parents. Sadly it can happen that way today, too, particularly with abuses that are hard to prove.''

"What happened to Joe?" Whitney asked.

"He escaped a second time. He didn't come to us. Not that I blamed him. However good our intentions, we had been instrumental in his being returned to those monsters. The authorities found him several months later in an alley. He'd been living off the streets. He was so malnourished that he'd caught pneumonia and just . . . died."

"Oh, no," Whitney said.

A tear escaped from Esther's eye. "It still makes me cry, Ms. West. I'm sorry."

Adam watched as Whitney put her arm around the older woman and hugged her. Her brandy eyes were full and beginning to overflow. She reached into her jacket pocket and produced tissue for them both.

"It's okay, Esther," Whitney said. "It makes me cry, too. Call me Whitney."

Esther looked into Whitney's face and smiled as she dabbed at her eyes.

"I found my second runaway a couple of months later," she began again after a moment. "Her name was Gina and she was thirteen. She was trying to talk the manager of a theater into hiring her as an usherette. He knew the identification card she had shown him that said she was eighteen was false. He went to his office. I heard him calling the police to come pick her up.

"I got her away before they showed. I told her right off I knew she was a runaway. It was her eyes, you see. She had that same sad, scared look that Joe had had. I told her she could stay with Jacob and me for as long as she liked, and we wouldn't ask any questions.

"She stayed. But she was jumpy. And leery. I found blankets missing from the linen closet, food from the kitchen. One night, after she'd been with us a few days, I peeked into her bedroom just to make sure she was all right and found her gone."

"She just left? Without a word?" Whitney asked.

"I was so frightened and worried for her. A girl that young, alone on the city streets at night. I prayed that she would be all right. I prayed that she would come back to us."

"Did she?"

"The next morning she came down to breakfast as though nothing had happened. I was stunned and enormously relieved. The next night I watched. Just as soon as she thought Jacob and I were asleep, Gina left her bedroom and went to sleep in the old toolshed at the back of the yard. When I looked in the toolshed, I found the extra blankets and Melanie, Gina's younger sister."

"And that's where the extra food had gone," Whitney guessed.

"Yes. Gina was afraid to tell us about Melanie. She had been betrayed by her adult caretakers so badly, she no longer felt she could trust anyone."

"How was she betrayed?" Whitney asked.

"Gina's new stepfather was making sexual advances to her. He threatened that if she didn't cooperate, he'd go to her little sister."

"Where was the girls' mother?" Whitney asked.

"She had remarried this man just months after the girls' natural father had died. Gina said her natural dad had loved her and her sister, but her mother had always been distant. When Gina told her mother about what the stepfather was trying to do, she screamed at Gina and beat her with a broom, accusing her of making it all up. She warned Gina that if she ever repeated such lies again, she'd kick her out of the house."

"What an incredible imbecile!" Whitney said. For the first time Adam heard anger in her normally mellow voice. Its fierceness surprised him.

"Yes, and it cost her her daughters. Jacob and I had learned our lesson with Joe. We couldn't risk returning the girls to that home. We talked it over and told Gina and Melanie that they were welcome to live with us for as long as they liked."

"Good for you," Whitney said immediately. Adam could tell she meant it, too.

"It was dangerous, of course, Whitney. If caught, we could be charged with kidnapping. But when I saw the tears of relief in Gina's eyes as she hugged her little sister and then us, I knew we were doing the right thing."

"You sure were," Whitney said, sending Esther a big smile. Adam rather felt at that moment that Esther and Whitney had forgotten he was in the room.

He didn't mind. He enjoyed watching the openness and honest warmth flowing between these two women. He had never seen respect or trust develop so fast. Whitney had that indefinable quality that invited both. He knew it was because of Whitney's presence here today that Esther was even telling her story.

"The girls' mother and stepfather lived in Kingston," Esther continued. "Gina had gotten herself and Melanie to Seattle by taking the ferry across Puget Sound. I realized the authorities might figure they came to Seattle when they didn't find them on the other side.

"I dyed the girls' hair red and cut it short. I bought them glasses with thick rims and plain lenses. I took them shopping for clothes with extra padding to make them look fatter. I told everyone that they were my sister's children and had come to live with me because she had passed away.

"Jacob made them dummy birth certificates with new names. Enrolling them in school was the difficult part, because they had no transcripts. Jacob explained that away by telling the principal that my sister had been an eccentric schoolteacher and had insisted upon teaching the girls at home."

"Did it work?" Whitney asked.

"Exceptionally well. Only then we were invaded."

"Invaded?" Adam repeated.

"Gina and her sister had been living on the street in a grocery-store carton for two days before she applied at that theater for a job. There were other street kids out there who knew about the girls. Word got around that they had found a safe, secure home. Soon they were showing up on our doorstep."

"More runaways?" Whitney guessed.

Esther nodded. "In a month's time we had eight of them bunking at the house. They needed food, shelter, a warm, safe place. Plus many of the youngsters had been traumatized by their brutalizing experiences and desperately needed counseling—and love. I couldn't turn them away."

"Of course you couldn't," Whitney said.

"By then I'd stopped going to our office and was staying home with the kids. Establishing new identities and integrating the girls into the family had not been an easy thing. We knew we couldn't do it with eight more kids. It was while I was trying to think of what to do that social services raided us."

"Raided you?" Whitney repeated, her voice clearly alarmed.

"We told the social-services worker that the eight kids huddled around sleeping bags in the living room were visiting friends of our daughters, Gina and Melanie.

"She looked at their faces and their clothes. The children were clean, but Jacob and I hadn't been able to afford new clothing for them. One by one she asked the kids their names and addresses. One by one they gave fictitious names and addresses. The social-services worker wrote down what they said and then she went away."

"She believed you?"

"Not for a minute. The kids told us. Their harsh experiences had taught them to read people very well, particularly people in authority."

"What happened?" Whitney asked.

"The social worker was back in an hour with two policemen to round up the kids. Only, by then the kids were gone, except for Gina and Melanie, of course. When the social worker asked where the other kids were, Jacob and I looked her straight in the eye and told her they had gone home. I never knew I could lie so straight-faced. Or that I could feel so proud doing it."

Whitney gave Esther another hug. "What did the social worker do?"

"Oh, she made some threats and talked the two police officers into watching the house for the next few days. But after that she gave up."

"And the kids?"

"As soon as the police left, they came back. Jacob sold our life-insurance policies to get the children new clothes and add another bedroom and bathroom to the house. But before the construction could begin, one of the policemen who had been with the social-services worker dropped in unannounced and caught us with all the kids at dinner one night."

"Oh, no," Whitney said. "What did you do?"

"Jacob stood up and told the policeman he would fight him if necessary to keep the children from being returned to the adults who had abused them. You must understand, Whitney, Jacob is only five-five, slenderly built and a very gentle man. He had never been in a fight before in his life. He knew he never had a chance when he stood up to that big, burly policeman. But I was never so proud of him. That night my Jacob became the tallest man in the world to me."

Adam watched as Esther wiped away a proud, bright tear from the corner of her eye. Without having ever met him, Adam envied Jacob Rubin very much at that moment. Whitney's eyes were swimming, too. She was not reticent about showing her feelings. Adam respected that in her, because he respected the feelings he was seeing.

"Please tell me your husband didn't have to fight the policeman," Whitney said.

"No, he didn't fight him. We had the policeman all wrong. His name was Patrick and he wanted to help. He had talked it over with his wife. They wanted to take one of our runaways into their home to raise with their children."

"To adopt the child as you adopted Gina and Melanie?" Whitney asked.

"No, Patrick drew the line at paper forging. He and his wife simply wanted to take care of one of the runaways and keep quiet about where he came from. A month later Patrick brought over another couple who wanted to give one of our runaways a home and were willing to keep our secret. And thus began the solution to our problem."

"You placed the runaways in unofficial foster homes," Whitney said.

"Yes. Not that it didn't present some significant problems. They needed schooling, and without birth certificates and transcripts, the public system was out. So I started conducting academic classes, as well as therapy sessions, here at the house. The foster parents dropped the kids off for their therapy sessions and schoolwork during the week and picked them up to return to their foster home for the night and weekends."

"What an ingenious plan," Whitney said appreciatively.

"Still, it seemed like we'd no sooner get our last runaway placed, when another would appear on the doorstep. Then one day one of those runaways was a young girl with long golden hair and big violet eyes—the most beautiful creature I have ever seen."

Adam shot forward in his chair. "Excuse me, Dr. Rubin. Are you saying that *Patrice* was one of your runaways?"

"Yes, Mr. Justice," Esther Rubin said, her dark eyes coming to rest fully, sadly, on his face. "And, without a doubt, my most difficult challenge of all."

Chapter Seven

"Why did you call Patrice your most difficult challenge?" Whitney asked while Adam was still trying to get over his surprise at what he had heard.

"Her beauty was like a magnet. It drew everyone who saw it. One glance and a smile, and the runaway boys at the house were tripping over themselves to do things for her. The first two couples who came to the house after she arrived actually got into a heated argument over who would get her. Nothing like that had ever happened before.

"Even my Jacob found himself captivated by her. He refused to let either of the would-be foster parents take her. He wanted to make Patrice one of our daughters, as we had Gina and Melanie. He was as smitten with Patrice as everyone else who saw her. For the first time since I started taking in runaways, I sensed we were in real danger."

"I don't understand what you mean by danger," Whitney said.

"How can I explain? With her beauty, with her angelic smile, with the soft melody of her voice, she went about enticing my Jacob away from us. When he got home each night, she would take him the newspaper, get him his slippers, ask him about his day. Jacob began ignoring me and our daughters, so eager was he to please the lovely creature who seemed to need him so badly as she sat at his feet looking up at him adoringly."

"How old was Patrice then?" Whitney asked.

"Barely twelve. An incredibly beautiful, needy innocent. It was a heady combination and an absolutely irresistible one to Jacob. To protect my family, I knew I had to do something."

"What did you do, Esther?"

"While Jacob was at work one day, I called up one of the couples who had seen Patrice and wanted her so badly. I told them to come get her."

"How did Patrice feel about that?" Whitney asked.

"When she met the couple and saw how they fawned over her, she seemed very happy and eager to go. I was floored. I thought she would be upset to leave Jacob, she seemed so attached to him. I didn't understand her, you see. If only I had, I wouldn't have made the dreadful mistakes I did."

"What mistakes?" Adam prompted, finding himself eager to hear about the childhood of the woman whom he had known so well yet so little.

"In eight weeks' time Patrice's foster mother returned her to me. We had never had one of our runaways returned before. Her foster mother felt very bad about it, but said she had to. Patrice was obsessive in her devotion to her foster father and seemed intent on stealing all his attention from his wife and natural daughter. Her foster mother was very uncomfortable with the situation."

"Patrice behaved toward him as she had toward your husband?" Adam asked.

"Exactly. What's more, she saw nothing wrong with her behavior. She told me she was just making sure her foster father loved her. When I asked about her foster mother and sister, Patrice told me that if they wanted his love, they should have gone after it as she had."

"She didn't care what her foster mother and sister thought of her?"

"No. Only the affection of the man of the house mattered to her."

"How very... odd," Whitney said.

"Yes. Patrice never spoke about what had driven her from her home, but it was very clear that wherever she had come from, she had been taught to play up to men and ignore women. She focused all her attention on the man of the house—whatever house she was in. I tried to talk to her about the danger she would be in if she made the wrong male her focus of her attention. I explained to her that a young girl as beautiful as she could be physically and emotionally preyed upon by the unscrupulous and unprincipled, who might choose to misinterpret her affection. I tried my best to impress upon her that she needed to learn to relate to men in a more reserved manner for her own protection."

"Did it make an impression?" Whitney asked.

"She laughed at my concern. She told me she knew how to handle men much better than I ever would. And the way she said it sent a chill down my spine, because I knew it was probably true."

"At twelve years old," Whitney mused, shaking her head. Adam heard the sadness in her voice and saw it reflected in her face, as well.

"I knew she would need many years of therapy to work her way through these harmful attitudes and behavior. Yet the harder I tried to get through to her, to make her understand this, the more she ignored me. I felt so incredibly helpless. And every day she stayed in my home, I had to watch her stealing all my husband's attention. I confess to you that although I said nothing to Jacob, I was about to admit defeat, call the authorities and let others deal with her."

"But you didn't," Whitney said.

Esther sighed. "No, thank God, it never came to that."

"How did you finally solve the problem?" Adam asked.

"I didn't. One day it solved itself, quite by accident."

"What happened, Esther?" Whitney inquired.

"I spilled milk on the kitchen floor while getting lunch for the kids and slipped in it, falling and breaking my wrist. I lay on the floor in terrible pain, trying not to cry out for fear of alarming the children."

Whitney said nothing but she rested her hand on Esther's arm. Esther returned the gesture with a small smile.

"My clumsiness proved to have a silver lining," she continued. "Suddenly there was Patrice leaning down to me. Out of all the children, she was the one who immediately came to my rescue. She helped me to a chair, got me some hot tea to drink, called Jacob and told him what happened. I was amazed at her presence of mind, her concern.

"Jacob came home and took me to the hospital for X rays. It was a bad break. It took nearly three months to heal. And every day it was Patrice who helped me to get around. She became my hands, seeing to the needs of the other children. She was so gentle and sweet to me—as angelic as her smile—displaying a side of her character I never dreamed existed."

"What made her change that way?" Adam asked.

"I think it was my weakness. I know that seems strange, but I think the fact that I needed help made her feel powerful, just like she felt when she wrapped men around her finger. Patrice liked to feel needed. It made her feel in control."

"What happened after your wrist healed?" Adam asked, fascinated to learn these things about Patrice and wondering how much more there was to know.

"I took my cue from her treatment of me while I was ill and never again assumed the mother or teacher role with her. I asked her advice. She liked the power of giving her opinion. I tried to make her feel needed in every way possible. We became friends."

"You must have been her first female friend," Whitney said.

"Yes. I began to have hope for her. I found a foster family who was already raising one of our runaways. I spoke to the mother—a lovely woman who I knew would understand how to make Patrice feel needed. I warned both parents that Patrice had difficulty understanding that love was more than the outward manifestation of affection. When I placed Patrice with them, I continued to see her thrice weekly in therapy to make sure things were going well."

"Were they?" Adam asked.

"Patrice was getting better at displaying more appropriate behavior toward her own sex. But she still needed the adoration of every man she met. Still, she came a long way in those years she spent with her foster family."

"Was Feldon the name of her foster parents?" Adam asked.

"No."

"Who was the family who reared her?"

"I'm sorry, Mr. Justice, but that is not a confidence I can share."

"How did she come to the Rubin house?"

"That also involves another whose identity I must keep confidential."

"Can you at least tell me if Patrice Feldon was her real name?"

"Yes. It was."

"Patrice left me a birth certificate under the name of Patrice Dulcinea Feldon, Dr. Rubin. It was a phony."

"That's because we could never find her real one. Jacob made that birth certificate for Patrice."

"How do you know that Patrice Dulcinea Feldon was her real name and August 2, 1964, was her real birth date?"

"Because she told us her name and the date of her birth when she first came to us at twelve."

"And the names of her parents that appear on the birth record?"

"Those are made-up names. Patrice could never give us the names of her real parents."

"Why not?"

"It was . . . beyond her ability."

"Why did you supply her with a birth certificate?"

"There's a ritual each youngster who comes to us here at the Rubin house goes through. No matter what name we give them through their growing years to protect them, when they reach their majority at eighteen and know their abusive legal parents or guardians no longer have dominion over them, they have the option to send for their real birth certificates and take a G.E.D. test using their real name."

"So they can reclaim their real names?" Whitney guessed.

"Yes. They use the results of the G.E.D. test in lieu of a high-school diploma to establish an educational record they can rely on to start them at a job or college."

"Patrice took a G.E.D. test using the birth certificate you made for her in the name of Feldon?" Adam asked.

"And did quite well on it, too. I was certain she'd go on to college when she left her foster home at eighteen."

"Do you prohibit your runaways from talking about their experiences at the Rubin house when they leave?" Adam inquired.

"No. Our graduates are discreet, of course. But they have shared the specifics of their upbringing at the Rubin house with their spouses. Some of the best foster parents we subsequently obtained were once the runaways we took care of here."

"Why didn't Patrice ever tell me about you and your husband?" Adam asked.

"I'm not surprised she didn't, Mr. Justice. Patrice was always very secretive. Whatever the home environment she left, she never once spoke of it, not in the entire six years she was in therapy with me. When I asked her, she would tell me she couldn't remember."

"Do you think she had amnesia?"

"No. I'm sure she remembered. Her statement about knowing how to handle men told me that. She only said she didn't remember because she didn't want to talk about it. That's the way it is with some of our children."

"Why is that?" Whitney asked.

"They have to learn to see themselves as wonderful, worthwhile human beings, deserving of care, attention, praise and love—the real kind, not the false attention some were made to think was real. Many children can't redefine themselves in a healthy way if they are made to dwell on how they were treated before. I believe Patrice was one of these."

"Did you ever hear from her after she left?" Adam inquired.

"Oh, yes. She sent Christmas cards every year. She never put a return address on her cards, though, so I couldn't write back. That was typical of her secretive streak. When her cards stopped coming seven years ago, I thought she simply had no time because she had become so focused on her new life. It happens. Jacob and I generally see it as a good sign. I never realized that in Patrice's case it was because she was dead.''

Esther paused after that statement, her eyes becoming sad as she looked down at her hands.

Adam was aware of the large room filling with quiet. He had a sudden image of Patrice as a young girl standing in this room, walking over to a sofa, sitting down. She was looking at him with that angelic smile on her face—the one that radiated the knowledge and power of her incredible beauty.

"Esther, you're still taking in runaways, aren't you?" Whitney asked.

Whitney's question extinguished the ghostly vision from Adam's mind and sharply refocused his attention on Esther's face.

"That's why you're afraid of accepting the money Patrice has left you," Whitney went on. "You're afraid if it gets out about what you're doing here, the authorities will stop you from continuing."

Esther nodded. "For the most part social-services workers are good-hearted souls. Over the years, we've worked with them to return runaways to their homes when it was the right thing to do. When it wasn't the right thing to do, those social workers have turned a blind eye to us, just like our policeman, Patrick, did. But if what we're doing becomes public— as it most surely would with the receipt of this money—these good people would no longer be able to pretend we aren't here, doing what we're doing. They'd have to close us down.''

"Esther, don't worry," Whitney assured as she took both the woman's hands into hers. "Mr. Justice and I won't let that happen. We'll think of some way to protect you and the kids.''

"MR. JUSTICE AND I WON'T let that happen?" Adam repeated as they drove away from the Rubin house.

"Well, what was I supposed to say, Adam? 'Sorry, Esther. After twenty-seven years and all you and your husband have sacrificed, you're just going to have to close your doors to the kids who need you so badly?' ''

"It may be what she'll have to do," Adam said. "We have to report what we've learned about the Rubins to Commissioner Snowe. Legally we have no power to keep the beneficiaries' names out of the court records when this probate comes to trial."

"I don't accept that, Adam. We're two smart attorneys. We should be able to think of something. Esther and Jacob are wonderful people, the kind who truly make a difference in this world. They take youngsters with no future and see that they get one. All they're asking is to be left alone so they can continue."

"You don't have to sell me, Whitney."

"I'm glad. I confess that I did have a few uncertain moments back there when I wondered if you were going to turn them in."

"As beneficiaries of Patrice's estate, the Rubins are my clients. I am not in the habit of 'turning in' my clients. Besides, I suspect they need to help those children as much as those children need to be helped. You realize it was not wise for you to have become so friendly with Esther Rubin."

"What are you talking about?" Whitney asked, surprised.

"You may find yourself representing blood heirs with interests directly opposed to the Rubins' on this matter."

"Just because I may end up representing another's interests doesn't mean I can't respect and admire the Rubins."

"But you know their secret. You could use that information as leverage to further your own clients' positions."

"Just a minute here. Are you suggesting I would blackmail the Rubins? Adam, how could you imagine I would do such a thing?"

He looked directly at her. For the first time Whitney saw a hint of something behind the cool look in Adam Justice's eyes—something warm and very blue. And then he smiled.

It was a small smile, but it changed his face so much. He suddenly looked younger and much less foreboding—and so damn devastatingly gorgeous—it took her breath away. A warmth began to rush through her body. His voice was at its deepest, smoothest.

"Actually I *was* having trouble imagining you doing such a thing, Whitney. But I had to bring it up to be sure. I wouldn't be doing my job if I didn't address all pertinent issues affecting my clients."

As Adam looked back at the road, Whitney swallowed and shook her head, trying her best to get her breath back.

"That's not what is going on here, Adam. You like what the Rubins are doing and you want to help. You don't fool me one bit."

"I wasn't aware I was trying to fool you, Whitney."

"No, I suppose not. But all that stiff formality you're encased in can be very misleading, Adam Justice, and I'm convinced you use it to your fullest advantage."

He said nothing in direct response. But as she watched his profile, the edge of his lip turned up. There was so much she wanted to know about him—so much that made her curious.

"Adam, how did you get that scar on your neck?"

The edge of his lip immediately fell back into its straight line. "A small accident."

"It doesn't look that small."

He said nothing in response.

"Was it long ago?"

"Yes."

She waited for some elaboration, but there was none. "You're not going to tell me about it, are you?"

"No."

"Not even if I agree to tell you about my tattoo in return?"

"You have a tattoo?"

"We have a deal?"

"No."

Despite his disclaimer, Whitney could see that the edge of his lip was rising again. She turned her attention back to the road, reminding herself that she'd promised herself that she'd remain nonchalant about her attraction to this man.

"We could petition Commissioner Snowe to see if she would be amenable to conducting this probate behind closed doors, Whitney. That way it might be possible to keep the names of the beneficiaries from becoming common knowledge."

"Do you think she'll go for that?"

"Not without more-compelling grounds."

"Then why did you bring it up?"

"Because we're two smart attorneys. We should be able to think of more-compelling grounds if we put our minds to it."

Whitney chuckled. "And there's another thing you do well."

"Which is?"

"Use my own words back at me."

He turned and smiled at her again, and she sighed, not nonchalantly at all.

The car phone rang. Adam picked it up. Whitney listened in on his half of the conversation.

"Yes, I've been out of cellular range conducting interviews," Adam said. "Who's there?"

Adam's part of the conversation disintegrated into nothing more than a few affirmative responses.

When he finally hung up, Whitney was ready with her question. "What's going on?"

"The Justice Inc. offices have been swamped this morning by newspeople and would-be blood heirs to the Patrice Feldon estate."

"So it's started already. Well, Commissioner Snowe warned us. I'd best get a fax off to the press notifying them that I'm the G.A.L. for the unknown heirs. That will get them off your firm's back. Looks like I'll be spending the next few days in the office interviewing the claimants."

"My secretary has shortened your time somewhat. He asked them to put down the full name and birth date of the Patrice Feldon they claimed to be related to. Only one could. He told the others to go home."

"What did he tell the one who could?"

"He's waiting in my office. If you wish to speak to him in confidence, a room will be made available for you."

"You've included me in your conversations with the beneficiaries—I intend to include you in my conversations with claimants. If he's a legitimate blood relation to Patrice, I'm sure we both want to see that he gets what is fair. I'm surprised you didn't understand that about me by now."

"I did. But I received the impression a little while ago that you would rather I not admit such personal knowledge about you."

"So what are you doing now?"

The side of his mouth curled upward. "Displaying admirable sensitivity."

Whitney laughed.

"CHAD BISTER," the man said in a voice that boomed as he held his hand out to Adam.

Bister was in his late thirties, nearly six-four, with the athletic build of a football player accentuated by a formfitting T-shirt and tight jeans. He had a deep tan, a bushy mustache, wavy blond hair, hazel eyes and the kind of smile a man wore when he knew he possessed the physical strength to break another man in half.

Adam took Chad Bister's hand but found that Bister kept his fingers splayed, preventing any firm contact. Bister quickly dropped Adam's hand and turned to Whitney, his eyes lighting up with that particular brand of speculation that predatory males used when they met an attractive woman. He was apparently sizing her up as a prospective sexual partner.

Adam was finding nothing about this man even remotely tolerable.

"And who might you be, little darlin'?" Bister asked in a smooth Southern drawl that had obviously just materialized for her benefit.

"This is Whitney West, an associate of mine," Adam said. "Ms. West is the court-appointed guardian for any possible unnamed heirs, Mr. Bister. She'll be conducting this interview. I am here as an observer."

"Well, little darlin', this is a pleasure," Bister oozed as he took her hand in his.

Whitney shot Adam a quick, speculative look. Adam knew she was probably surprised by the "associate" title he had given her.

He was a little surprised at it himself. He had deliberately used it to imply Whitney was one of his staff and, by inference, off bounds to Chad Bister.

Not that Bister was taking the hint. His eyes were devouring her from top to bottom, as his smile spread from ear to ear.

Adam was uncomfortable with Bister's obvious interest in Whitney—but even more uncomfortable with the feelings of jealousy it was provoking.

What had he once called it—a harmless flirtation? From the instant she had melted into his kiss and into his arms, it had become anything but harmless. It was hot.

He had set out to prove to her that she couldn't ignore the fact that he was a man. Problem was, now he couldn't ignore the fact that she was a woman.

And when he watched her with Danny D'Amico and Esther Rubin—saw the warm, genuine feelings overflowing from inside her—he found there were other emotions he couldn't ignore.

Whitney was making him feel things he hadn't felt in years. And they were feelings he would just as soon have done without.

Whitney finally reclaimed her hand from Bister's grasp and gestured him into a chair on the other side of the conference table. He ignored the one she gestured to and pulled up the chair next to hers.

"Mr. Bister—" Whitney began.

"'Chad,' please," he interrupted. His smile was all charm. "No need for formality now, is there?"

Adam could see Whitney's returning smile was courteous but lacked her normal warmth. If she was affected by the man's attention, it didn't show. For a woman with such a communicative face, she could obviously play it cool when the occasion called for it. He was not disappointed that she'd identified this interview as such an occasion. She had her pad and pen out, ready to take notes.

"Are you a resident of Seattle?" she asked.

Chad sat back in his chair and threw out his chest. "Born and raised. I gave my address and phone number and all that stuff to the secretary outside. Feel free to call me anytime, Whitney."

"For someone from Seattle, it's odd that you have a Southern accent."

Chad smiled. "Well, I did spend a few years working oil rigs down in Texas. I suppose I picked up a little accent."

Suppose nothing, Adam thought. This guy turned that phony accent off and on like an oily gusher.

"Are you married?" Whitney asked.

Another big smile. "Not currently."

"What do you do for a living?"

"I own a boat-renting-and-leasing company on Lake Washington with a couple of buddies."

"What is your company's name?"

"Washington's Water Wings. Our motto is We'll Get You Nice And Wet." The look in Chad's hazel eyes and the pointed inflection in his voice underlined that motto with overt sexual suggestion.

Whitney gave no sign that she had received his signal, however. She merely wrote down the name. Adam was rather intrigued to see she possessed this far more formal side than she had previously shown to him.

Her tone remained cool as she continued to question Chad. "You obviously came to Justice Inc. today with some expectation, Mr. Bister. What is it?"

"I expect to lay claim to my part of Patrice Feldon's thirty million dollars."

Chad smiled again. But this time it was the kind of smile that said, *See how honest I'm being?* Adam always mistrusted such smiles. On Chad Bister, he surmised, it was just as phony as his accent.

"How are you related to Patrice Feldon?" Whitney asked.

"She was my sister."

"Why do you believe that?"

Chad sat forward, resting his huge forearms on the conference table and his eyes on Whitney's face. "Thirty-two years ago my mama gave birth to her while my daddy was overseas in Saudi Arabia, supervising the construction of some oil wells.

Only problem was, my daddy only had one conjugal visit with mama while he was under that two-year contract with that oil company. That visit had been ten months before Patrice was born.''

Chad leaned back, an amused smile claiming his lips. ''Now, my daddy didn't take too kindly to my little sister coming into the world on that very suspicious schedule. He came right on home to have a heart-to-heart with Mama about the situation.''

''What happened?'' Whitney asked, her voice cool.

''Mama swore up and down that she had a ten-month pregnancy. It was kinda hard to swallow, seeing as how Patrice only weighed in at six pounds. Still, that didn't stop Mama from trying.''

''Your father didn't believe her?''

''Not hardly. My daddy ruled our home. He was an autocratic SOB under the best of circumstances. These were not the best of circumstances. I was only six then, but my ears still burn with the names he called her as he knocked her around.''

Chad paused to chuckle. Adam felt chilled by the flippant way in which he related this incident of his father striking his mother, as if it were some big joke.

''Anyhow, after Daddy vented his spleen,'' Chad continued, ''he grabbed the baby and tore out the door with her, saying he wasn't going to raise any bastard. When he came back a few hours later, it was without Patrice. He told Mama she'd never see her again, and he'd see to it she never cheated on him again, too. Mama collapsed into tears. Daddy made good on both his threats. Mama never even knew what happened to Patrice. She was never the same after that. She caught pneumonia a few years later and died.''

''Why didn't she report your father's physical abuse to the police?'' Whitney asked. ''They would have helped her find her baby. She could have divorced him.''

''Darlin', you're looking at this situation from the position of a women's libber of the '90s. This was more than thirty years ago. Women were a lot more subservient then. And when

I say my father ruled our home, I mean he *ruled*. He married my mama back in her rural village in Eastern Europe when she was sixteen and then brought her to America. My mother was too afraid of him to ever challenge his authority."

"But if your father really believed your mother had cheated on him, why didn't *he* divorce her?"

"Naw. He knew losing her baby was a much worse punishment—as was making her stay married to him and endure a thousand insults a day. He hired sourpuss female guards to watch her around the clock so she didn't get near another man. He went to prostitutes openly and rubbed her nose in it. No, the old man knew how to inflict the worst kind of punishment. Divorce would have been much too nice."

His mother's infidelity and the cruelty of his father's retaliation were bad enough to have to hear. But Adam found the way Chad Bister related this sad tale to be more than offensive.

"What happened to Patrice?" Whitney asked, her tone getting colder with every question.

"After Mama died, my daddy told me that he'd dumped Patrice on Denise Feldon, his divorced sister up in Spokane. He told his sister to raise the kid and change its last name to Feldon, because he wouldn't have it carrying his name. He hated his sister nearly as much as Patrice. He said they were a perfect match."

"What was the full name of his sister?" Whitney asked.

"Denise Dee Bister Feldon."

Whitney wrote it down. "And you believe the Patrice Feldon, whose estate Mr. Justice represents, is your sister who was raised by your aunt?"

"That's why you're talking to me, right? Because I knew her name was Patrice Dulcinea Feldon. And that she was born August 2, 1964."

"Patrice Dulcinea is an unusual name," Whitney said carefully. "How did your mother select it?"

"I don't know why she chose the name Patrice. But just before Mama died, she told me she called my sister Dulcinea be-

cause she had just read *Don Quixote,* and she felt a kinship to
the character Dulcinea.''

"Losing your mother at such a young age must have been
very hard on you," Whitney said, a note of sympathy entering her voice.

"What the hell. Every few months my daddy had a new
broad living at our place to fuss over me. They all felt sorry for
the kid without a mother. Thing was, the older I got, the
younger they started getting. That old bastard really lived it up.
Still, my mother got her revenge on him in the end.''

"Her revenge?" Whitney said. "What do you mean?"

"Daddy got real sick and needed a kidney transplant a few
years ago. The hospital asked me to come in to see if I would
be a suitable donor. Turned out our tissues didn't match at all.
You should have seen his face when they told him and he realized I wasn't his kid, either. He died waiting on a donor
match that never came through.''

"I'm sorry."

"Don't be, darlin'. The old bastard called me every obscen-
ity in the book when he found out I wasn't his. Told me to get
out, that he never wanted to see me again. Wrote me out of his
will the next day. I'm glad I didn't have a kidney to give him.''

Adam watched Whitney's face grow shuttered and remote.
"You never knew who your biological father was?" she asked
after a moment.

"I pretty much figured it out after that tissue-donor thing.
Daddy was dark. My mama was blond, fair. So am I. So was
Patrice. And so was this big, friendly mailman I remember
sitting in the kitchen having coffee with my mama and making her laugh. What a cliché, huh? My sister and I look like the
mailman.''

Chad's smile was big and engaging.

"How well did you know your aunt, Denise Feldon?"
Whitney asked, her voice even tighter.

"I didn't. Only time I ever even heard she existed was when
the old man mentioned that was where he'd dumped Patrice.''

"You never tried to see your aunt or your sister?"

"Once, when I was about twenty-five and found myself up in the Spokane area with some friends. I looked in the telephone directory. No Denise Feldon was listed. I called the Feldons that were in the directory, but no one knew a Denise or a Patrice. Could be they had moved by then."

"Mr. Bister—"

"'Chad,' darlin'. Please. We've already established that my last name is a mere formality anyway, right?"

"Right," Whitney said, her voice barely civil now. "Do you have documents of any kind concerning your sister's birth?"

"No, 'fraid not. I went through all my daddy's things after he kicked. I'm sure he destroyed her birth certificate. I sent a request to King County. They said they had no record. Of course, Daddy had a large chunk of change in the bank around the time Patrice was born. He probably bribed some babe down in records to pull Patrice's birth certificate and destroy it. He was like that."

"I hope you understand that it will be very difficult to substantiate your claim to the Patrice Feldon estate without some verifiable records, proving you are her brother."

Chad leaned closer to Whitney and flashed her his best ladies'-man smile. "Yeah, well, I kinda thought maybe you could help me find those records, darlin'. Believe me, I'll make it worth your while when I get my hands on Patrice's dough."

Whitney moved back. "To be frank, Mr. Bister, I'm not even sure that these records you speak of exist."

Chad leaned against the back in his chair, confident and easy. "Oh, they exist. I'm her brother. I can even describe her for you, if you need some convincing."

"I thought you said you only saw her as a baby? How could you possibly describe her?"

"She was a very distinctive baby. She was born with blond curls and violet eyes and she had a dark red birthmark on her upper thigh, right here. It looked just like a question mark, complete with the dot underneath it."

Adam sat forward. He had forgotten about that birthmark, until Chad Bister mentioned it. And where Chad was
pointing was its exact location.

Could it be that Chad wasn't lying after all?

Chapter Eight

"I don't know what to think, Adam," Whitney said as soon as Chad Bister had left. "He knows Patrice's full name, her date of birth, her coloring. And this awful story he tells about the relationship between his father and mother has a tragic ring of truth to it."

"So you believe him?"

She sighed, wishing she could deny it. "If he made up this story about a lost sister, he certainly didn't make himself look any too good in it. The only time he even admits showing any interest in his sister is when he just happened to be in Spokane with some friends and looked up the Feldon name in the telephone book."

"And now that he thinks she's left some money he can get his hands on," Adam added. "Still, he knew about the red birthmark on her thigh."

Whitney bit her lip. "I hate to say it, but it looks like I'll need to hire an investigator in order to have Chad Bister's story checked out."

Adam's eyes drew to her face. "Why should you 'hate' to say it, Whitney? Emotionalism has no place here. The only way to approach this situation is to clearly and calmly review the facts of his claim to determine if it is legitimate."

Whitney came forward in her seat. "Come on, Adam. Even when the claim is presented by a lowlife like Chad Bister?"

Adam was looking at her intently, his expression as smooth and controlled as his voice. "I believe Mr. Bister was doing his best to charm you. Am I to understand he failed?"

Whitney crossed her arms over her chest. "You think I'm charmed by a man who obviously tries to make every woman he meets?"

"Perhaps if he offered you a romantic gift—"

"I am not a woman who can be persuaded by gifts. Or by charm. I'm insulted that you should think so."

"Are you?"

"Bister has as much depth of feeling as an oil slick. You heard the way he talked about his parents' relationship with such a lack of human warmth. He was totally untouched by the pain and suffering in that nightmare marriage. And while we're on the subject of Chad Bister, I am not your associate, Adam Justice. What did you think you were doing introducing me that way? Protecting me from the Big Bad Wolf?"

"Something like that could have crossed my mind."

Whitney leaned across the conference table toward him. "Well, get your mind uncrossed. I told you before I can fight my own battles. I am not Little Red Riding Hood, and I've had my fill of overprotective, overbearing older brothers. It was downright irritating when I was sixteen. It's damn intolerable at thirty-two."

Adam smiled. "Rest assured, Whitney, I do not feel at all brotherly toward you."

His smile was dazzling, his eyes a warm liquid blue as they suddenly locked with hers.

Whitney's anger was swept away along with every ounce of breath from her lungs. She was vaguely aware of a pounding in her ears and knew it was her heart. Here she had just proclaimed that she couldn't be charmed, and Adam was charming her with just a look.

In the next moment he was beside her, his arms wrapped around her, kissing her with a gentle fervor that fired her blood. God, he smelled and tasted so good. Her whole body seemed to sigh in pleasure as she melted into the strength of his arms and heat of his lips.

His hands caressed her back in long, lingering sweeps.

Ever so slowly he began to feather kisses across her cheek and beneath her ear until finally he had turned her back to him, swept aside her hair and was kissing the sensitive skin of her neck. Exciting tendrils of warmth and desire dove down her spine.

He seemed to know exactly where and how to touch her. She closed her eyes and let herself go limp within the muscular arm that wrapped around her waist, anchoring her closely against his chest. He held her tightly to him, possessively. He whispered in her ear, the heat of his breath sending new waves of excitement down her spine.

"I thought I'd be able to keep this cool and light, Whitney. But now that I've kissed you and touched you, I know better. I want you. But I don't want complications. If you can accept this physical pleasure as just that and nothing more, then we can let this happen. If it is not enough, I will stop now."

She twisted around so she could see his face. He released his hold on her immediately and held her gaze instead. His eyes were so electric blue she felt their heat burning deep inside her.

"You can just turn it off?" she asked.

"I can control myself, Whitney. I suspect the strength of our physical attraction is as surprising to you as it is to me. I do not intend the heat of a moment to lead either of us into something we might regret later."

She stared at him and tried to assess what she was feeling. But the problem was that she was feeling so much—and so much of it was new—that it was difficult to assess it all. Only one thing was clear. She was disappointed he wanted her only physically. She understood they hardly knew each other, and she had no right to expect his feelings for her to be more than physical. But she did expect them to be more than physical— because she expected more from him. He wasn't a Chad Bister. He shouldn't be acting like one.

"I don't participate in relationships that are only physical," she said. "A woman and a man should be together because they deeply care for and respect each other. Without

such a mutual sharing of feelings, such an affair lacks...
heart."

Adam rose and went over to stand by the floor-to-ceiling
window. She watched his polished profile as he slipped his
hands into his pockets and calmly stared at the sunlit space
needle jabbing the brilliant blue Seattle sky.

A long moment passed in which the only sound she heard in
the quiet conference room was the slow thudding of her heart.
Then his deep, cool voice filled the still air.

"Your choice is a wise one, Whitney. I commend you for
it."

She knew he meant it, too. For some strange reason, that
brought a sudden wave of sadness into her heart.

A knock sounded on the conference-room door.

Adam walked over to answer it. When he opened the door,
Whitney got a glimpse of the face and form of an immacu-
lately dressed, stocky, sixtyish man with a gray white crew cut.

"Sorry to interrupt, sir, but A.J. left this message when you
were in conference with Mr. Bister. I made the earliest arrangements, assuming that would be your preference."

Whitney watched Adam reading the information the man
had handed him.

"This will be fine, Smithy. Good work."

"Thank you, sir."

Adam closed the door on the man and returned to the table. When he looked at Whitney again, it was his cool, distant regard that told her he had returned to an all-business
relationship. He'd said he could just turn it off. He was proving he could do just that.

And that brought another wave of sadness to her heart.

"Can your partner take care of the next group of claimants
to Patrice's estate that will no doubt show up tomorrow?" he
asked as he retook his chair.

"Why, what's up?"

"A.J. has gotten a strong lead on the Carmichaels."

"And you're planning on our going to see them tomorrow?"

"Our plane leaves tomorrow morning for Las Vegas. A car will be waiting for us at the airport. Overton is about sixty miles due east. We should make it there and be back on the late-afternoon plane."

"Who arranged for all that?"

"My secretary, the man at the door just now."

"He's your secretary? He looks and sounds like a drill sergeant in a civilian suit."

"You have a good eye. Smithy was a master sergeant in the army before he took his pension and I signed him up for service here at Justice Inc."

"An army master sergeant turned law secretary. What's his story?"

"Feel free to ask him."

"You don't know?"

"It wasn't necessary to request that information. His skills and qualifications got him the position. Will tomorrow prove feasible for you?"

"I'll talk to Jack to see if I can get him to rearrange his schedule. How long has Smithy worked for you?"

"Approximately five years."

"And you aren't curious about why he chose to be a secretary at a law firm as his second career?"

"You are an extremely persistent woman."

"Thank you."

"It was not a compliment."

"I know."

He didn't smile this time. Whitney didn't know she could miss a man's smile so much, so fast. Or that she could feel so disappointed when she realized she might never see him smile again.

It's better this way, she told herself. *He can't offer you what you really want.*

"When will you know about tomorrow?" Adam asked.

"As soon as I get back to the office and talk to Jack. I'm sure it will be all right. Jack is quite flexible about these things. Adam, did you ever suspect that Patrice was an abandoned or abused child?"

"No. She told me her parents had died when she was five and she'd been brought up in loving foster homes. I suppose all of us who met her had trouble seeing beyond her beauty to the truth."

"Because her beauty was so overwhelming," Whitney said musingly. "And so powerful. Maybe there wasn't a male born who could resist her."

The thought crossed Whitney's mind then that Adam would never have offered Patrice only a physical relationship. No, for Patrice they all offered whatever she wanted.

She swallowed the bitter taste of that thought and refocused her mind. If she had understood who Patrice was, where she had come from, how she had been raised, maybe things could have been different. Maybe—

"You have a very unusual look on your face, Whitney," Adam said, cutting into her thoughts. "Is something wrong?"

"No...nothing," she lied, wishing he didn't sound so concerned. She suddenly felt close to tears.

She told herself she needed time to think, to adjust to what she had learned, to absorb, to try to understand. She told herself it had nothing to do with her having to face the fact that she wanted this man in ways he didn't want her.

She rose to her feet. "I'd best take a taxi to my office so I can send that fax off to the press, letting them know I'm G.A.L. on the probate."

"I'll drive you," Adam said rising.

Whitney turned toward the door. "No. I'd rather take a taxi, thanks," she called over her shoulder. And with that she all but ran out of the conference room.

"HAVE YOU LEARNED any more about Whitney West?" Adam asked A.J., the moment she answered her phone.

"Nothing I haven't already told you. Why? Something happen?"

"I'm not sure," Adam said, remembering the sudden odd sound in Whitney's voice and the look in her eyes as she fled the conference room. "It might be nothing."

"I haven't made her background check a priority. I can rectify that. Just say the word."

The more Adam thought about his suspicions, the more they seemed groundless. Whitney was a sympathetic person. She was probably just feeling bad about what Patrice had gone through. Or she might have been disappointed about his offering her only a physical relationship.

That had been a mistake. He should have realized she wasn't a woman of casual affairs. But he had wanted so much for her to respond to him, he hadn't been thinking clearly. And now that she had responded to him, he wanted her even more.

But he couldn't have her. Not on his terms. Not on hers. *You do something right, or you don't do it at all.*

"Adam?" A.J.'s voice prodded. "Is knowing more about Whitney West a priority?"

"No, let the in-depth background check stay on the back burner for now," Adam said. "Finding out about Patrice should be your number-one priority. How is Piper doing on researching those stock certificates?"

"She and Gavin are working on it. She'll contact you directly when she has something to report. Frankly her assignment is easy compared to the one I have. Finding what unofficial foster family raised Patrice is proving to be a bear."

"You'll do it."

"I wish I had your confidence on this one. The Rubins are very protective of their foster families, and everyone who knows what the Rubins are doing are very protective of them. I'm going to have to employ some pretty devious methods to get any answers on this. Is it really important to know who this family was?"

"It's important for me to know everything I can about Patrice, A.J."

"Only because you're still trying to understand why she left you for Peter, right?"

"A.J.—"

"Adam, I've always known their decision to go away together puzzled you as well as hurt and angered you. I've been luckier. At least I knew that Peter left me for Patrice because he was as dazzled by her beauty, as was every other man who met her. Shall I tell you why I think Patrice left you for Peter?''

''I don't need to—''

''Adam, I need to say it. Peter was never half the man you are. But take it from one who knows. Sometimes women fall for that kind of heart-thudding surface charm that came so naturally to Peter, just as men fall for the kind of overwhelming physical beauty that Patrice possessed.''

''I know, A.J. It's not necessary to—''

''Let me get it all out, Adam. Please. Bottom line here is that Patrice was the kind of woman a man could have, but never hold. She lacked that important ingredient known as staying power. Drop this, Adam.''

''I can't, A.J. If I'm to safeguard Patrice's money against claimants such as Chad Bister, I'm going to need to know everything about her to make sure the rightful beneficiaries receive what she intended.''

''Let someone else look after their interests. You don't need to remain Patrice's executor and safeguard anything for anyone. You owe her nothing! For heaven's sake, even the new birth certificate she presented you with is a phony!''

Adam took a deep breath and let it out slowly. ''I've accepted the responsibility as executor of the estate.''

''You can go to the court this afternoon and have yourself excused. And you should.'' A.J. paused to sigh. ''But you won't. And I'm just wasting my breath trying to talk you out of it. And now that I've had my say, I'll shut up and get to work investigating this damn woman who screwed up your life since the moment she entered it and is still screwing it up, even seven years after her death.''

''COME IN, ADAM,'' Whitney said early the next morning as she swung open her front door. ''I'm not quite ready.''

Adam looked at her robe and slippers and decided that Whitney was gifted with understatement.

He stepped past her into the entry hall, and she closed the door behind him, yawning.

"I'm sorry, but I just don't operate at full throttle in the morning. Particularly when you're thirty minutes early."

"We have a schedule change. I tried to reach you on the cell phone a few minutes ago, but I didn't get an answer."

"I must have been in the shower. What's up?"

"We're taking a later flight. Danny D'Amico called my answering service this morning and asked us to drop by his home to meet with him and his mother as soon as possible."

Whitney's eyes seemed to open a bit at that news. "You think he's figured out who Patrice was and why she left them that money?"

"That could be the case."

"Go on into the living room and make yourself comfortable, Adam. I won't be long."

She whirled around and moved down the hallway, leaving the tantalizing scent of sweet bath oil in her wake.

One of the light oak floorboards squeaked beneath Adam's shoes as he walked into the living room. It was an older house, newly redecorated, the walls a freshly painted peach, the gingerbread strips at the middle and baseboard a contrasting persimmon. The drapes were a knotty weave of peach and cream.

The room displayed a warm, attractive openness, much like its owner.

Adam's eyes were drawn to the pictures adorning the mantel of the flagstone fireplace. He stepped up to them to get a closer look. The first two, faded from age, showed stiffly posed couples in old-fashioned clothes, obviously her grandparents.

The next was a candid shot of Whitney. She couldn't have been more than seven or eight. At first he saw only her, wearing a big, beautiful, open smile that seemed to draw the sun to her face, just as it did now. Then he looked to her two brothers, taller and older, on either side and her parents in the background.

A wave of surprised recognition swept through Adam.

"Some of these family photos are good enough to be mug shots," she said suddenly.

He turned to find her standing behind him. She was wearing a classic, tailored cream pantsuit with a light pink silk blouse. She looked crisp, cool, like a piece of peppermint candy.

"You're William T. West's daughter," he said, pointing to the family picture he had been studying. "Wild Bill West. The defender of the downtrodden. The legal Lancelot riding to the rescue of the poor and friendless."

A telltale gleam of pride entered her eyes as he repeated the media accolades that had been attributed to her celebrity-lawyer father over three decades.

"Most people don't recognize those earlier pictures of my father, before his hair turned white."

"His white hair is a distinctive trademark, yes, Whitney. But I first met your father when his hair still showed some of the color of yours—much as it is in this picture."

"You met my father?" she asked, clearly surprised at the news as she stepped closer to the mantel.

"Your father and mine were opposing counsel on a case. I was just a youngster then, but I remember it well. A landlord was trying to evict a tenant for nonpayment of rent. The media had blown the case all out of proportion, because the tenant was a one-armed veteran."

"And your father was representing the landlord and my father the tenant."

"Do you remember the case?"

"No, but I know my dad always represented the underdog. Go on."

"Your father found out that his client hadn't lost his arm in the line of duty, but as a result of a barroom brawl he'd been involved in after he was discharged from the service. He had been passing himself off as a war hero for years. Even his kids thought the Purple Heart he had bought in a pawnshop was one he had earned. Your father came to see my father one night at our home in order to try to work out a settlement that would allow the real story to be squashed."

"My father wasn't one to hide the truth."

"But in this case, he was right. When your father learned how the man had really lost his arm, he told my father. He didn't have to do that. My father probably never would have found out."

"But my father knew it was the right thing to do," Whitney said very matter-of-factly. "What was the settlement?"

"Your father paid for his client's back rent and quietly moved him out of the apartment and into an alcohol-detox center. He also paid for his client's treatment. My father agreed not to publicize the man's lies in order to avoid his personal disgrace in front of his family and friends. I'll never forget what my father said about yours that night as we watched him walk away."

"What?"

"He said that Wild Bill West wasn't just the best lawyer he'd gone up against, he was the best man. I'm sorry about his passing, Whitney. It was last year, wasn't it?"

Whitney nodded. "Yes. But your father was wrong, Adam. My dad may have been the best lawyer, but he wasn't the best man."

The words struck a discordant note in Adam's ears. "Excuse me, Whitney?"

"The best man is the guy who stays true to his wife and family. My dad got caught up in all the notoriety. He ended up having an affair with a socialite who thought it might be fun to sleep with a headline."

"Your parents divorced?"

"Yes. My mom told me that two people can hang together against anything as long as they have trust. But once trust goes, there's nothing of value left."

"Was their breakup hard on you?"

"Very. I loved both my parents. And I needed them both. After the divorce I hardly ever saw my dad."

"Still, a lot of him rubbed off on you. That has to be why your practice is geared toward representing those who don't have a lot of money to pay a lawyer."

"Yes, but it was my mother who taught me the important

lessons about love and putting family first. I was engaged to a guy named Skip a few years back. He's a successful developer of computer software, a regular Bill Gates. Except his attitude toward the law was, 'If it isn't making you lots of money, babe, why are you doing it?' "

Whitney had lowered her voice to a deep baritone when she mimicked Skip's voice. It made Adam want to smile.

"And Wild Bill West's daughter didn't approve," Adam said.

Whitney nodded. "Skip's attitude toward children was, 'Sure, babe, we'll have some if they'll make you happy.' Not exactly a rousing commitment to fatherhood."

Once again her voice had deepened to a baritone when she mimicked Skip.

"Still, if he hadn't had the annoying habit of laughing at all those wonderful old movies, where people stayed together forever, we might have worked out the other stuff. So, are you ever going to get married and have some kids?"

Adam's eyes dropped to his watch. "No. We'd best go."

"But I just put the coffee on."

"We'll get some later."

"You don't understand, Adam. I positively growl without my coffee. It won't take but a couple of minutes before it's ready."

"A couple of minutes will make us late."

"And being late, I'm sure, would violate the Adam Justice code of ethics."

"It would be discourteous."

"Same thing," Whitney said, but he noted she didn't say it disapprovingly. "Okay, but you've been warned. A disgruntled postal worker with an Uzi is nothing compared to me without my caffeine."

ALL THE WAY to Danny D'Amico's place, Whitney thought about Adam's quick and emphatic denial when she'd asked him if he would marry and have children.

She understood. All too well. The way Patrice had betrayed Adam had no doubt soured him on love and marriage for life.

Still, it was a shame it had to happen to such a man as Adam Justice. A caring man. An honest man.

As disappointed as she was that Adam had only offered her a physical relationship, she had to acknowledge that most men would have tried to get her into bed before admitting that they had no intentions other than the pursuit of physical pleasure.

But as Whitney was coming to realize more and more, Adam was nothing like most men.

Whitney hadn't formed any conscious expectations about what Danny D'Amico's house would look like, but when Adam turned into a long, circular driveway lined by imposing poplars and parked in front of a replica of a Greek temple, she definitely did a double take.

She did a triple take when the enormous front doors were answered by a snotty-looking woman in full maid's uniform.

"We have an appointment with Mr. Danford D'Amico," Adam said to the woman.

She nodded and turned to lead the way down an incredibly long, ostentatious hallway lined with marble busts on shoulder-high pedestals. At its end the maid opened a door. Whitney found herself outside again on a concrete pathway that led to a small, separate house at the rear of the large one.

"You go back there," the maid said. The look on her face clearly conveyed the message that she belonged to the big house, not the insignificant one at which she was pointing.

Adam and Whitney followed the path to the small cottage. Unlike the elaborate dwelling that dwarfed it, the cottage was very modest, with just a few wild rhododendron bushes marking its entry. Adam knocked on the door. Danny opened it immediately.

"Please come in, Mr. Justice, Ms. West."

"Call me Whitney," she said, sending Danny a warm smile.

The inside of the cottage was neat but small and sparsely furnished. Danny gestured toward an old checkered sofa shoved against a far wall. She and Adam obligingly took a seat on it. Danny remained standing.

"My mother will be out in a minute. It's the nurse's morning off, so it takes Mom a little longer to get it together."

"We don't mind waiting," Whitney said, shifting on the lumpy sofa while she wondered why Danny's mother needed a nurse.

"Your uncle owns the house at the front?" Adam asked.

"My grandfather," Danny answered. "My uncle lives in one of the wings with my aunt and cousins."

"And you and your mother live back here?" Whitney asked.

Danny shifted on his feet. "My grandfather lets us live in this cottage, buys our food, our clothes and sees to my mom's medical needs. Now that I work for my uncle, I get a few dollars in spending money."

Whitney didn't detect any pride in Danny's words, just a kind of resignation. She was decidedly annoyed at the difference in living quarters between his grandfather's opulent home and this cottage Danny and his mother had been relegated to. Couldn't his grandfather have found some space in his home for his daughter and grandson? He'd found space for his son and his family.

"Hello, I'm so sorry to keep you waiting," a woman's voice called cheerily as a wheelchair rolled into the room from the hallway adjacent to the small living room.

The woman sitting in the wheelchair was fortyish and wore a tentative smile on her badly scarred face. She was attired in a cheery, bright red blouse, and from her waist to her feet she was covered in a faded plaid throw. The way her eyes were unfocused and staring off at odd angles told Whitney immediately that her inability to walk was not her only physical disability.

A spear of sadness struck Whitney's heart.

Adam was on his feet in an instant and had stepped over to the wheelchair to lean down to take the woman's hand. Whitney was touched by his action. Very few people would have the presence of mind and sensitivity to offer such a courteous gesture.

"Mrs. D'Amico, I'm Adam Justice. Whitney West is also here."

"You have a capable-sounding voice, Mr. Justice," Mrs. D'Amico said. "It matches your handshake. May I shake Ms. West's hand also?"

Adam stepped aside, and Whitney moved to his vacated place next to the wheelchair. She took Mrs. D'Amico's hand within both of hers. "Call me Whitney. Unlike Mr. Justice, I'm very informal."

Mrs. D'Amico's smile broadened. "Me, too, Whitney. My first name is Beatrice. Please sit down and make yourselves comfortable. Has Danny gotten you refreshments?"

"I, uh, there might be some coffee—" Danny began.

"Please don't bother," Whitney said quickly, wishing to take the pressure off both Danny and his mother to offer them what little they had. "We don't need any coffee."

Whitney didn't miss the slight lifting of Adam's lips as he listened to that disclaimer.

He turned to the woman in the wheelchair. "Mrs. D'Amico, has your son had an opportunity to explain the reason for our getting in touch with you?"

"Yes, Mr. Justice. But I know no one by the name of Feldon or Waring."

"Did you check with other members of your family?"

"The only relatives left are those on my side of the family, Mr. Justice. No one friendly with them would be leaving anything to me or Danny," Mrs. D'Amico said. "My Danny should have carried his father's name, Thomas. But I named him Danford after my father in an effort to mend family fences. It was futile. None of my family ever approved of my marrying Thomas."

"Why was that, Beatrice?" Whitney asked.

"Just because he was poor and had no family. That's all they had against him, Whitney. You'd think he was a criminal the way they treated him. They even tried to make the accident into his fault."

"The accident?" Whitney asked.

"The one that took my Thomas, my sight and my ability to walk."

"When did it happen?" Whitney asked.

"Twenty years ago. Danny was only two months old when Thomas's only relative, a distant aunt, died and we flew to Phoenix to attend the funeral. We were on the airport bus coming home when our driver hit the back of a truck. Next thing I knew, my Thomas was dead and I could no longer see or walk."

"I'm so sorry, Beatrice," Whitney said, feeling the words acutely as she rested her hand on Beatrice's arm.

"Knowing my little baby had survived and needed me was all that kept me going."

"Did the authorities ever determine the cause of the accident?" Adam asked.

"The bus driver had been drinking. My father sued, but the airport bus service declared bankruptcy, so we never got anything. My father blamed Thomas for not having the money for a car to drive us home. Can you imagine? Such nonsense. Like money was the measure of a man. My Thomas was warm and kind—everything a real man should be. Go get the picture and show them, Danny."

"Aw, Mom, they don't want to see—"

"Danny, please. Go get the picture."

Danny shook his head in resignation as he left the room. As soon as the sound of his footsteps drifted away, Beatrice spoke again in a lowered voice. "I've hated bringing up my Danny here," she said. "I don't mind the indignities they put me through, shutting me up in these old servants' quarters. But the way Danny's own grandfather and uncle treat him, like some servant—" She stopped herself and sighed. "When he came home yesterday and told me about how you said this woman had left us some money, I hoped this was his chance to get out before they break his spirit. Has it all been a mistake?"

Before either Whitney or Adam could answer, Danny came back into the room, holding an eight-by-ten photo in a silver-filigree frame. He shook his head at Whitney unhappily.

"You have it there, Danny?" Beatrice said. "Let me feel the edges to make sure it's the right one."

Danny obediently handed his mother the framed photo. She felt the edges. "Yes, this is the one. Take a look, Whitney. It's our wedding picture taken twenty-two years ago."

Whitney gently took the photo out of Beatrice's hand. The woman in the wedding dress she would have recognized anywhere. It was the young, unscarred face Danny had given his mother in his family drawing. But the photo image of the man in the tuxedo by her side had been viciously slashed until it was unrecognizable.

A cold stone dropped into Whitney's stomach. She looked up to see the pain on Danny's face.

"Well, Whitney, what do you think?" Beatrice asked. "Isn't Danny the spitting image of his dad?"

"Actually, Beatrice," Whitney said carefully, "I think Danny has your big brown eyes and widow's peak."

"Really?"

"Yes, definitely, Mrs. D'Amico," Adam said in his formal, emphatic voice after a brief glimpse at the slashed photo. Whitney resisted a very strong impulse to give Adam a hug.

"I hope we haven't disappointed you," Whitney said.

"Oh my, no. I'm just surprised. My father and brother have both insisted over the years that Danny grew up to look exactly like his dad in that wedding picture."

Whitney wondered whether it had been his grandfather or his uncle who had ruined the picture of Danny's father. She was beginning to understand only too well the kind of indignities Danny had been subjected to while under their thumbs. And the more she understood, the angrier she got on both Beatrice's and Danny's behalf.

"Mr. D'Amico," Adam said, "in reference to Patrice Feldon—"

"Since we don't know her, I guess we don't get what she left, right?" Danny interrupted.

"On the contrary, Mr. D'Amico," Adam said. "Despite the fact that you did not know Patrice Feldon, her bequest to you is still valid. I am satisfied that you and your mother are the

Beatrice and Danford D'Amico that my client has selected to be beneficiaries of her estate.''

Surprise stole over Danny's face. "Really. We get it? How much, Mr. Justice?''

"Before probate costs and taxes and any debts are addressed, the amount comes to approximately ten million dollars.''

"Ten mil—" Danny's voice stopped dead as his eyes glassed over and his thin, gangly body collapsed into an old easy chair as though it had suddenly become jelly.

"Dear God, you are in heaven,'' Beatrice said on a heartfelt sigh as big, beautiful tears ran down her scarred face.

Chapter Nine

Adam led Whitney to their seats in first class on the plane headed for Las Vegas. She'd never flown first-class. Before she could even buckle up, the flight attendant was asking her if she'd like a cocktail. It was eleven-thirty in the morning.

"Irish coffee," she said without hesitation.

Adam ordered plain coffee. When their drinks came, Whitney raised hers to offer a toast. "To caffeine," she said. "Please don't let them ever discover that it causes cancer."

Adam sipped his coffee in salute.

"And to Beatrice and Danny D'Amico," Whitney added in a more serious tone. "May they take their ten million dollars and rub it in the noses of that nasty uncle and grandfather."

"They don't have the money yet," Adam said, his tone at its most formal. "The possibility always exists that they might not get it. A lawyer cannot afford to let her passions get the better of her."

Whitney took a big gulp of her drink. "Nonsense. A lawyer's passions are the best of her—or him. Without passion the law is just like decaf—lacking all its zip."

A small smile lifted his lips. "You have a lot more of your father in you than you've admitted, Whitney."

God, she was happy to see him smiling at her again. Too damn happy. Whitney felt a warming in her blood that she knew had nothing to do with either the caffeine or alcohol in her drink.

"Who did you hire to investigate Chad Bister's claim?" Adam asked after a moment.

"An investigative firm down the hall from Jack and me. They call themselves Checkmate. They're a bunch of gutsy divorced gals who learned how to be detectives the hard way."

"And what's the hard way?"

"Tracking down their own philandering husbands."

"This isn't that kind of case, Whitney."

"Still, I want them on it. Checkmate is just getting started and needs every break it can get. Many of the gals are single moms who count on the work to make ends meet."

"And what if they discover that Chad's claim is genuine?"

"Then I'll tell him he needs to engage an attorney to represent his interests."

"You won't represent him?"

"Of course I won't represent him. You had to ask?"

"No. I was just trying to display that admirable sensitivity you seem to appreciate so much."

The lift to his lips and the warmth in his eyes were devastating and set her blood to tingling all over again. Whitney downed the rest of her Irish coffee.

Adam Justice could sweep away all her nonchalance with a single smile. Thank God he wasn't the kind of man to take advantage of it.

"What do you know about this Huntley and Brinkley Carmichael we're going to see?" she asked.

"A.J. wasn't able to learn anything about them, which is unusual," he said.

"Their first names sound familiar, although I don't know why."

"Perhaps because the names are those of two famous newsmen, whose spot was called 'The Huntley-Brinkley Report.'"

"Yes, that rings a vague bell. What was their report about?"

"It focused on important world events and was widely respected and well-known. Unlike their namesakes, however, A.J. advises me that neither Huntley nor Brinkley Carmichael are showing up in the credit computers. And there is no telephone listing for them in Overton, Nevada."

"Then how will we know where to find them?"

"It's a small town. We're going to ask the only other Carmichaels living there—Kevin and Linda. Even if they aren't family, in that small a town it stands to reason that they would be familiar with someone else sharing their familial name."

"So you're thinking that if Huntley and Brinkley lived there at one time and have moved, Kevin and Linda probably know where. You've called, of course, to set up an appointment with them?"

"My secretary attempted to get the information over the phone, but Linda Carmichael informed him that she had never heard of me and she didn't discuss any business over the phone."

"That doesn't sound very promising."

"Still, when we arrive on their doorstep, it will be difficult to turn us away."

He said that with such confidence. And Whitney was sure he was right. She doubted anyone ever turned Adam Justice away. Especially not a woman.

Except, in the end, Patrice had, she reminded herself.

The more she learned about Adam, the more that fact surprised Whitney. How could Patrice have ever turned away from this man in favor of another, unless—

"Adam, may I ask you something?"

His lips lifted slightly. "Whitney West requesting permission to ask a question? Now, this is the kind of news that would have made 'The Huntley-Brinkley Report.'"

She indulged only a small smile in return, determined to keep her serious focus. "Were you true to Patrice when you were married?"

The upturned edges of Adam's lips slowly straightened. He was quiet for such a long moment that Whitney didn't think he was going to answer.

"Yes," he said finally.

"Did you ever suspect Patrice felt anything romantic toward Peter Danner before she left with him?"

"No."

"But she was in his company a lot?"

"Not to my knowledge."

"So her leaving was a total surprise?"

"Why are you asking these questions, Whitney?"

Whitney let out a little puff of impatience. "I guess I got carried away with a sudden urge to know what you're really feeling inside. I can't imagine what possessed me. Just forget it. I'm sure the urge will pass."

"Will it?"

It was his same cool, unemotional voice that had asked the question. But when she glanced in his direction, the look of clear blue sincerity in his eyes sent a small shock through her system.

"No, I rather doubt it will pass," she heard herself say. "Adam, why did you marry Patrice?"

"You met her, Whitney. Do you really have to ask?"

"I know her incredible beauty and angelic smile undoubtedly claimed all the male hearts within beating distance. But I want to know what she did that not only claimed your heart, but your hand, as well."

"Why is this important to you?"

"Because . . . I want to understand. No, I *need* to understand."

A long quiet moment passed. When Adam finally spoke, he stared straight ahead, and his deep voice was smooth and even.

"I fell in love with Patrice, because when we were together everything seemed possible. The world shimmered and soared out of control, unfettered by any confines of reason. I gave her my heart, my hand and everything else I possessed, because that's what a man does when he falls in love."

He said it so quietly, so calmly, so matter-of-factly. Whitney had not understood the depth of Adam Justice's feelings for Patrice until now. The truth of his every word hit her like a blow.

A woman who was loved like that by a man like this would have to be a fool to let him go. She would have never guessed Patrice was a fool.

"Adam, when I first met you, I believed that Patrice turned to another man because she discovered you didn't have a loyal and loving heart. But now I realize that isn't true. You loved her, right up to the end. I can't understand why she left you."

He said nothing in response, just stoically sipped his coffee.

Whitney read his silence with growing unease. Was her suspicion correct? Was it possible Adam didn't know why his wife had left, either?

OVERTON WAS a small desert town in a crescent-shaped valley near Lake Mead in southern Nevada. As Whitney and Adam rounded the road at the top of the surrounding mountain range, she caught her breath at the beautiful muted pastels of the desert palate spread out before her. The sky was a milky summer blue, the sands an eggshell white draped with golden yokes of mesquite. On the far-off horizon, a long lavender mesa gradually gave way to pink-tipped ridges.

It was cool inside the rental car, but when Whitney got out of it at the end of tiny Spur Lane, the September desert heat hit her square in the face. By the time they had walked up to the door of the modest mobile home where Kevin and Linda Carmichael lived, perspiration was streaming down Whitney's back.

A tall, skinny, fiftyish man with thinning hair opened the door in response to Adam's knock. He wore white cotton gloves, a baggy T-shirt and even baggier shorts. "Yes?"

"Kevin Carmichael?" Adam asked.

"That's me. Who are you?"

"My name is Adam Justice, Mr. Carmichael. I'm an attorney."

"Adam Justice? You have anything to do with that call my wife got yesterday?"

"Yes, Mr. Carmichael. Ms. West and I have just flown in from Washington State to see you and your wife. Do you have a few moments you can give us?"

Kevin scratched his receding chin with his white-gloved hand as his dark eyes studied Adam. "All the way from Washington State?'' he finally said. ''Well, I guess I can't send you back without at least a cool drink. Come on in.''

As they stepped indoors, Kevin shut the door behind them. Whitney didn't find the interior of the house that much cooler than it had been outside. She slipped off her light cotton jacket but still felt as though she was about to melt.

Kevin escorted them into the den and closed the door. The room was equipped with a noisy window air conditioner that managed a modest cooling. Kevin gestured toward the vinyl lime-colored couch in the corner and walked behind the portable bar with the simulated wood counter.

''Lemonade or orange juice?''

''Orange juice,'' Whitney said, taking a seat on the vinyl couch and immediately feeling herself stick to it.

''Just water,'' Adam said as he sat beside her.

Whitney thought it odd that Kevin didn't take off his gloves when he fixed their drinks. ''So what can I do you for?'' he asked as he set the drinks in front of them.

Whitney took a long drink of her orange juice while at the same time offering a quiet prayer of thanks for the blessed coolness of Washington State summers.

''Mr. Carmichael, do you know Patrice Feldon?'' Adam asked.

Kevin blinked at Adam in surprise. ''Patrice? Well, yes, of course I know Patrice. Wait a minute. Did she send you?''

''I'm here representing her interests,'' Whitney heard Adam say carefully.

''You'd better hold on, Mr. Justice,'' Kevin said making for the door. ''My wife is going to want to hear this, too. She's been waiting for word from Patrice for a long time now.''

Kevin had reached the door. He opened it and yelled, ''Linda. Someone is here about Patrice.''

A moment later a fortyish woman, wearing a cotton blouse, shorts and no shoes, entered the room, drying her hands with a dishcloth. She had short, dark hair, a pretty, round face and a happy smile.

''Patrice sent you?'' she asked eagerly.

Adam rose and introduced himself and Whitney.

"Please sit down, Mr. Justice," Linda said. "So, finally we get word. How is Patrice?"

"Mrs. Carmichael, I regret to inform you, but Patrice is dead," Adam said in his deeply formal voice.

Linda Carmichael sank onto the seat next to her husband. Whitney watched her face go through a reverse of those before-and-after pictures of a face-lift recipient. Instead of losing ten years, Linda aged ten. She slumped against her husband.

"Oh, no. When?"

"Seven years ago," Adam said.

"That's why she stopped coming by," Linda said on a long exhale of air. "All along I've been telling myself she was just too busy. I didn't want to think . . . damn."

Linda bit her bottom lip. Kevin wrapped an arm around his wife's waist as a tear escaped from the corner of her eye.

"I'm very sorry, Linda," Whitney said.

Kevin looked accusingly at Adam. "I thought you said Patrice sent you."

"No, I said I represent her interests, Mr. Carmichael, and I do," Adam replied calmly. "I'm executor of Patrice's estate. I'm looking for two beneficiaries she has named in her will. I believe you can help me find them."

Linda's sigh was deep and sad. "Patrice didn't have any family. Sorry, Mr. Justice. We can't help. Doctors Esther and Jacob Rubin of Seattle might be able to assist you. I have their telephone number around here somewhere."

"Ms. West and I have already spoken to Dr. Esther Rubin," Adam said. "I think these beneficiaries might be relatives of yours. Their names are Huntley and Brinkley Carmichael."

Kevin and Linda Carmichael looked at each other and then at Adam. For a moment neither of them spoke. Then Linda leaned forward. "Patrice made Huntley and Brinkley beneficiaries in her will?"

"That's correct."

"How did she do it? I mean, did she just say give Huntley and Brinkley such and such amount of money?"

"It would be inappropriate of me to discuss the particulars with anyone other than the beneficiaries," Adam said. "Can you tell me where I might find them?"

Kevin smiled as he rose to his feet and helped his wife to hers. "We can do better than that, Mr. Justice. We can take you to them."

Adam and Whitney followed the couple down the hallway to the back of the house. Kevin pushed open the screen door and stepped out onto a short, shaded patio. In a portable Doughboy swimming pool, a young boy and girl squealed and splashed each other.

"There are Huntley and Brinkley Carmichael, Mr. Justice," Kevin said, a big, proud smile on his face. "Our children."

ADAM WAS SITTING back in the hot den with Whitney and Linda a few minutes later. Kevin had stayed outside to supervise the children. Linda had filled Whitney's glass with more orange juice and Adam's with more iced water. She sat on the lime vinyl sofa across from them and sipped lemonade.

"I should have guessed Patrice would do something like this," Linda said. "Not that I expected her to die, of course. Never that. But since she has, I can see her leaving what she had to the kids. She knew Kevin's disability pension wouldn't let us give them what we once hoped to."

"Your husband is disabled?" Whitney asked.

"He got both his hands caught in a printing press at the metropolitan newspaper he worked at ten years ago. They had to amputate at the wrist."

"He manages very well. I never would have known," Whitney said.

"They fitted him with prostheses. He's gotten so good with them he can fool people. Patrice mentioned the Rubins in her will, too, didn't she?"

"It would be inappropriate of me to discuss—"

"You don't have to worry, Mr. Justice. I know all about Jacob and Esther and what they do. And what they meant to Patrice."

"How do you know this, Linda?" Whitney asked.

"I used to live up in Seattle near the Rubins. My folks used to drive some of the kids to swimming pools during the summer. I was the one who brought Patrice to them."

"You brought Patrice to the Rubins?" Whitney repeated, leaning forward. "From where?"

"Now, there's a good question, Ms. West."

"Please call me Whitney. It's extremely important for us to know about this, Linda. Where did Patrice come from?"

Linda took another sip of her lemonade as her eyes drew to Whitney's. There was a strange look on her face. "Patrice didn't come from anywhere."

"What do you mean?" Whitney asked.

"Patrice was always a bit of a mystery, even to those of us who knew her best."

"How did you meet her?" Whitney asked.

"In a way I'm never likely to forget."

"Please tell us."

Linda sighed. "Well, now that she's dead, I don't suppose it matters."

"Yes?" Whitney said, putting all her encouragement in her tone.

Linda took another long sip of her lemonade and set the glass on the table. She leaned forward, resting her elbows on her knees. "I had just turned twenty-two. I was living up in Seattle with my folks. I was walking home alone late at night after going to a show. I was pulling my coat a little tighter around me when suddenly I saw her out of the corner of my eye."

"Patrice?" Whitney asked.

"Yes. She was standing against a lighted store window, looking inside just like she was window-shopping. No shoes. Her dress and sweater badly torn, what was left of a red silk scarf tied around her waist. She was covered in dirt and dried blood."

"What did you do?" Whitney asked.

"The Rubins were just down the block. My folks had confided their secret to me the year before, so I knew they took in abused kids. And if ever there looked like a kid who had been abused, it was Patrice. I walked up to her, draped my coat around her and told her I would help her. She said nothing, just kept staring into the store window like I wasn't there.

"She offered no resistance when I took her to the Rubin house. Esther and I put her in a warm tub to wash the dirt and blood off her skin and hair. The soles of her feet were abraded and bleeding. She was developing some bad bruises on her arms and legs, but Esther found no other injuries.

"Esther was worried about shock. I called my folks and told them I was staying at the Rubins'. Esther put Patrice in a pair of pajamas and tucked her into bed. I lay beside her and held her hand. She never moved nor made a peep the entire night."

"And in the morning?" Whitney asked.

"When I woke, she was standing beside the bed looking at me. Her hair was a mass of golden curls falling to her waist. Her eyes were huge violet orbs. For a moment, I swear to God, I thought she was an angel."

"What did she say?" Adam asked.

"She told me her name was Patrice Dulcinea Feldon and that she was twelve years old. She was very emphatic about it, even spelled her name and recited her birth date several times. I asked her how she came to be standing in front of the store window. She just kept repeating, 'I wasn't supposed to be there.' When I asked her about her mother and father, she said she didn't remember having a mother or father or any family."

"What about the bruises and blood and the state of her clothes?"

"She just kept answering 'I wasn't supposed to be there' to every question. That's all she ever said."

"Esther and Jacob must have looked for someone she belonged to," Whitney said.

"A policeman friend of the Rubins ran the name Feldon through their files. Nothing. He looked through all the police reports in the area that night. Still nothing. Esther checked for her birth certificate in county records throughout the state so she could get the names of her parents and an address. But there was no birth certificate for her there. Everywhere Esther looked, she came up empty.''

"And you found out no more?'' Whitney asked.

"No. She wasn't really friendly to me at first. It wasn't until later, when Esther placed her in one of those unofficial foster homes and she came to the Rubin house for her therapy sessions, that we got to know each other.''

"You were in therapy at the Rubin house?'' Whitney asked.

"I had a bad experience with a boyfriend who beat me up. I was a mess there for a while. Both Esther and Patrice helped me to get through it.''

"Who was the foster family that raised Patrice?'' Adam asked.

"I wouldn't tell, Mr. Justice, even if I knew, which I don't. Esther is as protective of her foster parents as she is of the children she places in their homes.''

"You must have kept in contact with Patrice, Linda,'' Whitney said. "She knew about your children.''

A quiet smile stole across Linda's lips. "Yes. She knew about my Huntley and Brinkley, better than anyone.''

"Why do you say that?'' Whitney asked.

"When Patrice turned eighteen, she came to see me. I had met and married Kevin by then. She still looked like an angel with all that golden hair and that angelic smile. I told her that Kevin and I had been trying to have a child and that when we did, I hoped I had a daughter who looked just like her.

"I saw her off and on during the next few years. It was always without warning when she'd show up at the door. That was Patrice—unpredictable in so many ways. One day she pressed me about why I hadn't had that daughter I had talked about.

"That's when I told her about how I'd tried all the fertility drugs. Nothing was working. The fertility doctor that I had spent our savings on said there was no hope. I had no fertile eggs left.''

"An early menopause?'' Whitney asked.

"He didn't know. Anyway, Patrice explained that she was working with a scientist who had developed a new fertility process using donor eggs that was very successful. There were no negative side effects, and the research was reaching the stage where the next step was to be human trials. She asked me if I wanted her to arrange for me to be in the first of the trials."

"And you agreed?"

"Agreed? I jumped at it. Kevin had lost his hands by then. We were so despondent and in need of hope. But then Patrice called me and told me that there would be a delay in going forward with the project. She told me she would be in touch and not to lose hope.

"But nearly a whole year went by, and I didn't even hear from her. And then, when I finally did, it was so strange. She called me and told me everything was set. She was express-mailing me some pills that I was to take each morning and night for two months. She gave Kevin the name of a lab that would collect his sperm over the same period. She said there was no cost involved. She had gotten us into a trial, and everything was covered.

"The unlabeled bottle of pills arrived in a brown-paper envelope. When the two months were up, airplane tickets to British Columbia appeared in the mail along with a note from Patrice that said a representative of this pharmaceutical firm would meet us at the airport."

"What pharmaceutical firm was that, Mrs. Carmichael?" Adam asked.

"Let me think. Emerson? No, Emery. That was it," Linda replied. "Emery Pharmaceuticals."

Whitney and Adam exchanged glances as Linda went on.

"A nice young woman from Emery Pharmaceuticals met us at the airport and said we had to hurry because the fresh embryos had arrived and would not be viable for long. She drove Kevin and me right to their lab. They drew my blood, tested it, examined me from head to toe and then artificially implanted me with the embryos. Then they gave me more pills to take for the next eight weeks, and Kevin and I were on the next plane back."

"So fast?" Whitney asked.

"Yes, and I was not reassured by the rapidity, Whitney. The quick-in-and-quick-out treatment was unsettling. Still, eight weeks later my doctor in Las Vegas confirmed my pregnancy and declared it a miracle. Seven months later I gave birth to my miracles—my little girl, Huntley, and my little boy, Brinkley."

"They're fraternal twins?" Whitney asked.

"Both donor embryos I was given made it to term. My babies turned seven and a half years old last week."

"Seven and a half? Patrice must have placed them in her will right after they were born," Whitney said, mostly to herself.

"She didn't have to do it," Linda said. "She'd already given me the greatest gift of all—my children. How much did she set aside for them?"

"A third of her estate," Adam said. "How much they actually receive will depend on what debts arise and whether the will withstands challenges from possible blood heirs."

"Well, if there isn't enough to start a college fund, it won't matter. It's the generosity of her gesture that counts."

"Providing that the will is upheld and debts are not substantial, there should be enough for college for Huntley and Brinkley, Mrs. Carmichael," Adam said. "Patrice's estate is worth in excess of thirty million dollars."

Linda Carmichael dropped her glass of lemonade. About the same time it was crashing to the floor, a loud commotion arose from the other side of the den door and it burst open.

Huntley and Brinkley Carmichael came charging into the room, squealing in delight as Kevin growled and chased them.

They were still in their wet bathing suits, their damp dark hair drawn back off their smiling faces as their quick little bodies eluded their father. They were beautiful children, obviously well loved and cared for, glowing with good health and humor.

But when Whitney looked into their laughing eyes, her heart sank sadly inside her chest.

Chapter Ten

"It's me, Jack," Whitney said glumly into the telephone receiver from her room at the Luxor Hotel in Las Vegas.

"Whitney? What's wrong?"

"Nothing," Whitney lied, trying to imbue her voice with a little more animation. "I just wanted to call to let you know we didn't get back from Overton in time to catch the plane. I'll be spending the night in Las Vegas."

"And...?" Jack said suggestively.

Whitney realized that her attempt to lighten her tone hadn't succeeded. She normally didn't keep secrets from Jack. And she admitted to herself that if this one concerned anyone else but Adam, she would have confided in her partner.

But this one did concern Adam, and that changed everything. She didn't examine the reason for that too closely. She was afraid to scrutinize it too carefully.

"I'm just tired, Jack," she lied again.

"Just... tired?" Jack repeated.

"It's been a long day, and you know what a lousy traveler I am. Plus I've just spent next month's mortgage payment at a hotel boutique buying an outfit so I'd have something to wear to dinner tonight."

"Just a minute. Did I hear right? Whitney West went to a hotel boutique to buy a dress? The same Whitney West—whose clothes are so old the tags inside them read Made In America—blew a bundle on a new outfit? Uh-oh."

"What's with the 'uh-oh'?" Whitney said, immediately on the defensive. "I've been known to buy something new once in a while."

"Once in a very *great* while—and then only if there was a man involved. The last time you splurged on an outfit it was for Skip. Oh, no. Wait a minute. Don't tell me you're falling for Adam Justice."

Whitney chuckled at the note of overblown abhorrence Jack had deliberately put in his voice. She knew now that he wasn't serious.

"What's happened to your standards?" Jack asked, his tone rising in unmitigated horror. "This Justice guy represents *corporations!* He'll take you to business banquets on your dates! Do you know how many boring speeches you'll have to listen to? How much overbaked chicken you're going to be forced to eat? And that will be only the beginning. Those people are into that networking thing. You'll be dragged to all their indigestible events. Have you ever tasted raw fish and sesame seaweed?"

Whitney's chuckle burst into a laugh.

"And that's not the worst of it," Jack continued, his dramatics deliberately exaggerated. "He's sure to invite all his corporate clients to the wedding. These guys give the worst presents. You'll be up to your cupboards in silver finger bowls and tea sets!"

Whitney laughed heartily. When she finally got herself back under control, she blew Jack a kiss. "Thank you, partner. I needed that."

"Yeah, well, I hope you're going to tell me someday about whatever it is we're not talking about tonight."

Whitney knew then that she hadn't fooled Jack. She should have realized he would see right through her. He always did.

"I hope I'm going to tell you about it someday, too," she said simply.

"So, now do you want to hear how my day went?" Jack asked.

"By all means. How did your day go?"

"Well, first you should know that the Checkmate Detective Agency has discovered that Chad Bister's parents did indeed have the kind of marriage he described. What's more, his mother gave birth to a baby girl who his father dumped on an aunt by the name of Denise Dee Bister Feldon to raise."

"Was the baby's name Patrice?"

"They don't know."

"What happened to her?"

"It seems both the aunt and the baby left Spokane a year later and haven't been heard from since."

"Damn. I hate to think he's Patrice's brother."

"Yeah, this Bister guy is a real loser. Checkmate says he's been married four times, the last three wives claiming physical, as well as mental, cruelty when they divorced him. Apparently some old school buddies let him in as a partner at that water-wings company because he couldn't keep a job."

"Did you get any other contenders knocking on the doors today?"

"Did I. Thirty-five people showed up at the office, all claiming to be Patrice's blood relatives."

"Thirty-five? You're kidding."

"I wish I were. The vultures started to flock in the second Isabel opened the doors this morning. Obviously they had all watched the TV last night, and every station ran the news that our firm was responsible for identifying possible blood heirs. I've been tied up interviewing them and looking over their proofs all day."

"Jack, I'm sorry. I should have been there helping you handle those people."

"Well, at least our regular caseload is light. And Isabel is a wonder, as you know."

"How many claimants did you get through?"

"All but three."

"That's great. Any real contenders in the bunch?"

"No. Unlike Chad Bister, none knew her middle name or birth date. Those who offered a plausible excuse for not knowing couldn't offer any personal information about Patrice that would help to substantiate their kinship. Personally

I think anyone with the family name of Feldon thinks it's worth showing up and taking a shot. Thirty million dollars is an enticing target. Which reminds me, you should know Fred Dykstra wormed his way into seeing me by passing himself off as a claimant."

"You kicked him out, of course."

"And it felt good doing it, too."

"What has the local news coverage been like today?"

"Loaded with speculation, but mainly just a rehash of Dykstra's news-beat spot. They keep running pictures of Justice and even dug up one of you from your law-school days."

"Oh, no. I hate those pictures of me. My face looks so full and my hair so bushy. I'm a dead ringer for Fred Flintstone."

"Actually the *Seattle Times* reprint came out with a big ink blot over your right eye. Now you look like Fred Flintstone with an eye patch."

"Thanks so much, Jack. That makes me feel much better."

Jack chuckled. "They haven't been able to come up with a picture of Patrice, which seems a little odd. You'd think a looker like her would have posed a lot."

"Yes, you would, wouldn't you?" Whitney mused. "Still, it's just as well they're not running her picture. If they did, anyone who ever thought they ever looked like her would be showing up at our door. At least you only have three more wannabe millionaires to interview."

"Until the next influx."

"The next influx?"

"Another six called in for appointments. And who knows how many more will show up at the door tomorrow."

"I'll be in on the morning flight. After a change of clothes, I promise the office will be my next stop."

"You may want to avoid coming through the front door. In addition to the people claiming to be Patrice's long-lost relatives, we've circled the wagons against a bunch of bloodthirsty reporters determined to scalp everyone with insolent questions."

"I appreciate the warning. I'll park on the next block and come in the service entrance. Jack, you've really been great to take this on for me today."

"And it will all be back in your hands tomorrow, partner. This is definitely not my kind of case."

Whitney recognized that new tone in Jack's voice. "Uh-oh. What happened? Did one of the female claimants proposition you so you'd validate her as a blood heir?"

"'Proposition' is putting it lightly. She started to strip right in front of me when I asked her for her credentials. And believe me, Whitney, she had all the, uh, credentials. I tell you the temptation is more than any red-blooded man can take. I had to call Isabel in to the rescue."

Whitney laughed as she got a mental flash of their stout, matronly secretary running into Jack's office to pull out a half-naked lady intent on compromising Jack's ethics.

A knock came at the door.

"Got to go, Jack. I'll see you tomorrow. Be sure to lock your doors tonight. You never know. Ms. All the Credentials might have gotten your home address."

Whitney was still chuckling in response to Jack's resultant groan when she went to answer the door.

ADAM THOUGHT he had known the extent of Patrice's betrayal. This afternoon had taught him otherwise. It was a lesson he could have done without. His thoughts were buried far into a bleak past when Whitney opened the door. But the sight of her swiftly brought him back to the present.

The golden lights in her brandy eyes told him something had amused her. She had done something to those laughing eyes that made them look darker and something to her mouth that made it look softer. Her hair was swept up on top of her head and fastened with a pearl barrette that matched the tiny pearls piercing her ears. Her jade silk dress was simply cut and fit to perfection.

"You look very nice," he said, and recognized the comment was a major understatement, even for him.

"Thank you. I'd tell you how you look, but it would probably just turn your head."

The edges of his lips curled upward. He liked knowing that she approved of what she saw when she looked at him. He realized most women did. But not since Patrice had a particular woman's approval meant something to him.

Since Patrice. No, he didn't want to think any more about Patrice tonight. For one night at least he wanted a respite from the unhappy past.

"Where are we eating?" Whitney asked as she snatched up an evening bag and checked for her key card.

"I made reservations at The Isis."

"Of course," she said, closing the door to her room and turning to face him. The lights were dancing once again in her eyes. "The most formal restaurant in the place. I should have guessed."

He got a tantalizing whiff of her enticing perfume. Images of slipping that silk dress off her lovely cream shoulders and making love to her filled his thoughts.

He knew he had it within his power to spend such a night with her. The right words, the right touch, and he could ignite them both until their physical needs overcame all objections. But in the morning she would wake up remembering she needed more than he could give, and she would feel cheated.

He knew what it was like to feel cheated. He would not make her feel that way. He would keep his distance and simply enjoy her company tonight, and tomorrow neither of them would have to regret anything.

They sipped drinks in the lounge, and he watched her eyes dance with mischief as she told about cutting school early in order to sneak into courtrooms so she could see and hear her father arguing a case.

"He wasn't living with us anymore and he was always so busy he often missed his weekends with my brothers and me," she explained. "It hurt. My brothers finally just gave up on him. But I was more stubborn. I'd watch the newspapers to see when one of his highly publicized cases would go to trial. I knew I could always catch him at the courthouse."

"Wouldn't you get in trouble for skipping school?"

"Yes, but I risked it to be with him. Once in a while he'd take me out for a root-beer float at the end of a trial and talk to me about why he had won or lost. He always believed he had to win. When he lost, he'd cry and tell me to never become a lawyer. He felt so deeply about his clients and doing right by them."

"You seem to have some very good memories of your father."

"He put his career before us, and that hurt a lot. But some of the fondest memories of my childhood are of those rare afternoons of root-beer floats with my dad."

After drinks they stepped through golden gilded doors into the dining room. Over pheasant and white wine, he told her about how he and his sister had sat around the formal dining table of his attorney parents and listened to how precedents were set and the best way for corporate investment portfolios to be diversified.

She chuckled. "And I bet even as a kid you came to dinner dressed in a white shirt, coat and tie."

"The tie was optional until I was ten."

Her chuckle deepened into a warm, mellow laugh that made him smile.

"They were grooming us both to become lawyers and take over the firm they started," Adam explained. "I was drawn to it from the first."

"But A.J. didn't become a lawyer," Whitney said.

"A.J. spent several of her younger years in a hospital bed. She saw herself pursuing a more physically active career, which is one of the reasons why she decided to become a private investigator."

"Why was your sister in the hospital?"

"She had cancer."

"And the doctors beat it?"

"No, she beat it."

Adam watched as a glow of respect formed in the center of Whitney's eyes. "And A.J. stands for courage," she said, repeating his earlier words, a new understanding in her tone.

"Speaking of A.J.," Adam said, "she's found a newspaper story on the accident Danny and his mother were in twenty years ago. Five people were killed and three survived—Danny, his mother and a teenage boy. The bus driver had not only been drinking, he was also carrying a stolen wallet with an ID he'd used to get the job. They never did find out who he was."

As soon as Adam had said it, he was sorry. They had both been able to forget the case for a while. Now it was back in the fore with all its problems and plaguing questions.

Whitney looked away and finished her last sip of wine. When her eyes rose to his again, they held a different expression.

"We have to talk about Huntley and Brinkley Carmichael."

Adam finished the last of his wine. He didn't drink often. He could feel the alcohol he'd already consumed running warm through his blood. Still, he knew the relaxing evening was over.

"I need to talk about them," Whitney pressed.

Adam signaled the waiter for the check.

"I'm acting in my professional capacity as G.A.L. now, Adam. Please understand, I can't ignore what Huntley and Brinkley represent."

No, of course she couldn't. In her place he wouldn't be able to, either.

"Not here," he said.

"Then back in my room."

"As you wish."

As he walked her back to her room, his eyes followed the gentle sway of her hips. He thought about how he would have liked this evening to have ended. And it definitely wasn't on the subject matter she had chosen to end it. When she closed the door to her room behind them, she pointed toward the phone.

"An after-dinner drink?"

"Not for me," he replied.

She rested her hand on the receiver and then removed it and turned away. He didn't think she wanted any more to drink, either.

He looked at her averted face and then to her hands. They were flitting by her sides, nervous and uncomfortable. He could see that no matter how much she felt it was necessary, broaching this subject matter was difficult for her.

She finally faced him. "I have to know what you intend to do about Huntley and Brinkley, Adam."

"They are beneficiaries in Patrice's will. I intend to see that they receive a third of her estate."

"That's *all?*"

"You say that as though you think there should be something else, Whitney."

She was trying to remain businesslike and in control, but Adam could see a sadness creeping into her eyes and settling around her mouth.

"You know whose children they are," she said.

"They are Linda and Kevin Carmichael's children," Adam said carefully.

"Linda Carmichael may have given birth to Huntley and Brinkley, but they both have very distinctive violet eyes," Whitney said. "Patrice donated her own eggs."

Adam said nothing. There was nothing to say.

"She never told you," Whitney said.

"No."

"And she donated her eggs during the time you were married."

"Yes."

"Adam, I don't understand this at all. She told me you'd make a great father. She told me you two were trying to have children. How could she give away her eggs without telling you? Those children could have been yours!"

Her face was so sad, so beautiful. Knowing she was sad for him filled Adam with a guilty kind of pleasure that he knew should bring him shame but brought him satisfaction instead.

He got up and went over to her because he couldn't stay away. He wrapped his arms around her and gently drew her to him, intending comfort.

She sighed and slipped her arms around his neck, sliding her soft breasts and belly against him in a purely female gesture of invitation that at once startled him and spoke directly to everything in him that was male.

And everything in him that was male was answering. He claimed her soft mouth in hot, urgent kisses as he crushed her body to him. She tasted and felt so good, so impossibly good. He knew this woman had the capacity to make him forget every other—even Patrice—if only for a while. And he wanted her to help him forget, even if it was only this one day of painful revelations.

His hands pulled up the skirt of her dress and found her silky panties beneath it. He cupped the warm softness of her bottom. She arched against him with a sharp intake of breath.

And then, for one crystal-clear moment, the madness receded and he realized what he was doing. Calling upon every ounce of control he possessed, he released her and stepped back.

Her face was now flushed and beautiful and far from sad. And the way her eyes were looking into his . . .

His blood beat faster. He took another deep breath and another step backward and prayed for strength. This was going to kill him to say and do, but he was going to say and do it. He was not going to use her this way.

"This has been a shock for you, Whitney. I can see that. I know what a very sympathetic person you are. I will not stay here and take advantage of this situation."

And with that he turned away from all the beckoning warmth of her and fled the room, just as fast as his resolve would take him.

FRED DYKSTRA WAS not happy. Following up on the Patrice Feldon story was proving impossible, and every day that passed his producer got more impatient.

He almost wished he'd never eavesdropped on dear old Dwight Errent and Tiffany's tête-à-tête in the courthouse cafeteria and gotten the story in the first place.

Even masquerading as a blood heir at the law offices of Novak and West hadn't helped. He'd pumped the other contenders to the title of long-lost blood heir that he found in the waiting room and discovered they were as phony as he. And not only had Jack Novak recognized him immediately, but the lawyer had physically shoved him out the door.

The power of the press just didn't seem to impress some people.

There was nothing to do but go back to the Justice Inc. offices and keep a close lookout to see who showed up there. Maybe he'd get lucky. He'd better. He needed more on this story. And he needed it quickly.

WHITNEY WAS YAWNING openly as Adam drove her home from the SEATAC airport. She had not slept well at all the night before. It was all Adam Justice's fault. He'd left her tossing and turning and much too excited to sleep.

She kept telling herself she was glad he'd left her room when he had before either of them had done something they would certainly have regretted. And she didn't kid herself. She knew she had been well on her way to doing just that.

It wasn't just his great looks and intelligence that made this man so impossible to resist. It was the way he faced and lived with Patrice's betrayal. He was strong in ways most men couldn't even imagine.

And he was so damn honorable. He knew she'd been ready to make love to him the night before. But he hadn't taken advantage. He'd told her he wouldn't and when it came right down to it, he was true to his word.

She appreciated the fact that he behaved like the gentleman he was. But she very much resented the fact that he looked so well rested. He could have at least had the decency to suffer a little insomnia, too.

"Adam, I have to tell Commissioner Snowe about Huntley and Brinkley being Patrice's biological children. You represent them as named beneficiaries, but I represent them, too, as G.A.L. for the blood heirs."

"We'll both tell Snowe, Whitney," Adam said. "But we have to add the disclaimer that it is only our belief."

"You don't doubt it?"

"No, and I'm sure Kevin and Linda know. But Commissioner Snowe has neither seen Patrice's eyes nor those of the children. When Patrice donated her eggs, she must have done it at a local lab that sent them on to Vancouver in British Columbia for fertilization. There should be a way to track the paperwork. I'll put A.J. on it."

"What do you think Commissioner Snowe will do when she learns about them?" Whitney asked.

"Patrice states that she has no children in her will. She obviously gave up all rights to her eggs at the time she donated them. She leaves a third of her estate to Huntley and Brinkley. I believe Commissioner Snowe will consider them adequately provided for. If your opinion as G.A.L. is that they should receive a larger split, I'm sure Snowe will be open to any arguments you present."

"I don't intend to present anything except a plea to conduct this probate behind closed doors," Whitney said. "Learning of Huntley and Brinkley Carmichael's real parentage should be sufficient grounds to convince Snowe."

"That's unlikely," Adam said.

"She has to understand the kind of headlines that would follow should the truth get out," Whitney protested.

"Such headlines could embarrass no one but me. I doubt Commissioner Snowe will consider my discomfort sufficient grounds for concealment."

Whitney had to admit he was probably right. Frustration for many things began to flower inside her. "Damn."

"What's wrong?" Adam asked in his cool, unemotional tone.

"What's wrong? What's right? I keep telling myself Patrice must have had a dreadful time during her early years. She probably was subjected to terrible abuse before Linda found her and Esther took her in. She likely thought what she was doing for Linda was a way to repay her earlier kindness. But to have never even discussed giving away her eggs with you ... to have just done it ... like you didn't matter at all."

Adam pulled up in front of Whitney's house and cut the engine. He turned to her. "You're angry at Patrice."

Whitney laughed, but there was no mirth in the sound. "Angry? I'm furious. If she weren't dead, I'd be tempted to wring her neck."

Whitney snatched at the handle and pushed against the passenger door.

The gentle pressure of his hand on her shoulder was enough to stop her from getting out of the car.

"Don't be angry. It will only hurt you."

She turned toward him, resenting his calm, steady voice in the face of her currently upset state.

"How would you know, Adam? You never get angry."

His other hand rose to feather his fingers lightly through her hair, sending a warm, tingling feeling through the nerve endings down her spine.

"I get angry," he said.

The admission surprised her. She turned more fully toward him, resting her back on the passenger door, her fury dissipating with every second she gazed at the warm look in his eyes.

"How is it you never show that anger, Adam?"

"I've learned that anger's energy is much more useful when it is leashed and controlled."

She looked into his calm, handsome face and was amazed anew at how strong he was. She found herself responding with a warm rush of feelings to that strength and the deep, beautiful cadence of his voice and the gentle touch of his hand.

Very slowly he began to lean toward her. Her heart began to pound; her breathing began to quicken. He was going to kiss her again. And she wanted him to. Oh God, how she wanted him to!

The passenger door suddenly pulled away from Whitney and she nearly fell backward out of the car. She probably would have taken a tumble onto the pavement if Adam hadn't quickly caught hold of her shoulders and held her steady.

"Whitney West?"

Whitney swung around on the car seat toward the gray-faced man who had called out her name and now held open the passenger door.

"Who are you?" Whitney demanded of the stranger. She was thoroughly angered by both his interruption and the manner in which he had achieved it.

"Detective-Sergeant Ryson, King County Sheriff's Office," he said in an authoritarian tone, flashing his badge while still holding on to the door. "Would you please step out of the car?"

Whitney moved to the edge of the seat and felt Adam's hands immediately releasing her. She scrambled out of the car, startled by the man's identity and his somber-voiced request. Once on her feet, Whitney saw there was a heavyset man standing behind Sergeant Ryson. He flashed her his badge.

"Detective Ferkel, ma'am."

"What do you want with me?" Whitney asked.

"We need to talk to you regarding an investigation, Ms. West," Ryson said. "I suggest we go inside."

Ryson gestured toward Whitney's house.

Adam had gotten out of the car and come to stand next to Whitney.

"What is this all about, Sergeant?" he asked.

"We intend to talk with Ms. West privately, Mr. Justice. We can do this inside her home now, or we can do this inside the sheriff's office, also now."

Adam and Sergeant Ryson faced each other. Whitney watched as something changed in Adam's stance and demeanor. It reminded her of the way Adam had looked when he faced Edgar Kirkbin—formidable and forbidding. She understood now what he had said about leashed anger.

The palpable tension between Adam and this sergeant alarmed Whitney. Adam's expression and tone were perfectly controlled, but the emphatic quality in his deep voice sent a warning vibration down her spine.

"Sergeant Ryson," he said, "Ms. West has a very busy schedule today. If you wish to talk to her, call her office and make an appointment."

"What are you afraid of, Justice?" Ryson asked, a daring taunt clear in the curl of his mouth and words. "What she'll tell us? Or what *we'll* tell her?"

Watching Adam face this sergeant, Whitney didn't know how she could have ever doubted that he got angry. She was seeing it so clearly now. Oh, yes, it was ultracontrolled. But it was also as cold as ice and scary as hell. She didn't know what was going on between these two men, but she did know it was time for her to step in between them.

If Adam had left any room. He hadn't.

She moved closer to him and stared up into his face, pressing for his attention. "It's all right, Adam. I appreciate your concern, but I'll handle this. Thank you for the ride home."

Adam paused in his response just long enough to make Whitney's nerves dance. Finally he stepped back. "As you wish."

He pivoted and circled back to the driver's seat of the Jaguar. She waited until he drove away before turning up the sidewalk to her home.

Once she and the detectives were inside and she had closed the door, she turned to Detective-Sergeant Ryson, crossing her arms over her chest.

"Now, Sergeant, what in the hell is all this about?"

"Wouldn't you rather have this conversation in the living room, where we can all sit down?"

"No, Sergeant. I don't extend the welcoming mat to anyone who resorts to yanking open a passenger door to get my attention."

"But you were about to extend the welcoming mat to a murderer."

"What are you talking about?"

"Patrice Feldon was murdered by Adam Justice, that man who you were just about to invite inside your home."

The sergeant's words sent a shiver through Whitney. She uncrossed her arms. "I don't believe you."

"The crash that killed Patrice Feldon and her lover, Peter Danner, seven years ago was no accident."

"There's been nothing in the papers—"

"We've been keeping the investigation quiet until we had the goods on him."

Whitney's mind was racing over the facts she possessed, and the conclusion she was reaching rejected everything she was hearing from this detective.

Adam Justice was no killer. He was an honorable man. A gentle man. A caring man.

"If you had any so-called *goods* on Adam, you would have arrested him."

"The only reason we haven't arrested him, Ms. West, is because we don't have everything we need yet. Which is why I'm here. Detective Ferkel and I need to ask you some questions."

"I can't help you."

"You can tell us everything Patrice told you about Justice that day she left her will with you. You realize, of course, that the reason she prepared it was because she knew Justice was dangerous and had already threatened to kill her."

"I know nothing of the sort. The day Patrice gave me the envelope containing her will, she told me Adam Justice was wonderful and that she was in love with him."

"Then why was she running away from him in fear of her life not six months later?"

"She wasn't in fear of her life. She had met and fallen in love with someone else."

"You don't believe that any more than I do, Ms. West."

The more she had gotten to know Adam, the harder that part *was* to believe. Still, Whitney had no intention of admitting any doubts to this thoroughly disagreeable man.

"Don't presume to tell me what I believe, Sergeant."

"Well, then I'll tell you what I believe. Patrice was scared to death of Justice. When Peter Danner agreed to take her away from him and protect her from her pseudohusband, she jumped at the chance. The only trouble was Peter Danner couldn't make good on his promises."

"That's absurd."

"Is it? Justice fixed Danner's car so he'd lose control and the two of them would plunge to their deaths."

"Adam wouldn't do such a thing."

"Why? Because you two just spent a cozy night together in Las Vegas?"

Whitney was taking a very strong dislike to this detective-sergeant. A very strong dislike.

"I don't like being followed."

"Then maybe you should stay out of the company of murderers."

"You're throwing around a lot of accusations, Sergeant, but you haven't given me any proof that Adam was involved in Patrice's death. And until you have such proof, you can just get the hell out of here."

Ryson smiled as he headed for the door. It was not a nice smile. "Don't make the mistake of falling for the man, Ms. West. The last woman who did ended up dead."

Chapter Eleven

Adam punched in Whitney's office number. He had no idea what Sergeant Ryson had said to her the day before when he'd dropped her off at her place, but he could guess. When a secretary who identified herself as Isabel put him directly through, he knew at least Whitney wouldn't refuse his call.

"Hi, Adam," Whitney said a second later. "I'm so glad you called. What's up?"

Adam tried not to feel so pleased with the warmth in her tone as he imbued his own with cool formality. "Our first debtor claimant to Patrice's money has come forward."

"Uh-oh," Whitney said. "Who is it?"

"Stanford Carver, an attorney representing this claimant, is waiting in my outer office, insisting on telling me in person. Would you care to sit in?"

"You know I would."

"How long will it take you to get here?"

"I just interviewed my last bogus claimant for the day. I can be there in half an hour at the most."

"I'll stall him."

"Adam?"

"Yes?"

"Sergeant Ryson is an idiot. Why don't you slap a slander suit on him?"

Adam quickly squashed the leap of satisfaction that sprang up at hearing her unqualified belief in his innocence.

"He has to hurt my reputation first, Whitney. As you know, slander is about injury. And since you have obviously failed to take his accusations seriously, you leave me with no grounds."

"So, what you're saying is, it's all my fault you can't go after him?"

He heard the smile in her voice and imagined those mischievous golden lights collecting in her brandy eyes.

"Yes, Ms. West," he said in his most formal tone. "Perhaps the next time you might try to be more cooperative when someone accuses me of murder."

Her answer was a warm laugh that circled in a snug little ring around his heart.

"MR. JUSTICE, MS. WEST," Stanford Carver said in a quick, sharp voice as he took the chair next to Whitney's in front of Adam's desk after Adam had performed the introductions.

Carver was a tall, slender, well-dressed man with thinning brown hair, a long, bony nose and deep-set eyes that darted around Adam's office, clearly assessing it for prestige value.

Carver didn't offer his hand for a shake and Adam retook his seat without offering his.

"My secretary tells me you represent a debtor claimant against the Patrice Feldon estate," Adam said.

"That's right," Carver replied. The words shot out of his mouth like from a pop gun, loud and fast. "I'm the chief inhouse attorney for Crowe-Cromwell, a major pharmaceutical company headquartered in Olympia."

"I've heard of Crowe-Cromwell," Adam said.

"Of course you have," Carver replied. "We've been on the leading edge of the latest in medical research for four decades."

There was a pompousness about this man that was beginning to get on Adam's nerves.

"What is Crowe-Cromwell's interest in the Patrice Feldon estate?" Adam asked, careful to keep his voice cool and unemotional.

Carver leaned over the side of his chair and reached into his briefcase to pull out a dark brown, accordion-type cardboard file. He got up and placed it on the desk in front of Adam. Then Carver sat down again and leaned back in his chair as if his actions had given Adam his answer.

Adam made no move to open the cardboard file, but maintained steady eye contact with the man. "Mr. Carver, I have a very busy schedule. I would appreciate your stating your business."

Carver motioned to the file he had placed before Adam. "It's all in there, Justice."

"What, Mr. Carver?"

A frown of impatience formed on Carver's brow. "All you have to do is read the file."

Adam rose. "Mr. Carver, I don't intend to read about the reason for your visit. If you don't wish to discuss it, this meeting is over."

Carver looked distinctly put out. Adam understood that the man had wanted Adam to rummage through the material in the cardboard file, no doubt intending the discovery process to create some form of suspense or dramatics.

The fact that Adam refused to be orchestrated in such a manner was not sitting well with Carver. He was obviously a man used to dominating and receiving deference in return.

He came forward in his chair with undisguised irritation.

"All right, Justice. You want the cold, hard facts? I'll give them to you."

Adam sat back down.

"Patrice Feldon worked for Crowe-Cromwell in our research-and-development lab for nearly three years."

"What was the full name of the Patrice Feldon who worked for Crowe-Cromwell?" Adam asked.

"Patrice Dulcinea Feldon, born August 2, 1964," Carver said, shooting out his answer. "And you and I both know that information has not gotten into the news. There's only one way I could have known it."

"Go on."

"During her last year with Crowe-Cromwell, Patrice Feldon performed as an assistant to Dr. Lydon Miller, one of Crowe-Cromwell's top research scientists. Her position was a sensitive one. It necessitated our giving her a top-security clearance."

"Are you saying Patrice was given a government security clearance?" Adam asked.

"A top-security clearance is also an in-house term with us," Carver said. "Our security team is manned by some ex-Feds and it's just as thorough as the FBI's. Patrice Feldon's fingerprints were run through all the right computers to check for any prior criminal acts. She came up clean—otherwise, we would never have let her on the lot to the R-and-D wing."

"All right. You checked her background. Then what?"

"Then one day, nine years ago, she failed to show up for work. No notice. No nothing."

"Why did Patrice do that, Mr. Carver?" Whitney asked.

Carver turned to her. "The department manager believed she was despondent over the death of the research scientist she had been assisting."

"The Dr. Lydon Miller you spoke of?"

"Yes. He lost his wife to cancer. It unbalanced him mentally. He committed suicide."

"That's...tragic," Whitney said. "I can understand how Patrice could have been so distraught that she stopped going to work."

"That isn't why she stopped going," Carver said, no sympathy in his tone.

Whitney leaned forward. "Then why did she?"

"The answers are all in those records sitting in front of Justice. All you have to do is read them."

"All you have to do is come to the point, Mr. Carver," Adam said, still making no move to read the indicated records. "Neither Ms. West nor I are fond of having our time wasted."

Pink bands slashed into Carver's cheeks. A frown dug a trough in his forehead.

"The point is that when Patrice Feldon was assisting Dr. Miller that last year before his death, Dr. Miller was working on a revolutionary new fertility process, better than anything anyone else had on the market. He had just finished his final experiments and entered his data into the computer when his wife died, and he made that tragic decision to take his own life. Naturally the whole R-and-D section was stunned by his death. It wasn't until after Dr. Miller's funeral that his department head even thought of looking. And that's when he discovered it.''

"Discovered what?" Whitney asked.

"That Dr. Miller's formula for his new fertility process and all his research data had been deleted from the computer data base."

"Why would he have done that?" Whitney asked.

"*He* didn't."

"How can you be so certain?"

"Because the computer records showed the files had been cleaned out the day *after* Dr. Miller's death."

"And you think it was Patrice Feldon who did it," Adam said.

"Damn right we do."

"But why?" Whitney asked.

"Because she was the only other person with access to Dr. Miller's computer code and, therefore, the missing files."

"No, I mean why would she destroy his work?" Whitney said.

Carver's jaw locked. "She didn't destroy his work. She copied his formula and all the test results onto floppy disks. Then she wiped Crowe-Cromwell's data base clean so that when she sold the fertility formula, we wouldn't be able to compete with the company that marketed it. That bitch robbed us blind."

"I resent the use of that word in reference to a human female, Mr. Carver," Whitney said, her warm voice cooled considerably. "'Bitch' is a term for a dog, not a woman."

Carver's jaw clenched even more as the pink bands on his cheeks flashed red. He was clearly upset to be receiving this verbal dressing-down from Whitney. He obviously thought himself too exalted a personage to have to put up with criticism from anyone.

Adam almost smiled at the way Whitney looked Carver directly in his arrogant eye, just as if she were ready to spit in it. He wasn't surprised to see it was Carver who looked away first.

"If Patrice Feldon stole this formula as you say, Mr. Carver," Adam began, "why didn't Crowe-Cromwell prosecute her?"

"Because by the time we realized the files were gone, so was she."

"Still, you could have taken action," Adam said.

"We didn't know she intended to sell the formula. We thought Dr. Miller's death had unbalanced her, too, and that was the reason she had destroyed the files."

"And when did you decide that wasn't the case?"

"When Emery Pharmaceuticals started marketing our product."

"If you were so sure that Patrice sold them your formula, why didn't you take legal action then?"

"Normally we would have placed the facts of such a theft in the hands of the authorities and let them take it from there. But our senior management was in a very precarious position at the time with regards to a proxy fight. The bad publicity of such a theft would undoubtedly have led to accusations of sloppy management and undermined our chairman's efforts to maintain his leadership role. We simply couldn't afford to go public with the matter."

"So you hushed it up?" Whitney said.

"We didn't know where Patrice Feldon had gone. We assumed it was somewhere in Canada, since she'd sold the formula to a Canadian company. We had no idea the company had paid her in stock. We thought she had a fistful of cash in hand and a lot of foreign land in which to disappear. Based on that we figured the chances of locating and prosecuting her were slim. We chose not to broadcast the theft."

"But you're willing to do so now?" Whitney asked.

"Now we have the evidence tying her to the Vancouver pharmaceutical firm who she sold the formula to and who marketed our fertility drug."

"What records do you have verifying that Dr. Lydon Miller was working on the fertility process you describe?"

"I can produce the sworn affidavits of half a dozen of Dr. Miller's fellow scientists at Crowe-Cromwell. I also have these two internal company memoranda," Carver said, getting up and slipping his hand inside the folder on Adam's desk to pull out a couple of sheets. He passed them to Adam before resuming his seat.

Adam perused the memoranda. Both carried Dr. Miller's signature and were dated nine years previously. They were enthusiastic reports about the results he was achieving with a new process of embryonic implant.

In both memoranda Dr. Miller was asking for more money to go forward with the experiments. In the later memorandum the request was almost a plea. It spoke of having had to arrange with a Dr. McGrory for the test subjects. Adam passed the documents on to Whitney as he directed a question to Carver.

"Does this McGrory—the person who Dr. Miller mentions briefly in one of these memoranda—work for Crowe-Cromwell?"

Carver shifted uneasily in his chair. "No, he's a professor at the University of Washington. The men were friends."

"Is the purpose of this visit to tell us you are going public with this matter now?" Adam asked.

Carver turned to Whitney. "Justice and I have a few private items to discuss. You'll have to excuse us."

"Ms. West stays," Adam said before Whitney had a chance to respond.

Carver turned to him, a bead of irritation digging across his forehead. "This is a very sensitive matter, Justice."

"Ms. West stays," Adam repeated.

Carver looked decidedly put out with Adam's uncompromising stand. He shifted some more in his seat before resuming. "All right. As we at Crowe-Cromwell see it, there's no reason to give all the particulars on this sensitive matter to the press, not if an equitable accommodation can be reached."

"Equitable accommodation?" Adam repeated.

Carver leaned forward. "We know she made you the executor of her estate, so it's really pretty simple. You recognize our claim as sole debtor and hand over the stock. In return, we see to it that your fees are covered with a special bonus for speed and efficiency."

"A special bonus?"

"The stock clearly belongs to us. We're going to get it. Why subject the courts and everyone else concerned to a useless, protracted and costly probate? I'm authorized to offer you a quarter million to handle this matter expeditiously. This is in addition to your normal fees, of course. What do you say, Justice?"

"Mr. Carver, you have not yet submitted a claim against Ms. Feldon's estate. Until you do, there is no way for me to assess its merits."

Carver's voice rose in disbelief. "Assess its merits? Haven't you been listening? Patrice Feldon stole our secret formula. Then she turned around and sold it to Emery Pharmaceuticals. Every penny in her estate belongs to us."

"What proof do you have that Patrice Feldon took your formula?" Adam asked.

"Proof? The proof is the fact that she ended up with all that stock in that Canadian pharmaceutical firm that came out with Crowe-Cromwell's fertility drug."

"That stock is not proof, Mr. Carver."

"The hell it isn't. What is this, Justice, a shakedown? You want half a million? Three-quarters?"

"What I want, Mr. Carver, is to see that Patrice Feldon's estate is properly executed."

Carver lunged out of his chair, rested his knuckles on Adam's desktop and leaned his tall frame toward Adam menacingly. "Don't jerk me around, Justice. You don't handle this right, you can count on the newspapers getting the complete story from us."

"And why should that concern me, Mr. Carver?"

"Oh, the truth might prove a little embarrassing to Crowe-Cromwell, but it will prove a lot more than embarrassing to you. No one is going to believe you didn't know who she re-

ally was and what she had done when you married her under
that alias. On the contrary, after we get through, everyone will
know you were in on this theft and fraud. Your name won't be
worth spit, I guarantee it. And neither will this law practice.
You have twenty-four hours to make the right decision,
Justice.''

And with that, Stanford Carver stomped out of the room
and slammed the door behind him.

"I'VE BEEN OVER this stuff so many times I'm getting cross-
eyed," Whitney said, looking up from studying the contents
of the cardboard file that Carver had left. "Haven't you seen
enough yet?"

Adam held up his hand, not taking his eyes off what he was
reading. "Just a minute, Whitney. I have this one last document to review."

Whitney leaned an elbow across the black leather sofa in the
corner of Adam's office, her feet tucked beneath her. It was a
room full of natural light, bordered on two sides by floor-to-
ceiling windows, its steel-and-leather furniture clean, crisply
modern, functional. There were no plants, pictures or any
other touch that might have lent something of a personal nature.

To Whitney this room was a perfect outward manifestation
of the man beside her. But it reflected none of what she knew
he was inside. None of the humor. The gentleness. The
warmth.

She studied his clean, strong features—a man's features,
nothing boyish about them. His lustrous black hair was rich
and straight and full, like a lion's mane.

But he was a lion who didn't waste his energies on roaring.

No matter how much Stanford Carver had tried to manip-
ulate, intimidate or provoke him, Adam had remained perfectly cool and calm and in control.

Finally Adam set the document with the others on the glass
coffee table. He ignored the last triangle of chicken sandwich
and instead swallowed the remainder of the cold coffee in his

cup—the remnants of the late lunch his secretary had brought for them both. He leaned against the sofa's back.

"The birth date of Patrice Dulcinea Feldon is the same as that on the birth certificate Patrice left with her will," Adam said.

"It looks like her handwriting on the application form," Whitney added. "The photo they took for the employee ID looks like her. The documentation of Miller's suicide and Patrice's job abandonment seems pretty thorough, too."

"Agreed," Adam said. "Carver ties Patrice to Crowe-Cromwell, and the stock in her estate ties her to Emery Pharmaceuticals. At this point in time those are the two strongest points to his case."

"If this claim Carver has made is true, it would explain why Patrice was using an alias when you met her. She was hiding her identity so Crowe-Cromwell wouldn't find her."

"That occurred to me, too."

"Linda Carmichael said Patrice worked with a scientist developing a new fertility process. And then Patrice arranged for Linda to be the recipient of donated embryos implanted by Emery Pharmaceuticals in conjunction with their new fertility process. If Carver finds out about Linda and the children—"

"Yes, Whitney, I know. Still, at this point we are not obliged to tell him, and the company has offered nothing to substantiate that this Dr. Miller ever produced such a fertility process—much less that Patrice stole the formula for it."

The intercom on Adam's desk buzzed.

Adam got up, walked over to it and pressed the button to connect him with his secretary. "Yes?"

"Piper Lane and Gavin Yeagher are here to see you, Adam."

"Good. Send them in."

He turned to Whitney. "They wouldn't have come unless they had some news."

Whitney quickly slipped her feet into her shoes and stood, turning her attention to the couple entering the office.

The woman was very well-groomed, with shining titian hair drawn to the top of her head and arresting turquoise eyes beneath thick bangs. Behind her was a very casually dressed lumberjack-size man, with unruly wavy brown hair, deep brown eyes and the beginnings of a scraggly beard. Whitney thought they made quite a contrast—she so neatly groomed, and he so unruly and unkept.

"Piper Lane, Gavin Yeagher, this is Whitney West," Adam said.

Piper stepped forward and offered her hand and a smile. Whitney liked the firm shake and straight look of the woman right away. Then Gavin took Whitney's hand and treated her to a charming lopsided grin that revealed two very deep dimples.

"You'll have to excuse Gavin," Piper said to Whitney with a conspiratorial wink. "He thinks the grizzly-bear look is in."

Gavin released Whitney's hand and turned to Piper, both dimples in clear evidence as he stroked the week-old growth spiking out of his chin.

"Most women tell me I'm more like a big, cuddly teddy bear."

"Until the next morning, when they sober up and discover their face is red and sore from those whiskers," Piper said, a dash of merriment in her turquoise eyes. "Do the female population of Seattle a favor and get a razor, Gavin."

Gavin chuckled easily at the ribbing.

"So what is it you've learned?" Adam asked, gesturing them to seats around the conversation area where he and Whitney had been studying the Crowe-Cromwell records.

"Very little with respect to who Patrice Feldon was," Piper answered as she took a seat in one of the black leather chairs across from the sofa. "There is no birth date for a Patrice Dulcinea Feldon in any county in Washington State for the last thirty-five years. But I did find that there was a Patrice Anne Waring born in Seattle on February 4, 1964."

"Are you saying she really was Patrice Anne Waring?" Whitney asked as she sat again on the sofa.

"No, Patrice Anne Waring was a crib death at two months old. Patrice Feldon apparently wrote for her birth certificate and used it to take a G.E.D. test that allowed her to enroll at UW under that name just a couple of months before Adam met her."

"How did she know about Patrice Waring?" Whitney asked.

"Probably by reading the name and birth date off her tombstone," Piper said. "It's really not that difficult to get someone else's birth certificate and, with it, take on another identity."

"Is that all you've found out so far?" Adam asked.

"About Patrice's background," Piper said. "But since you called and left that message about your visit from Stanford Carver, I started inquiries at the Crowe-Cromwell lab in Olympia. So far, nothing. They're a tight-knit group, and no one's talking. Our best lead is this Dr. Grover McGrory that Miller mentioned in his memorandum. I've set up a luncheon meeting with you and him tomorrow at Elliott's Oyster House, Pier 56."

"Good." Adam turned to Gavin. "Find out anything about the stock?"

"Yes," Gavin said, resting one scuffed boot over the knee of his other leg. He had taken the chair next to Piper's. His blue jeans were very worn and frayed at the bottom. Whitney had a hard time picturing Gavin as the financial guru Adam had described. The guy didn't look as if he had that proverbial dime to his name.

"Before we get into the matter of this stock, Adam, I'm curious as to why Patrice prepared a will instead of placing her assets into the kind of trust that could pass to her beneficiaries without all this probate cost and state intervention. When I think of all the time and money wasted—"

Adam held up a hand. "You're right, Gavin. I always recommend trusts to my clients."

"How is it, then, that Patrice didn't listen to your advice?"

"She didn't ask for my advice. Now, what have you found out about that stock?"

Gavin draped his hands, which looked more to Whitney like rough clubs, over the arms of his chair and leaned his hefty bulk against the back. "Nine years ago Emery Pharmaceuticals was barely making it, rumored to be going under. And then, suddenly—miraculously, by some accounts—they came out with a revolutionary new fertility process based on embryo implant. It was far more advanced and superior to anything else anywhere in the world."

"Is there a big market for such a fertility process?"

"Very big, particularly here in the States. Baby boomers who delayed having children to get educated and establish careers are now trying to make up for lost time. Those who experience fertility problems—and there are a lot of them—are reaching for whatever help they can get. Emery's process has a ninety-nine percent success rate and boasts no side effects, unlike other drugs that have been linked to cancer."

"Sounds like a winning combination," Whitney said.

"Which explains why the company has grown by leaps and bounds. Today it's a major pharmaceutical concern, with yearly sales in the multimillions."

"And all because of this new fertility process?" Adam asked.

"It certainly was what jump-started their corporate engine nine years ago."

"What's it going to take to find out if their research scientists developed such a process?"

"Well, unlike other companies, pharmaceuticals spend a big chunk of their profits on research and development. The competition is stiff, so they're very secretive about what they're doing. The only way for Piper and me to find out anything is to fly up there and do some poking around the skeletons in their R-and-D closet. Which is why we're on a flight leaving in two hours."

"Is there any reason Emery couldn't have come up with the process on their own?" Adam asked. "They could have. But the stock that was issued to Patrice was preferred stock. It's generally only issued to officers of the company or capital-supplying investors."

"I doubt Patrice had any money to invest," Whitney said.

"Still, if she had that fertility formula to offer them," Gavin said, "it was better than money."

"I'M NOT LOOKING FORWARD to telling Commissioner Snowe about the Crowe-Cromwell claim," Whitney said to Adam as they entered the elevator in the hallway outside the Justice Inc. office. "I really hate the idea of Crowe-Cromwell getting that money instead of the D'Amicos and the Rubins and the Carmichaels—even if it does technically belong to them."

"They don't have it yet," Adam said as he pressed the button for the garage level. "We still have a lot of facts to gather before coming to any final conclusions. Sorting out what happened nine years ago and Patrice's part in it is going to take time. And I have no intention of introducing Crowe-Cromwell's claim to Commissioner Snowe until Carver fills out the proper paperwork."

"Since he gave you twenty-four hours to accept his deal that means he's not intending to file until tomorrow. So what do we do in the interim?" Whitney asked as they stepped off the elevator.

"While Piper and Gavin fly to Vancouver to see what they can learn from Emery Pharmaceuticals, I suggest we—"

"Talk to me," A.J.'s voice said suddenly from behind Adam, finishing his sentence.

Adam turned, surprised to see his sister, but not surprised he hadn't heard her. A.J. could move as silently as a whisper when she wanted to.

Adam introduced Whitney.

"I've been hearing a lot about you lately, A.J.," Whitney said, her tone warm.

"And I've been hearing a lot about you," A.J. said. Adam noted that his sister's manner and tone seemed excessively formal for the occasion.

She quickly turned back to him. "We need to talk, Adam."

Adam felt a vague sense of unease collecting in the pit of his stomach. "You've learned something?" he asked.

"I've found the foster family who raised Patrice," A.J. said.

Adam smiled. "I had no doubts you would."

A.J. did not smile back.

"What's wrong?" Adam asked, his previous uneasiness growing appreciably in light of his sister's continued formality.

A.J. glanced over at Whitney.

"You can speak freely, A.J.," Adam said, sensing his sister's hesitation.

The elevator doors opened, and a bunch of workers from other offices in the building began to pile out into the underground garage on their way to their cars.

"Not here," A.J. said, after a quick glance at the group.

"Shall we go back up to the office?" Adam asked.

"No. I'll meet you at your place."

And with that, A.J. turned and walked away.

Adam watched his sister disappear into her Jeep Cherokee at the end of a row of parked cars.

"What's wrong?" Whitney asked beside him.

"I don't know, but something has upset her. Whatever it is, it must relate to her finding that foster home. I'd like you to be there to hear what she has to say."

"But the question is, will A.J. want me there?"

Adam turned to Whitney, surprised by her question. "Why should she object? She knows I will not keep something from you that is germane to this investigation. You might as well learn what she's found out now instead of later."

Whitney said nothing in response. Adam was certain he understood her hesitation.

"A.J. isn't generally so abrupt, Whitney. Don't take it personally. Something is bothering her."

"Yes." She paused to sigh. "Obviously. As you say, I might as well find out now. I'll follow you in my car."

Whitney turned to go.

Adam reached out to take her arm, halting her retreat. "Ride with me. I'll bring you back here later."

She looked up at him, surprise in her eyes.

He understood her surprise. All day long he'd resisted saying or doing anything that wasn't in keeping with the businesslike behavior she had a right to expect of him. Still, he had almost kissed her in the car the morning before when he drove her home. And now, as he looked into her face tilted up to his, his arms ached to hold her.

He shouldn't have asked her to ride with him. He shouldn't be touching her. He should be keeping his distance. He shouldn't be wondering what it would have been like two nights ago if he hadn't walked out of her hotel room.

He shouldn't be, but he was.

"Come ride with me, Whitney," he said again.

Before she could say the words that would remind them both of all the good reasons why she shouldn't, he urged her over to the passenger side and opened the door to the Jaguar, helping her inside and closing the door behind her.

She could have protested. If she had, he told himself he would have backed off immediately. But she hadn't protested, and he was halfway to convincing himself that she wanted this as much as he.

She was quiet on the drive to his home. He was quiet, too, reflecting on this step he had just taken toward violating their agreement. He knew he could still stop this. He knew it wasn't too late. He could still drive her back to her car tonight.

He knew he wasn't going to.

He passed through the security gate and drove up to his house. A.J. was already parked in the driveway. He had been so preoccupied with thoughts of Whitney that he had nearly forgotten he was meeting A.J. here. And why.

He remembered now. And with the memory came a renewed sense of foreboding as he reflected on A.J.'s somber demeanor.

He left the Jaguar at the front curb. When they were all in the house, he closed the door behind them and led the way into the living room, flipping on the lights. He gestured toward the white silk sectional sofa. Whitney sat, but A.J. headed for the portable bar to immediately mix some drinks.

Adam's unease continued to mount. His sister rarely drank.

A disturbing quiet descended on the room, broken only by the click of ice cubes and the pouring of liquor. A.J. filled three glasses and handed the first to Whitney.

"Campari and soda, right?"

Whitney took the glass from her with a startled glance. "Yes, that's what I prefer, but how did you—"

A.J. turned to Adam. "And your favorite, straight Smirnoff on the rocks."

Adam took the drink and the lick of apprehension that went with it.

A.J. raised her glass for the toast. "To honesty, loyalty and love—the three dying arts," she said. Adam and Whitney only took a sip in response to the toast. A.J. drained her glass.

Adam put his drink down on the black onyx coffee table. "A.J., what is it? What did you learn?"

She faced him fully. "The names of Patrice Feldon's foster parents are Marla and Lydon Miller."

"Lydon Miller?" Adam said. "As in Dr. Lydon Miller, the scientist at Crowe-Cromwell?"

"The very same. Patrice was raised by the Millers until she was eighteen. She went off to the University of Puget Sound, received an undergraduate degree under the name of Feldon and went to work for her foster father as his assistant at Crowe-Cromwell."

"That ties her to Crowe-Cromwell even more strongly," Whitney said, resting her drink on the coffee table.

Adam nodded. "This news is far from palatable in terms of the beneficiaries, A.J. But I don't see the necessity of washing it down with a drink."

"That's because I haven't ted you the least palatable part of it yet. Patrice wasn't the only one of the Rubins' runaways that the Millers took in and raised. Three years before, they accepted a thirteen-year-old boy by the name of Peter Danner."

A.J.'s words hacked through Adam's memories like a machete, slashing and shredding their previous meanings.

Peter Danner. A.J.'s fiancé. Patrice's lover.

"Yes, Adam," A.J. said. "Patrice and Peter played us both for fools from the start. They didn't meet through us, five months before she ran off with him, as they both pretended. They had known each other from childhood."

Adam could barely believe how completely he had been duped. Up until now, he'd looked upon his year of marriage to Patrice before Peter had come along as idyllic. But now he knew all the time it had been Patrice and Peter.

The phone began to ring. Adam ignored it.

He reached for his drink instead.

Chapter Twelve

Whitney watched Adam's face as he calmly sipped his drink. As usual no emotion reflected in his strong, stoic features. But she could imagine what he must be feeling. Her heart pitched painfully.

A.J. silenced the ringing telephone.

"It's Octavia," she said, handing the receiver to Adam.

When Adam took the phone, A.J. turned to Whitney. "Walk me out," she said.

It was more of a summons than an invitation. Whitney got up and followed A.J. outside.

A warm night breeze whispered through the trees as they walked slowly toward the Jeep.

"Wouldn't you prefer to take a taxi home, A.J.?" Whitney asked, breaking the uncomfortable silence that had stretched between them.

"There's no cause for concern. Unlike yours and Adam's, my glass was filled with plain water."

"Of course. I should have realized you had better sense."

A.J. stopped when she reached her Jeep, then turned to face Whitney. She crossed her arms over her chest. Her tone was cool and impersonal. "Not your first error in judgment on this matter, is it?"

Whitney had been expecting this. A.J. was strikingly similar to her brother in many ways—the same black hair, the same pale blue eyes, the same uncompromising look in them. When

A.J.'s eyes had met Whitney's tonight, Whitney knew it was all over. She had been found out.

"So, are you going to tell Adam or am I?" A.J. asked.

Whitney took a deep breath and slowly let it out. "I'll tell him."

"When?"

"Tonight. I'm sorry, A.J. I couldn't tell him before."

A.J.'s uncompromising look did not change. Neither did the cool tone of her voice. "You couldn't be *honest?*"

"He would never have let me be the G.A.L. for the unnamed heirs on the case."

"You've never been about money or publicity before. I would have thought this kind of subterfuge beneath you."

"I had to know about Patrice. I had to understand why she did what she did . . . to me."

A.J. uncrossed her arms. "Did to *you?* What did Patrice do to you?"

Whitney said nothing, mostly because she didn't know how to begin to explain to this strong woman what it was like to be so weak-minded and foolish.

"Does this have anything to do with a man?" A.J. asked after a moment.

Her understanding startled Whitney. "Yes."

"A man. Of course. What else? I should have guessed."

A.J.'s face and tone softened with those words, telling Whitney very clearly that as strong as she might be, A.J. was a woman who had suffered from something very similar.

Whitney rested her hand on A.J.'s arm to let her know she understood. "At least when Patrice took the man I loved, she did it openly."

A.J. shook her head. Her tone was decidedly disappointed. "I'm sorry to hear it."

"Sorry to hear it?" Whitney repeated, removing her hand, certain she must have heard wrong.

"Yes, Whitney. I hoped what you had to tell Adam about Patrice would be completely descriptive of the callous disregard and contempt she had for the feelings of others."

"You hoped?" Whitney echoed, still surprised at this reaction.

"Adam needs to hear the worst."

"He's already heard the worst," Whitney said.

"Has he? When she left him for Peter, that should have done it. Hearing about Huntley and Brinkley Carmichael should have done it. Learning tonight that Patrice lied to him from the start about her and Peter should have done it. But I'm not sure any of it has."

"Done it? Done what? A.J., what are you talking about?"

"Whitney, do you care for my brother as much as he cares for you?"

"Cares for me? How do you know he cares anything for me?"

"You're the first woman he has brought to his home since Patrice left it. Do you understand? The first one in *seven years*. Not even his female law partners have been invited here. When he drove up here with you tonight, I knew. Don't you see? That's why I didn't tell him about you and Patrice back there just now. That's why I'm giving you this chance to tell him yourself."

A warm, exciting rush washed through Whitney. Adam cared for her—enough to bring her to his home. She'd had no idea what his inviting her here tonight meant.

"I realized that for the first time there was hope he'd be able to put the past behind him and extinguish the torch for that damn woman," A.J. continued.

Whitney's warm rush quickly trickled to a complete stop.

"The torch for...you don't mean he still cares for Patrice?" Whitney said. "No, A.J. That's impossible. He hates her."

"Hates her? He hasn't shown any interest in another woman in seven years. Does that sound like hate to you?"

"She hurt him. Her betrayal made him lose faith in love."

"Lose faith? Whitney, open your eyes. Look at his house— his black-and-white house. It wasn't that way when he first brought her here. It was full of bright, beautiful color. But she couldn't see the color. All she could see was gray. She was—"

"Color-blind," Whitney said, understanding dawning. "That's right. I remember now. Patrice was color-blind."

"And that's why he ripped all the color out of his house—and his life—and replaced it with black and white. For her."

"She did talk about having the house redone," Whitney said. "Getting rid of the busy wallpaper. Covering the furniture in white silk. Putting in the black marble floors."

"Only she didn't stay around long enough to do it," A.J. said. "So Adam changed it for her. After she was gone. After she had run away with Peter."

"Afterward?" Whitney said.

"Yes, Whitney. Afterward. He made it a shrine to her. Does that sound to you like a man who's lost faith in love? Or does that sound like a man who will always be hopelessly in love with that damn dead woman."

Whitney licked dry lips. "No, A.J., that's not possible. Not after all he's learned. He can't still . . . love her."

"I'd like to think you're right, Whitney. I'd like to think that finally the truth about her has broken the yoke of her hold on his heart. But I have to warn you. Adam has a loyal heart. Too damn loyal for his own good."

"ADAM, I JUST HEARD from my contact in the sheriff's office," Octavia said over the phone. "They found your golden cross and neck chain in the wreckage. They tracked them back to the jeweler. They know Patrice gave them to you."

"I should have realized I lost them there," Adam said, relieved that A.J. had suggested Whitney walk her to her Jeep. This was not a conversation he would have been comfortable conducting in front of either A.J. or Whitney. "Well, now at least we know why Sergeant Ryson has been paying me so much attention."

"There's more, Adam. Ryson got approval to send the golden chain and cross and the remnants from the wreckage back to the FBI forensic team for a more extensive evaluation. The reports are due back anytime. Adam, I have to ask. If what they have is enough to convince a judge to issue a search warrant, what will they find?"

"I'll take care of it, Octavia," Adam said carefully.

Octavia sighed. "Oh, hell, I knew it. You never threw it away. For your sake, for both our sakes, get rid of it, Adam. Tonight. Now. And if Ryson shows up with a warrant of any kind, call me. Do not try to do this alone. You know an attorney who represents himself has a fool for a client."

"I'll be in touch," Adam said before hanging up the phone.

Adam got up slowly and walked into his study. He made directly for his desk. He opened the bottom drawer. He reached beneath the family album, beneath the stack of his law-review honors, to the very bottom. He found what he had been seeking, removed it and closed the drawer.

Carefully he unwrapped the crystal picture frame. He stared at the picture of the woman it held, the incomparable woman.

Large, velvety, violet eyes set in a heart-shaped face. Porcelain skin surrounded by thick golden curls. And that angelic-looking smile.

All too beautiful to be real.

"Oh, God, it's true," Whitney's voice said from the doorway.

Adam looked up with a start. He hadn't heard her come in. When he saw the look of utter dismay on her face, he was astounded. He set Patrice's picture on the desk and went to her. With every step he took toward her, she seemed to grow sadder.

"Whitney, what's wrong? What's happened?"

"A.J. was right. You've kept Patrice's picture all this time because you've never stopped loving her. Even now, after all you've learned, you still love her."

"A.J. told you that?" Adam asked, more than surprised that his sister would share such a confidence with Whitney. He could think of only one reason why A.J. would. He was so fascinated with that discovery that for a moment it made him miss the anger and hurt in Whitney's voice.

"Were Patrice to walk into this room this minute, you would forgive her, wouldn't you? You're just like Michael and all the others—still worshiping at the altar of her beauty."

The message in her words immediately grabbed his attention.

"What are you talking about, Whitney? What others? Who's Michael?"

"You want to know about Michael? Fine, I'll tell you. Michael was my fiancé, my first love, the man I would be spending my life with if Patrice hadn't happened along. Yes, Adam. I knew Patrice long before she waltzed into my office that day and asked me to hold that envelope for you. I knew her long before you two even met."

A dozen emotions marched through Adam, anger and disappointment leading the charge. He took Whitney's shoulders within his hands and stared hard into her eyes.

"You lied to me about knowing Patrice?"

She stared back, meeting his gaze squarely. He could see the stiff pride keeping her spine and shoulders erect.

"Just because I didn't tell you everything doesn't mean I lied to you. I'm not accusing you of lying to me because you neglected to mention you still love her. You want to know about me and Patrice? Well, that's fine, because I'm ready to tell you all about it."

Adam kept his tone cool, but just barely. "You're *ready?*"

Hurt filled her eyes. "Unless you're too angry to listen."

Adam's anger fled in the face of Whitney's words and the sadness in her eyes. Gently he drew her over to the couch in the corner of his study. He urged her to take a seat and sat beside her. When she attempted to move away, he followed and lightly wrapped his arm around her shoulders.

"I'm ready to listen, Whitney."

Her body was stiff, ungiving, but at least she didn't pull away. She looked down at her hands as she began.

"Patrice and I became roommates during my second semester at the University of Puget Sound. She was there under the name of Feldon, going for her degree, just as A.J. told you. I was there with my leg in a cast—a skiing accident that had occurred over the Christmas holidays. She was so helpful and kind as I hobbled around. I never imagined she could do anything cruel."

Whitney paused as a small, unhappy sigh escaped her lips.

"Is this where Michael comes in?" Adam guessed.

Whitney nodded. "He was a teaching assistant. We had met the first semester and had become engaged. We were planning to marry as soon as the school year ended. He didn't come back with me after our skiing trip over the Christmas holidays. He stayed with his folks to help out with his older brother's wedding.

"I was attending college on a scholarship. But I was ready to give up college and my dreams of a career in law to stay home and be his wife. I fell for Michael heart and soul, as one does for a first love. We even had the names picked out for the children we planned to have.

"I told Patrice all about him long before I introduced them. I considered her my friend, my confidante, the sister I never had. And then she repaid my affection and friendship by deliberately going after Michael the moment she laid eyes on him."

Whitney paused to flash Adam a look. "Oh, I know what you're thinking. You're thinking it was Michael and not Patrice who made the first move. You're wrong. I watched Michael when he met Patrice. He looked at her with appreciation as men do with a woman that beautiful. But when he looked back at me, the light of love was still burning brightly in his eyes.

"I realize now that's what Patrice couldn't forgive. Even after seeing her perfection, Michael still preferred me. From that moment on she made Michael her conquest, determined to win him. It didn't take her long. Three weeks later Michael broke off our engagement.

"I was bewildered, heartbroken by what I had watched taking place right before my eyes. I told myself that Patrice must have immediately fallen in love with Michael and not been able to help herself. I believed that Michael's response proved they were meant to be together. I neither blamed nor reproached them. But I couldn't stay around and watch them together anymore.

"I moved out of the dorm room I shared with Patrice into an apartment by myself and nursed my broken heart. Almost immediately afterward she came to see me. She told me she missed our talks. She said she'd break up with Michael if I'd move back in with her.

"At first I didn't understand. I thought that she felt so bad about losing our friendship that she was willing to give up the man she loved to make amends. When I told her that I could never accept such a sacrifice from her, she laughed and told me it wasn't a sacrifice. She said she didn't love Michael. She never had.

"I was angrier at her than I had been at anyone in my life. 'If you really want him, I'll send him back to you,' she said, as though her offer should square things between us and make everything all right."

"She never understood how much she hurt you," Adam said.

"She didn't know what it was to love."

Adam rubbed Whitney's shoulder gently, understanding that despite how long ago this was, she could still remember the pain. He felt her body relaxing against him, responding to his touch, to his understanding, as she went on.

"Even though I told her it was all over between me and Michael, she sent him back to me. The next morning he was on my doorstep, begging my forgiveness, talking about being temporarily led astray by lust, assuring me Patrice had come after him. He professed his undying love for me."

"How did you feel about that, Whitney?"

"I felt that if Michael had really loved me, he would have resisted Patrice. What good was his love without his loyalty? I had received a final warning that if I didn't bring my grades up by semester's end, I would lose my scholarship. I threw Michael and his apologies and pledges out the door and buried myself in schoolwork.

"When I received my grades after finals and found I had brought my grade-point average up enough to retain the scholarship, it felt wonderful to reclaim my dream of becoming a lawyer."

"And Michael?"

"I never saw Michael again. Mutual friends told me he had left the university to continue his graduate studies elsewhere."

"And Patrice?"

"I ran into her several more times during my undergraduate years. Each time she greeted me with open friendship, just as though the Michael episode had never happened."

"And you, Whitney? How did you greet her?"

"By then I had focused my sights on law school too strongly to acknowledge my weakness and folly of having come so close to giving it all up for that damn faithless man."

Adam gently stroked Whitney's hair. "Do you still think about him?"

"Only to count myself lucky that the Patrice episode had happened before Michael and I had married and had kids and I ended up with a hole in my heart like my mother."

"Did you ever tell Patrice how you felt about her callous disregard of your feelings in going after Michael?"

"No. She never intended it, of course, but she really did me a favor in showing me that I couldn't count on Michael. I didn't want to ever be put in the position of thanking her for that painful episode. The few times we had coffee together, she filled the conversation with unsolicited advice on the kind of law I should practice. The last time we were together, she told me that one day she'd come to see me when I became a lawyer. And one day she did—the day she gave me that envelope to hold for you."

"You mean she just walked into your office one day after not seeing you since undergraduate school?"

"And treated me like her bosom buddy from college. She told me she had married the man who was the perfect husband and would be the perfect father. I remember thinking that now that she knew what love was, she'd understand and apologize for what she had done to me. But she didn't speak of it at all. And I let her walk out that day without ever even mentioning Michael's name."

"And you've regretted that because you never understood why she did it," Adam said.

"Not then. But I think I know now. Michael's reserved response when he first met Patrice must have proved too enticing a challenge for her to resist. Like Esther described and I had observed, every other man she'd met had immediately fallen at her feet. She felt slighted when he didn't immediately bestow what she felt was her due. That's why she set out to get it."

"You're probably right," Adam agreed.

"After meeting you and experiencing the sophisticated formality you exude so naturally, I became certain that's why Patrice fell so hard for you, too."

"I remember when you first commented to that effect," Adam said. "It brought to mind the way Patrice had openly flirted with me the night we met—despite the fact that we were both with other dates."

"Yes, she couldn't resist conquering your implacable reserve," Whitney said. "However, it wasn't until Esther spoke of how she had been raised that I began to understand how ingrained such behavior was to her. She never knew how much she had shattered my faith in the enduring quality of love."

Whitney paused to look up into his face. "I thought that was what her betrayal had done to you, too, Adam. I thought I understood your reaction because I understood mine. But that isn't what happened to you. You never lost your faith in love, because you never lost your love for her."

Adam rose and brought Whitney with him, wrapping an arm around her shoulder and directing her toward the desk. "Come here. I want to show you something."

She didn't resist, but she didn't look too eager to even come near the picture of Patrice that lay there.

Adam released his hold on Whitney and picked up the picture. He took off the felt backing on the frame and slipped out the photograph. He turned it over. Whitney stared at the note written on the back of the photo in Patrice's flowery handwriting. She read it aloud.

"Adam,

Peter and I will be in Canada by the time you read this. I know our deciding to go away together will come as a surprise.

I would have told you in person if I could. But I couldn't. I was afraid of what you would say and do.

Peter loves me and needs me. I need to feel needed, Adam.

I must go now. Have a good life.

                                                    Patrice."

"This is how you found out?" Whitney said. "She left you this note on the back of her picture?"

"It was lying on the kitchen counter when I came home that day she left me."

"*Have a good life.* What an imbecilic thing to say! Her words are so damn cold and unfeeling. You're sure you had no warning that there was anything going on between them?"

"None."

"Adam, please tell me you don't love her anymore."

"What I feel for Patrice is not love, Whitney."

"It's not hate, either," she said.

"No, it's not hate."

"You still have strong emotion tying you to her."

"Yes."

"You're so damn honest, it's scary."

"Thank you."

"It wasn't a compliment."

He smiled. "I know."

Their eyes locked for a long moment. Whitney was consumed with a breathless heat. She dropped her gaze. "What is this map scribbled beneath her note?"

"Nothing of importance," Adam said as he gently took the photo out of her hands and laid it back on the desk. His hands cupped the sides of her cheeks as he tilted her face up to his.

"Whitney, being around you and trying to pretend that there is nothing but a business relationship between us has been more than uncomfortable. It's been dishonest. I can't deny my feelings for you."

"Your feelings for me, Adam?"

There was an eagerness in her voice and face that poured through him like hot rain.

He caressed her cheeks and ran his fingers down her neck and across her shoulders, aware of the quiver of her skin beneath his touch. He could feel the excitement leaping inside him and hear the growing huskiness of his voice.

"Yes, Whitney. I want you to be mine—all mine. Stay with me tonight."

The hopeful look died in her eyes. Adam was certain he understood why.

"I'm not talking about a physical affair. I'm talking about an affair of the heart. I care for you, respect you, admire you. I won't make you any undying-love pledges. We both know what they're worth. And I'm not a man who repeats his mistakes. But for every minute you choose to spend in my arms, I do promise you this. You will feel cherished."

His hands ran down the sides of her arms to her waist. He gently drew her body up against his.

"Well cherished," he said as he took her lips with his.

Whitney eagerly met the hot claim of his kiss, his touch. Her senses reeled at the warm, wonderful scent of him, the feel of his hard body holding hers so closely, the beautiful word, *cherish,* on his lips.

Adam picked her up and carried her to his bedroom, his lips raining hungry, burning kisses across her face and down her throat.

He laid her gently on the black satin bed comforter and locked her eyes with his as his hands strayed to her hair, down her arms and over her breasts with intimate, loving sweeps that sent exciting shivers up and down her spine and legs.

She dropped her head back with a delicious sigh and gave herself up to the incredible, incendiary sensations of his touch. As he removed her blouse and bra, she could feel the cool satin at her back and his cool hands on her naked skin. Both were in delicious contrast to the hot intensity of his look riveting her eyes to his. He slowly bent down to kiss her.

It was a deep, hungry kiss that drove all reason out of mind and runnels of excitement through her belly. And all the while his hands—his strong, gentle hands—were touching her skin, telling her how much he cherished her. She could feel it in his fingers, his lips, his every focused caress.

"Tonight, Whitney," he said, his voice a branding whisper against her skin, "you are all mine."

She thrilled at the possessive tone of his words. He continued to hold her eyes captive as he leaned down to softly lick her nipples, setting off small explosions inside her. She jolted at the force of them and could see his eyes smoldering in response.

His hand slid beneath her skirt, up her inner thigh. She arched her back eagerly as his mouth closed greedily over her nipple. His fingers slipped inside her panties to softly caress her.

She shivered as an electrifying wave of pleasure shot through her. Again and again it rippled through her as his fingers played and teased her soft folds beneath her curls.

And through it all, he held her gaze a willing slave to his, just as her body had become a willing slave to his touch.

She tingled from head to toe, streaming with sensations. She said his name over and over until she had no breath to speak at all. His gentle caresses became bolder, harder, faster. He nipped at her nipples. The heat swelled through her breasts and belly until she was on fire and arching helplessly against him and crying out.

And the intensity of her feelings was right there in his beautiful pale blue eyes, reflecting them, heightening them.

She exploded with a burst of passion so sharp and so sweet she didn't believe it possible. And she didn't just feel it inside her body. She watched it happening in his eyes, first the roaring flash of the flame, then the burning embers.

She lay back against the cool satin, breathless, basking in the glowing heat still reflecting in his eyes.

"You are all mine, Whitney," he repeated.

She was all his. She could see it in his eyes, feel it in her heart.

He stood to take off his clothes, once again never moving his eyes from hers. She watched him shed his suit, shirt and tie with a growing wonder at the magnificent body being uncovered.

She had felt the physical strength of his arms. But his suits had hidden the well-developed muscles of his shoulders and smooth mountains of his chest wall now swelling in the light. The corded scar that snaked down his neck to stop just above his heart added yet another dimension of strength and mystery rather than detracted from the perfection of his form.

Another time she would ask again about that scar. But not tonight. Tonight she did not want to talk. Tonight she only wanted to feel. Him.

He lay beside her and slipped off the rest of her dress, garter belt, nylons and panties, touching and kissing every part of her he exposed with his gentle caresses.

And never once did he drop his eyes from hers.

He kissed her ears, her neck, her breasts, her nipples, until every inch of her was warm and humming. She had never been loved like this—with such a sweet, focused intensity. Her body never felt so wanton or willing.

He rolled onto his back, bringing her with him.

She straddled his waist, reveling in the way he kept kissing and touching her, never letting the physical contact between them break, just as he never let his eyes move from hers. He slipped his hands over the globes of her bottom and stroked her intimately. She moaned in pleasure as the wet heat soared through her once more. She called to him. Hungrily he took her mouth as he came to her.

He filled her completely. He was part of her and she was part of him, as close as two human beings could become. She felt it in every cell of her being as their rhythms matched, as they rolled together on the bed in the celebration of the physical joy they gave to each other.

It wasn't until many hours later, when she lay wrapped in his warm, strong arms, that she allowed herself to face the truth. She loved him.

She could see now that she had been falling in love with him all along. She had just been afraid to face it. And with good cause. Here she had finally found the man she could count on, as well as love, and he could not love her in return.

I won't make you any undying-love pledges. We both know what they're worth.

Yes, once she had thought them worthless. But now she knew that if *this* man gave her such a pledge, he would keep it.

But she also knew he would give her no such pledge. *I'm not a man who repeats his mistakes.*

This was all she would ever have of him. These moments in his arms. That beautiful word *cherish* on his lips.

Maybe it would be enough. Maybe she could make it enough.

FRED DYKSTRA SLIPPED into the back seat of the limousine and closed the door behind him.

"You have it?" he asked.

Carver handed him a single piece of paper. When Dykstra reached for the thick manila envelope, however, Carver held it back.

"I'll send you the proof an hour before your TV spot tomorrow, Dykstra. Not a moment sooner."

Fred's eyes riveted on the paper he was reading, then rose to the man sitting beside him. "You're going to be supplying me proof of *this?*"

"I'm not supplying it. You are getting it from an anonymous source. Remember, anonymous."

Dykstra didn't like the stubborn look on Carver's face. In truth he hadn't liked the looks of the guy from the first. Ever since he'd cornered Crowe-Cromwell's big-league lawyer coming out of the Justice Inc. offices that morning, he hadn't been sure who had captured whom.

"Look, Carver, my refusing to name my source won't fool Justice. He's going to know you're the one supplying me with this stuff."

"Even if he does, there is nothing he can do."

"Nothing? I don't call suing both our heads off for slander nothing. I need that proof. Now."

Carver snatched the sheet of paper out of Dykstra's hands. "It appears I was wrong in selecting you for this exclusive. I'm sure there are reporters at other stations who will be eager to air this news tomorrow."

Dykstra was sure there were, too. What's more, his producer would skin him alive if he reneged on this story, particularly after his bragging to her about it all day. But if Carver's proof didn't come in on time, she'd have to cancel his segment. And it might just make her mad enough to cancel it permanently.

A thin slick of sweat coated Dykstra's palms as he licked lips gone very dry.

"Well?" Carver asked.

Dykstra snatched back the sheet of paper. Then he shouldered open the passenger door and lunged out of Carver's limousine before either of them could change their minds.

Chapter Thirteen

"I appreciate your coming here directly from the airport," Adam said as he poured coffee into Gavin's and Piper's cups. They had drawn up bar stools to the island in Adam's kitchen, where Whitney already sat sipping her morning coffee.

Normally Adam would have insisted on meeting Gavin and Piper at the office. He wasn't in the habit of inviting anyone into his home.

But when they had called from the airport at 5:00 a.m. with news that couldn't wait, he decided that he'd break a few rules rather than yank the warm, soft woman snuggled next to him out of bed and rush them both to the office.

It was just as well he hadn't tried. Whitney was definitely not an early riser. Even with all his coaxing, she had barely made it dressed and into the kitchen before Piper and Gavin were ringing the doorbell.

"I wish I could tell you what we found out was good news, but it isn't," Piper began. "And there is no way to sugarcoat this. Patrice did go to Emery Pharmaceuticals nine years ago and offer them a computer disk that contained the formula for a revolutionary new fertility process. She also handed over data from five years of clinical studies, all showing that the formula resulted in no negative side effects."

"Are you saying that Emery just exchanged the formula for their stock, no questions asked?" Adam said.

"They were in serious financial trouble, Adam," Gavin explained. "Once their scientists had checked out the fertility formula's efficacy and they determined the process hadn't been patented, they knew purchasing it wouldn't be violating any laws. To them it was a question of grabbing the opportunity the fertility process represented or going under as a company. It wasn't a difficult decision.''

"They had to know that breakthroughs like that didn't just happen," Adam said. "They had to know that a regular research lab had developed the process."

"Patrice told them that her scientist father had developed the process in his home lab before his death. She assured them it was hers to sell."

"And they believed her?" Whitney asked.

Piper shrugged. "Why not? There was no patent around to call her a liar. She was holding out this lifeboat of a formula, the difference between their going under and surviving."

"So they took it and disregarded their doubts," Adam said.

"There's more," Gavin said. "Part of the agreement Patrice made with Emery was that close friends of hers—Kevin and Linda Carmichael of Overton, Nevada—be the first in their human trials."

"We know about them," Adam said.

"Yes, but what you may not know is that Patrice insisted on her own embryos being used for Linda."

"Wait a minute," Whitney said. "Did you say Patrice's *embryos?* I thought it was just her eggs?"

"No, in Emery's process, the egg is fertilized in a fertile female's womb. The donor is given a special drug to stabilize the embryo against implant shock before it is removed and introduced into the infertile female's uterus, who has also taken the drug."

"Was Patrice inseminated with Kevin Carmichael's sperm?" Whitney asked.

"No, not Kevin's," Piper admitted. "Emery tested his sperm and found his count was too low. When they told Patrice, she said not to worry, that she would arrange for another donor's sperm."

"Emery didn't ask whose, and she didn't volunteer," Gavin said. "Adam, I'm sorry. I really pushed for this answer, but it wasn't any use."

Adam had been expecting news such as this since the moment he'd met Huntley and Brinkley Carmichael.

"It's all right, Gavin," he said. "I know whose sperm she used."

Adam felt Whitney's eyes coming to rest on his face. The room grew very quiet for a moment—uncomfortably so—as no one asked for elaboration.

Gavin got to his feet. "That's the bad news, Adam. Sorry, but it looks like Crowe-Cromwell's claim is going to hold. Piper and I will see ourselves out."

When the echoes of the front door closing faded away, Whitney's eyes drew to Adam's face. Her voice was heartbreakingly sad. "Adam, she didn't just give away her eggs—she gave away your children."

Adam went to Whitney and slipped his arm over her shoulders, hugging her to him. "No, Whitney. Huntley and Brinkley Carmichael aren't my children."

"Adam, they must be. She conceived them during the time you two were together."

"Yes, but I didn't father them."

She lifted her sad eyes up to his. "How can you be so sure?"

Adam took a long, deep breath and let it out. "I suspected the truth the moment I saw Huntley and Brinkley. The shape of the girl's chin, the boy's forehead. When A.J. confirmed Patrice and Peter's long-term relationship, I was sure. If Danny D'Amico had projected what Patrice and Peter's children would have looked like, he would have drawn the faces of Huntley and Brinkley."

"Peter Danner was their father? Patrice was sleeping with him even that early in her relationship with you?"

"I very much doubt she got his sperm by artificial insemination."

Whitney let out a long sigh. "It's unbelievable. She was totally amoral about so many things, and yet she picked such worthy beneficiaries. I'll never understand her, Adam."

Adam gave Whitney's shoulders another squeeze before letting her go. "Come on. You need another cup of coffee."

"Yes. Please," she said.

He filled her cup and she took a healthy gulp.

"Carver will file his debtor's claim today, won't he?" she asked.

"Yes."

"Will you fight it?"

"I can't without a reason."

"I would think the Rubins and D'Amicos and the Carmichaels would be reason enough."

"I meant a legal reason, Whitney. I'd like to see Patrice's named beneficiaries get that money just as much as you."

Whitney sighed. "Sorry, Adam, I know you do. I shouldn't have said that. My brain batteries are always this low in the morning. The caffeine should be kicking in soon and recharging them. I hope."

She drank the second cup and stretched into a very sleepy yawn. He watched the morning light streaming softly over her long, flowing hair, setting fire to its dark, silky strands.

He'd been demanding and greedy during their night together. He'd been so hungry for her, he had allowed her very little rest. But she hadn't complained. Quite the contrary. She had met his passion with an eagerness and hunger that surprised him.

But then this woman always managed to surprise him. He had begun to wonder who was going to exhaust whom. And when they had finally fallen asleep, he'd found it equally satisfying and pleasing to wake up with her in his arms.

"And you make coffee perfect, too," she said, smiling, her eyes suddenly rising to his as though she knew he had been watching her and thinking of their night together.

Her smile brought the sun over to him, filling the dark, cold and empty spaces Patrice had left inside him. This felt so good. Too good.

He looked away. These were dangerous reactions, dangerous feelings he was having for her.

He consoled himself with the fact that they were transitory. He wasn't a man who repeated his mistakes.

The thought brought unfinished business back to his mind. He looked at his watch. "Before I drive you to your car, Whitney, I would like to take care of something."

She nodded her response. When he left the kitchen for the study, she was right behind him, just as though she suspected what that something might be. He didn't try to stop her. It seemed right to him that she be a part of this.

He walked over to the fireplace and picked up a box of matches on the mantel. He returned to the desk and drew out one of the matches, striking it against the side. He picked up the picture of Patrice he had left lying there the night before.

"I should have burned this seven years ago," he said, bringing the flame toward the bottom edge of the picture.

"Not so fast, Justice," Ryson's voice yelled suddenly, startling them both. Adam whirled in the direction of the doorway to see the sergeant stepping inside the room.

"Get that, Ferkel," Ryson said.

Adam blew out the match and faced Ryson. When Ferkel tried to take the photo, however, Adam held it away from him.

"It's against the law to break into a man's home, Sergeant," he said in his cool, even tone.

"We didn't break in. We knocked and called out. The door was open. Lane and Yeagher must not have closed it properly when they left a few minutes ago."

"The door was closed when I walked by it a moment ago," Adam said, "and no one knocked or called out just now. You tried the door, found it unlocked and let yourselves in."

"You're mistaken," Ryson said. "Get the photo, Ferkel."

"I'll have a look at your warrant first," Adam said coolly.

Ryson stepped forward and produced the warrant, the sarcastic smirk he'd been wearing the whole time still intact on his lips.

Adam read the warrant, then glanced at the signature. Jenkins. Of course. Adam knew Jenkins was one of those self-proclaimed law-and-order judges who signed anything a policeman put before him.

Adam handed over the picture of Patrice. Ryson immediately took it out of Ferkel's hands and read the message on the back.

"Well, this cooks it for you, Justice," he said, smirking once more. "In her own words and handwriting, Patrice admits to being afraid of you."

"That's not what she says at all, and you know it," Whitney protested. Ryson ignored her, directing all his attention toward Adam.

"Why did you lie to us about destroying the note?"

"I never said I destroyed her note," Adam said, keeping his tone even.

"Of course you did."

"If you think back, Sergeant, you'll remember I merely asked Detective Ferkel here if he would have kept such a note."

Ryson's brow furrowed. "That's not what I remember, nor what I'll put into my report."

"Then your report will be inaccurate," Adam said calmly. "This looks like a map scribbled beneath her note here. Did you draw out their route so you could follow them?"

"How would I know what route they would take?"

"There are only a few ways to Canada from here. I'll check this diagram against a road map. Search the place, Ferkel," Ryson commanded.

"You'd better not break anything," Whitney warned. "I'm a witness as to the condition of Mr. Justice's home."

Ryson's smirk widened. "I'm quaking in my boots."

Adam watched the fire enter Whitney's eyes with a touch of amusement. But amusement quickly turned to alarm when the hands by her sides balled into fists and she started toward Ryson.

He was afraid that all that passion he loved in her so much was about to get the better of her good judgment. Adam stepped forward quickly to intercept her and fit his hand into the small of her back.

"I'll drive you to your car now, Whitney," he said.

And with that, Adam urged her firmly toward the door and out of the house.

"I wish you'd stop riding in to rescue me," she said with clear irritation as he opened the passenger door.

"Rescue you, nothing. I saw that look in your eye. I was trying to rescue Ryson."

That brought a reluctant smile to her lips, just as he hoped it would.

"I wasn't going to give him a piece of my fist, just a piece of my...philosophy."

"Of course," Adam said, stifling his grin as he circled around to the driver's side.

They were two blocks beyond the security gates when he noticed the familiar brown Chevy pulling in behind them.

"Why are they hounding you?" Whitney asked, the frustration coming through in her tone as she swung around and noticed the tail. "Even a fool could tell you are not the kind of man who would hurt another—much less a woman."

"I appreciate your vote for acquittal. When the case comes to trial, I'll see what I can do about getting you on the jury."

"You don't seriously believe they can make a case?"

"You should understand this, Whitney. I seriously believe they are going to try."

"And they are seriously going to fail. You had nothing to do with their deaths. Patrice and Peter died in an accident."

Whitney's words had carried her complete conviction. Adam didn't say anything in response. There was nothing to say. Unless he told her the truth. And he was hoping like hell he was never going to be forced to do that.

"WELL, I SEE YOU'VE taken care of the wannabe millionaires for this morning," Jack said as he slipped into the chair in front of Whitney's desk. "Hey, you're smiling. What're you reading?"

"Finally some good news," Whitney said. "Checkmate's tracked Chad Bister's sister and aunt to Australia. They're both still there and still alive. What's more, they found out Bister used to be a technician at a local medical lab—the same lab Patrice went to to donate her embryos for shipment to Emery Pharmaceuticals in Vancouver. That's how he knew that personal information about her. The creep was lying the entire time."

"Does it really matter, Whitney? From what you've told me about Crowe-Cromwell, it's clear that they're going to beat out the beneficiaries and everyone else and take all the money."

Whitney dropped the report on her desk and sunk back into her chair. "You're right, of course."

Jack leaned forward in his chair, resting his elbows on his knees. "Is the problem you've been wrestling with Patrice? Or is it Justice?"

"Yes," Whitney answered on a long, heavy sigh.

Jack shook his head. "Both of them? Terrific. This is worse than I thought."

"The sheriff's office believes Adam killed her and her lover, Jack. They were at his place this morning with a search warrant."

"What? Why didn't you tell me this sooner?"

"Because their suspicions are too damn preposterous to take seriously for a second. Adam is gentle, kind. He never would have hurt Patrice or anyone. He's . . . wonderful."

"Well, I'll be damned. You *have* fallen for him."

Whitney knew there was no point in denying it. "Yes."

Jack got up and circled her desk. He leaned against its edge and took Whitney's hands into his. His voice was gentle. "As in 'to have and to hold'?"

"I'm afraid so."

Jack grinned down at her. "And I had a bet with Isabel you were going to end up an old maid."

"You're in no danger of losing that bet, Jack."

"You can't be saying what I think you're saying."

"I can. I am."

"Whitney, if you want this guy for keeps and he's not on board with the idea, bail out now while you still can with some shreds of your self-confidence left. I've been in these one-sided love affairs. They'll rip you up inside."

"We're still working together on the case."

"Forget the case. You never should have gotten mixed up in this crazy probate in the first place. Best thing you could do now is get Commissioner Snowe on the phone and tell her you've changed your mind and want to resign as G.A.L."

"I've never quit a case in my life, Jack."

"This is not quitting, Whitney. This is a strategic, mid-course correction. Only a fool keeps heading up a road with a Dead End sign posted on it."

A Dead End sign. Yes, Jack was right. Adam's words the night before about not giving her a love pledge had been just that. But what Jack was suggesting would mean she would never see Adam again. Never. And that was such an awfully long time.

Isabel poked her head around the open door. "You told me to remind you of your luncheon at Elliott's."

Whitney's eyes shot to her watch. "Whoops." She bolted out of the chair. "I have to go, Jack."

"*Have to,* Whitney?"

"All right, I *want* to see this case through to the end."

"Justice is going to be at this luncheon, isn't he?"

"Don't worry. I'll keep a cool head."

"It's the other parts of you I was concerned about," Jack said, but he followed his admonition with a teasing smile. "Will you at least promise me one thing, Whitney?"

"What?"

"That you won't let Justice hurt you. From everything they tell me down at the men's club, he's in great physical shape. If I have to call him out, the guy's going to kill me."

"Bless you, Jack, for making me smile." Whitney blew him a kiss on her way out the door.

ADAM FORMALLY EXTENDED his hand to Dr. Grover McGrory, only to have it slapped in a very casual returning salute. McGrory presented nothing even remotely similar to the image of the dignified, scholarly professor. His stocky body was layered in what could have easily been taken for rags on a street person. His receding salt-and-pepper hair curled across his shoulders. He had five golden hoops piercing his left ear and dark hair growing out of a wart on his chin.

McGrory first ordered an imported bottle of beer—with specific instructions to serve it in the bottle—and then the most expensive item on the menu.

The moment the beer arrived, he upended the bottle, emptied its contents down his throat, let out a satisfied burp and slumped back in his chair.

"Okay, Ms. West, Mr. Justice, you have a choice to make. Which do you want? A nice tale about Lydon Miller or the truth?"

"The truth, of course, Dr. McGrory," Adam said.

"It will cost you," McGrory said.

"And what is your going rate for the truth?" Adam asked, careful to keep the disdain out of his tone.

McGrory folded his arms firmly over his chest. "This is not a shakedown, Justice. I know your reputation for honesty and fair dealing. It's the reason I'm here. The only payment I'll require is your silence."

"Silence about what?"

"You'll both have to give me your word you will not tell anyone what I tell you."

"And why would you require such silence?" Adam asked.

"You won't understand why until you hear my story. And you won't hear my story unless you agree to my price. That's the deal. Yea or nay?"

Adam studied the professor's face. He could tell this man wanted to get something off his chest. He was more than curious as to what it might be. "All right, Dr. McGrory, you have my word."

"And mine, too," Whitney said, following Adam's lead.

McGrory unfolded his arms and leaned forward. He stared at his hands as he picked at the short, stubby nails on the ends of his short stubby fingers. He cleared his throat twice before he began.

"Lydon and I went way back. We met at one of these scientific conventions nearly three decades ago and hit it off right away. He was a hell of a scientist and a damn good guy—far too good for the likes of Crowe-Cromwell. He should have quit those freezer-burned brain-suckers. He wanted to, too."

"He told you that?" Adam asked.

"All the time. Oh, the company was great to him when he first joined it. But those last few years the management got it into their heads that youth was the answer and started replacing everyone with kids right out of college. They treated Lydon like he was some old fogey. In his forties, with one of the greatest brains in research, and they considered him washed-up! They kept slashing his budget, reducing his staff, trying to force him to resign. If he hadn't had another three years on his contract, the damn yuppie management would have thrown him out."

"If they wanted him out, and he wanted to leave, why didn't both sides just agree to terminate their contract?" Adam asked.

"Because Lydon had to hold on to his employee health plan. With his wife, Marla, being so ill from the cancer and needing all those expensive treatments, Lydon had no choice but to stay. He could never have afforded her care on his own."

"Did he talk to you about this fertility process he was supposed to have been working on at the time of his death?" Whitney asked.

"All the time. He was very excited about its potential, although the company didn't share that enthusiasm. Lydon's requests for additional assistants, equipment, supplies and test subjects all fell on deaf ears. He finally had to build an open-air habitat at the back of his own home to house the test animals. At that time all he had was his son and one lab assistant to help him."

"His son?"

"Peter. A foster kid he raised. He raised a daughter, too. I never met her, but he told me once she was his lab assistant. He never told Crowe-Cromwell she was his foster kid, though."

"Why not?" Whitney asked.

"They had this thing against family members working together. Anyway, without Peter's help in building the habitat, and his foster daughter's willingness to work all those extra unpaid hours, it would never have happened. As it was, Lydon had to come to me for the test animals. I arranged for several zoos to loan us infertile female chimpanzees. I promised them that they would be well cared for, and any offspring would be returned along with their mothers. My reputation as an animal-rights activist was sufficient to reassure them. They loaned us six chimps. We returned twelve.''

"Each one conceived and carried to term?" Whitney asked.

"Without a single negative side effect. Lydon's fertility process was a great success—the crown of his career. And then, suddenly, Marla died and Lydon was blown up along with his boat on the small lake in back of his house.''

McGrory picked up the empty beer bottle and looked at it as though he wished it were a can he could crush.

"It must have been an unbelievable shock for you to learn of his suicide," Whitney said, her voice turning soft with understanding.

McGrory's eyes rose to her face. " 'Unbelievable' is right, Ms. West, particularly in light of the conversation we had the day before.''

"What conversation?" Whitney asked.

"It was at Marla's funeral. Lydon pulled me aside. He was so scared, he was shaking. He told me the management at Crowe-Cromwell had threatened him, and someone in a truck had run him off the road on the way to the services.''

"Did he tell you why Crowe-Cromwell had threatened him?" Adam asked.

"No, we got interrupted by a couple of people offering their condolences. I didn't get a chance to talk to him privately anymore that day. When I dropped by his place the next morning to find out what it was all about, I saw him getting on his boat out on the pier. I called out to him. He must not have heard me over the engine. I was just about to turn away when I saw the explosion.''

McGrory dropped his eyes and took a long pause before he went on. "It was awful, terrible—the bolting flames, the billowing smoke and then the steady rain of nothing but ashes.

The police wouldn't even have known Lydon had gotten on that boat if I hadn't seen him. They found a suicide note inside the house that said he was too despondent over his wife's death to go on. I never believed it.''

"What do you believe, Dr. McGrory?'' Adam asked.

"Believe? It's what I *know.* Lydon had mourned Marla's passing quietly and gradually over the many years of her illness. He'd prepared himself. He would never have committed suicide over it.''

"Are you saying that you think—'' Whitney began.

"I'm saying that those bastards at Crowe-Cromwell killed him,'' McGrory finished. "They rigged his boat to blow. I know it. You can't quote me, though. I'm not eager to end up as a short paragraph in the obituary column, the victim of yet another convenient *suicide.*''

"WHAT DO YOU THINK, Adam?'' Whitney asked as they walked back to their cars in the restaurant parking lot.

"I think Dr. McGrory's dramatic flair has been overfed from watching too many nice people turning into monsters on made-for-TV movies.''

"Sorry, Adam, but not in my kindest moment would I ever describe Carver as 'nice people,''' Whitney said. "Besides, I think McGrory's allegations bring an entirely different perspective to the events of nine years ago.''

"You're taking his suspicions seriously?''

"Oh, I recognize the fact that McGrory didn't like what Crowe-Cromwell had done to his friend and may have an ax to grind. But Patrice did tell Emery Pharmaceuticals that her father had developed his formula in a home lab and, at least for part of the process, McGrory seems to bear that story out.''

"Still, Miller was an employee of Crowe-Cromwell, and any discovery he produced—even one he worked on partially at home—was still their property.''

"What if Miller was angry about that? What if he told the management to go suck eggs when they wanted him to turn over the formula? What if that's why they threatened him?''

"Whitney, they had the law on their side. As long as he was under contract to them, they called the shots. They had no reason to threaten him. And in those memos from Dr. Miller that Carver showed us, he expressed eagerness—not reluctance—to share the fruits of his discovery, despite his having had to shoulder some of the expense to produce it."

"True, but I can't shake the feeling that there is something odd about Dr. Miller's suicide following so soon after his being threatened by them and nearly run off the road."

"Still, what McGrory proposes is not logical. When an employee proves a problem for a corporation, they find a way to terminate him legally—they don't physically rub him out like some 1920s gangster," Adam said.

"A 1920s gangster would have dropped him in the lake with cement shoes. These 1990s corporate types blew him up so nothing but his ashes reached the water."

"Whitney, there was no reason for Crowe-Cromwell to have gotten rid of Dr. Miller. He had just developed a new fertility process that would make them a lot of money, remember?"

"Well, maybe it's just the criminal bent to my mind, but I can't discount McGrory's version as easily as you," Whitney said. "Oh, look. There's that damn Chevy again. Do you see who the police have behind the wheel? What is this, some kind of sick joke?"

Adam swung around at Whitney's words to see where she was pointing. Sure enough, the brown Chevy was pulling up to the curb, not thirty feet in front of them. And behind the wheel was a woman in a black veil.

Adam felt a jolt of familiarity.

The veil was moving as though the shadowed eyes behind it were searching for something—or someone. Adam knew it was him.

"She's not with the police," he said, coming to that conclusion quickly and surely.

"Then who—?" Whitney began.

"I don't know who she is, but I intend to find out."

Adam started at a run for the Chevy. The motion must have caught her eye. The veil flipped in his direction. Then she gunned the engine, and the Chevy took off with a roar and a screech of tires, with Adam just inches from its bumper.

Adam quickly changed direction and raced to his car. He found Whitney had anticipated the move and was there waiting. They jumped inside, and he took off after the Chevy.

The woman with the black veil had a good head start. But Adam pressed the Jaguar into some tight turns, and after a dozen blocks, they had closed the distance considerably. The Chevy was two cars ahead. Just as Adam was making his move to pass and get alongside, the light went against them and the cars in both lanes before them braked.

Adam screeched to a halt, watching the brown Chevy speed away.

"What's wrong with these damn drivers?" Whitney said beside him. "The light was barely yellow. They could have gone through."

Adam tried not to smile as he picked up the phone and punched in A.J.'s number. The second she answered, he told her he needed the registered owner's name and gave her the license-plate number. She told him to hang on.

Adam didn't bother trying to pursue the Chevy. It was long gone. He headed back to the restaurant parking lot where they had left Whitney's car. He was just pulling behind it when A.J. came back on the line.

"The Chevy is registered to a Eugenia Miller of 222 Wood-lawn Place, Seattle."

"Miller," Adam repeated. "A relative of Dr. Lydon Miller?"

"His mother," A.J. answered.

"What is Lydon Miller's mother doing following me?" Adam asked aloud, already pulling away from the parking lot and heading for Woodlawn Place.

"It would be some trick if she were," A.J. said. "Eugenia Miller died four years ago."

WHITNEY STOOD next to Adam as he rang the doorbell of the small clapboard home at 222 Woodlawn Place for the third time. The Chevy was in the driveway. The heavy drapes at the front window had quivered after the first ring. It was clear that the woman in the veil was inside watching them. But no one was answering the ringing summons.

"Let's go call the police from the car phone," Adam said in what was obviously a purposely loud voice.

Whitney understood the real message in his words and turned with him to step off the porch and head back to his Jaguar at the curb. They were halfway there when she heard the front door open behind them and then the squeak of the screen door.

"Wait. Please," a high, pleading voice called out to them.

Whitney and Adam turned to see a small, frail-looking figure clad in a black dress standing in the doorway, a veil completely covering her head.

They walked back to the porch. "Who are you?" Adam asked.

"Not out here," she said. She stepped back from the doorway, leaning heavily on her cane.

Whitney and Adam ascended the porch again and accepted the invitation to go inside.

She led them into a dark, cool living room, where no lamps were lit. The only light was the little sun shining through the slit in the drapes.

Whitney bumped into a chair arm and wondered how the woman saw her way with that black veil over her face. Whitney's own mother constantly complained about needing more light for her older eyes.

"Sit down," the woman said, gesturing toward a couch.

"First I'll have to see the couch," Adam said, moving over to the window to pull the heavy drape back and let in more light.

"Please, not too much," the woman pleaded. "I have sensitive eyes."

Sensitive to too much light? Whitney decided that was the first time she'd heard someone over fifty complain of that.

Adam obligingly only opened the drape halfway.

Whitney could now make out the doilies lining the arms of the old-fashioned furniture. It was a little-old-lady's home, all right. And the extra light shining in from the window picked up the outline of the silver strands of hair beneath the black lace of the woman before them.

"Who are you?" Adam asked.

"I'm Eugenia Miller."

"Eugenia Miller?" Adam repeated in a voice that Whitney found remarkably noncommittal, considering they both knew the woman was lying.

"Lydon Miller was my son."

"You were at the funeral of Patrice and Peter," Adam said.

"Yes."

"Why are you following me?"

The woman calling herself Eugenia Miller leaned heavily on her cane. She appeared to be staring up at Adam while she considered his question. Whitney unobtrusively edged a little closer to her side.

"All right, Mr. Justice," she said. "I'll tell you. I believe Crowe-Cromwell killed my son. I also believe they may have been responsible for the deaths of Patrice and Peter."

"Those are rather amazing statements. And neither explains why you've been following me."

Whitney moved even closer, as the veiled woman's attention remained focused on Adam.

"I know you loved Patrice, Mr. Justice. When the police found their bodies, I knew you'd investigate her death until you found out the truth. That's why I've been following you. You see, all I want to know is the truth."

"That's all Ms. West and I want to know, too," Adam said.

Whitney lunged for the veil. "Let's start by finding out who you really are," she said.

She grabbed the top of the lace and gave it a yank. She got an uncomfortable jolt when both the veil and a silver wig ended up in her hand.

Whitney had prepared herself for a surprise. But that didn't keep her from staring in astonishment at the person she had just unveiled.

Chapter Fourteen

"You had no right to do that!"

Adam watched Whitney step back from the harsh words and the person shouting them.

And no wonder. Gone was the high, frail-sounding voice. And gone, too, was the frail-appearing woman who had needed to walk with a cane. In her place Adam found himself confronted with a short and very angry bald man.

"Who are you?" Adam demanded.

"I don't have to tell you," he said, holding the cane up as though he might use it if Adam came any closer.

"No, maybe you don't have to tell us," Adam said, as a growing suspicion took hold. "You're Dr. Lydon Miller, aren't you?"

All the umbrage seemed to deflate from the short, bald man as an unhappy groan escaped his lips. He dropped the cane, sank into the nearest chair and put his head in his hands.

"You're Lydon Miller?" Whitney asked, stepping closer. "But you're supposed to be dead!"

"I am dead," the bald man grumbled unhappily. "Now for sure. How did you know who I was?"

"I didn't for certain, Dr. Miller," Adam said. "Until Ms. West unveiled you just now."

"You recognized me?"

"Let's just say I recognized, from the dramatic act Mc-Grory put on for us at lunch today, that it was just his word alone that put you on that blown-up boat. If he hadn't told the police he had seen you get on it, they might have looked more closely at the debris and found it didn't include a body."

"This is incredible," Whitney said. "You and McGrory faked your death nine years ago. Why, Dr. Miller?"

Lydon dropped his hands and looked up at Whitney. "You'd better sit down, Ms. West. You, too, Mr. Justice. There are no abbreviated versions to this story."

Adam waited for Whitney to sit on the couch across from Miller. Then he sat beside her and gave his attention to the little bald man dressed in women's clothing.

"Most of what McGrory told you is true," Miller said. "My relationship with Crowe-Cromwell had gone downhill fast during those last years when Marla was so ill. They had shoved me into the smallest, least-equipped lab and had saddled me with one inept assistant after another.

"The only saving grace was they left me alone. I was working on this fertility drug, synthesized from natural substances. The first few experiments had looked very promising, but for reasons I couldn't fathom, I was having difficulty replicating the earlier results.

"Then, when Patrice graduated from college, I got a friend in personnel to hire and assign her to me. It was while I was training Patrice on how to enter the data from the lab charts into the computer that I discovered all the mistakes the other lab assistants had made. By the time we corrected the entries for the last couple of years, I realized that my formula wasn't flawed. It was just that the data had been improperly entered and analyzed. The process was working!

"I was so excited I immediately sent a covering memo with a summary of the results to my supervisor, telling him I needed a larger budget for more experiments. He scribbled a note on the top of my memo instructing me to submit the proper forms and sent everything back. I could tell he never even looked at the results of my work.

"I submitted all the required paperwork to him and waited. And waited some more. I wrote two more memos asking about the status. When I still got no reply, I stopped writing memos and built my own habitat for my primate subjects. Dr. Mc-

Grory supplied them. Patrice helped me with the embryo transplants. The results surpassed even my expectations. Two years later I walked into my supervisor's office and told him I had developed a new, foolproof, perfectly safe fertility method. I demanded he tell top management about it or I would.

"My supervisor finally looked over my data and called a meeting of the board of directors. The next morning I proudly presented the results of my work and submitted an IND to be filed with the FDA to begin to test the process with people."

"What's an IND?" Adam asked.

"Investigation new drug application. It's the next step after preclinical testing. But they didn't file my IND. Instead, the board of directors sent me a memo ordering me to stop all further experimentation and shelve my fertility process."

"Why?" Whitney asked.

"Because Crowe-Cromwell had just gotten approval from the FDA to release a new fertility drug on the market. Of course, that drug had only proved thirty percent effective on women previously labeled infertile and came equipped with serious side effects, including a staggering increase in ovarian cancer. But they didn't care. All they cared about was recouping what they had spent on R and D for the drug."

"I don't understand," Whitney said. "You presented them with a new, safe process, with no side effects, that was far more effective. Why didn't they just pull the other drug and wait until your process was approved by the FDA?"

"Because it took eleven years and close to two hundred million dollars to get their other drug approved. Crowe-Cromwell wanted their two hundred million back in drug sales before they submitted anything new."

"So, for the sake of money, they were ready to unleash a seriously flawed drug on women desperate enough to take it because of their desire to conceive? That's despicable," Whitney said.

"And that is what I told them, Ms. West. I had to watch my wife die of cancer. I didn't want it happening to other women. I told them I wasn't going to shelve my formula until they had recouped their money. I told them I was going ahead with my process and getting it out to the women who could use it."

"What did they say, Dr. Miller?" Adam asked.

"They told me it wasn't my formula, it was theirs. Their big-shot lawyer, Stanford Carver, sent me a threatening letter which said if I violated my contract by saying anything about my new fertility process to anyone outside the company, I would be fired, all health benefits to my dying wife would immediately be cut off and they would see to it that I was prosecuted and disgraced in every scientific circle.

"I left the office in a daze, clutching all those horrible memos in my hands, and went to the hospital to see my wife. I kept thinking 'I'll read these to Marla and we'll figure out what to do, just like always.' I was so stunned by their threats, I had even forgotten that the cancer that was taking my Marla's life had long ago taken away her capacity to participate in those warm, intimate talks we had once shared.

"Patrice and Peter found me crying next to her hospital bed many hours later that night. They took me home. The next day, when I arrived at work, I found my supervisor had locked me out of my lab, and Patrice had been reassigned to another researcher.

"They put me at an empty desk in a corner of the steno pool. It didn't even have a phone. They were doing everything they could to show me how powerless I was against them. When the hospital called that afternoon to tell me my Marla was gone, one of the stenographers had to relay the news.

"That was when I swore on the sacred memory of my wife that somehow I would get my fertility process out of Crowe-Cromwell's hands and into the hands of the women who needed it. I called the FDA. But the secretary insisted on first knowing my name and the name of the firm I worked for before she would even take a message for someone to call me back.

"I gave her what she demanded. When no one contacted me, I called back the next day. That same secretary said she had checked with Crowe-Cromwell, and they'd told her I was mentally disturbed due to the recent death of my wife. They told her to ignore me.

"Later that day on the way to my wife's funeral, a truck ran my car off the road. I landed in a ditch, and my car had to be towed out. I can't prove it, but I believe it was someone from Crowe-Cromwell driving that truck. I didn't know whether they were trying to scare me or kill me. When I confided what happened to Grover McGrory at the funeral, he took me aside and told me I should disappear for a while, just in case. That's when I got the idea of faking my own death. Grover agreed to help me with it and tell the police he had seen me get on my boat before it blew up."

"What about Patrice and Peter?" Whitney said.

"I told them the truth, but made sure they were far away at the time I was supposedly killing myself, so there would be no question of their being in on it, should I get caught."

"And McGrory?" Adam asked.

"He knew I'd swear to the police I jumped over the side before the boat blew and convince them that I duped him, as well as everyone else. And you'd best understand, I will, too. I won't repay his friendship by implicating him in this."

"We don't want to hurt you or your friend, Dr. Miller," Whitney said, her tone highlighting the meaning in her words.

Miller sighed. "It didn't matter that Crowe-Cromwell had locked me out of my lab. I knew my formula by heart. I had copied all my data from the clinical trials onto computer disks. I had them at home, since I did so much of my work there.

"At my direction Patrice took the disks and flew to Vancouver to meet with a reputable pharmaceutical company that I knew was going through some rough times. I was certain they'd recognize the formula's worth and use it. I was disappointed, however, when Patrice returned and told me she had exchanged it for stock. I wanted it given away, not sold."

"Did she tell you why she took the stock?" Adam asked.

"She took it for me. She felt I deserved to get something for all my effort. I told her that discovering the process and getting it out to women was all the reward I needed, and I didn't want the stock. I told her to give it back."

"But she didn't," Whitney said.

"She said if I refused to benefit from it, she knew other people she could give it to who would. I tried to tell her how dangerous it was for her to be associated with that stock when Emery Pharmaceuticals came out with my process. But she wouldn't listen. She said she had abandoned her job with Crowe-Cromwell, and there was nothing they could do. And then Peter went and pulled that damn stupid stunt."

"What stunt?" Adam asked.

"He wanted revenge on Crowe-Cromwell for their treatment of me. He wrote a letter to them saying that he had the formula and the computer disks with the research data, and it would cost them two million to get them back.

"Of course it didn't work. Crowe-Cromwell turned the letter over to the police, and they arrested Peter for extortion. The instant I found out, I called Patrice and told her to pack her things immediately and disappear. I warned her that Crowe-Cromwell would be after her, too. I wouldn't let her off the phone until she promised me. I warned her not to get in touch with Peter, since they would be looking for her to do that."

"Had Crowe-Cromwell discovered your foster-parent relationship to Patrice?" Whitney asked.

Miller shook his head. "No, but they found out Peter was my foster son when he made my funeral arrangements. And all Patrice's co-workers knew that she and Peter were lovers. They were bound to believe she was in on it with him."

"Neither you nor Patrice destroyed the formula or clinical data from Crowe-Cromwell's computer?" Adam asked.

"No, of course not. We didn't want the process destroyed. We wanted it used."

"It was just another lie we were told," Whitney said, exchanging glances with Adam.

"My mother had Alzheimer's for many years before she died," Miller continued. "I came here to hide. Dressed in women's clothing, I became her nurse. The only ones who knew I was still alive were Grover, Peter and Patrice. I pretended to be my mother when I arranged for Peter's lawyer.

"Then Crowe-Cromwell's big-shot attorney, that Stanford Carver guy, told Peter they'd drop the charges against him if he turned over the computer disks and signed a statement admitting his guilt to theft and extortion and fully disclosing Patrice's role in both."

"How did Peter respond to their offer?" Adam asked.

"He refused it. He said he never had the disks and Patrice had nothing to do with any of it. It took nearly eighteen months for his case to go to trial, the first six months of which he spent in jail while I tried to make his bail. When I finally got him out, he went looking for Patrice.

"When he found out she had changed her name to Waring and married you, Mr. Justice, he was very upset. He loved her from the first moment he saw her. Maria and I explained to Peter that Patrice's early experiences had seriously impaired her ability to love. We immediately sent him to school in Europe to separate them. The day he returned was the day Patrice was graduated from college. He presented her with an engagement ring. She refused him. Still, he never gave up.

"I know he went to see Patrice the day after you returned from your honeymoon. She agreed to meet with him secretly during that next year as he waited to go to trial.

"Then, right before he was scheduled to go to court, the prosecuting attorney told him if he pled guilty to a lesser charge, the extortion charge would be dropped and he'd be credited with time served and his debt would be paid. Peter took the deal."

"And that's when he presented himself to my sister and pretended to court her—just so he could have an excuse to openly be around Patrice," Adam said.

"And in the end, Mr. Justice, it afforded him nothing. Patrice still did not return his love."

"She left me for him."

"Patrice didn't leave you for Peter. Patrice left because Crowe-Cromwell was hot on their trail."

"What are you talking about?" Adam asked.

"The minute Emery Pharmaceuticals patented their new fertility process, Crowe-Cromwell knew Peter and Patrice had been responsible for their getting it. Peter came home that day to find Carver and two big, tough-looking guys pounding on his door, demanding to be let in, yelling they had a warrant for his arrest. Only Peter didn't think they were policemen.

"Peter got away before they caught sight of him and went to see Patrice. He knew his open pursuit of your sister over the previous five months was sure to be discovered and lead Crowe-Cromwell right to Patrice and her new identity. He convinced her they both had to disappear.

"They called me from your place that day, Mr. Justice, to tell me that they were leaving for Canada and why. They told me I wasn't to worry if I didn't hear from them for a while. When the years went by and no news came, I thought they were still afraid to get in touch. It wasn't until I heard that their bodies had been discovered in that seven-year-old car wreck that I understood why word never came. I kept thinking about Peter's description of those men pounding on his door that day. I know you loved Patrice. I was sure you'd investigate until you found out the truth. That's why I've been following you. I had to know if it was really an accident, or if those monsters at Crowe-Cromwell caught up with them and . . ."

"Crowe-Cromwell didn't kill Peter and Patrice, Dr. Miller."

"How can you know?"

Adam took a very deep breath and let it out. What he had feared most over the past seven years was now facing him.

"Because I killed them," Adam said.

Chapter Fifteen

Whitney couldn't believe what she was hearing. She felt as though a cold black hole had opened up inside her and was swallowing all the warmth in her body.

"Adam, no."

He turned to look at her. The sadness in his eyes stopped her heart stock-still.

"Whitney, I'm sorry. I would have spared you this if I could."

Adam turned back to Dr. Miller, and Whitney heard that cool, formal cadence of his voice as though it were coming from a great distance.

"A colleague and I returned to the house to pick up some papers I needed for a case going to court that afternoon," Adam said. "We walked into the kitchen and found Patrice's note.

"I couldn't believe she'd been carrying on with Peter Danner behind my back. I was angry, determined to confront her face-to-face. I was certain they couldn't have much of a head start. My colleague offered to assist by calling a close friend of hers, who was a Native American chief. She secured her friend's permission for us to take a secret route through his tribal lands in order to make up for the head start Peter and Patrice had.

"The shortcut allowed us to catch up with them just as they were starting up a narrow mountain road. I beeped my horn to attract their attention. Peter must have recognized my car, but instead of pulling over, he gunned the engine of his Porsche and burned rubber up that mountain.

"I was right behind him. We flew up that dangerous, winding, narrow strip without a whit of sense. My colleague was in the passenger seat. She tried to get me to slow down, but I wouldn't listen. I had let my anger take over, and it was all I heeded. And then, suddenly, I saw the Porsche miss a tight turn and sail over the side of the cliff.

"I slammed on the brakes, screeched to a stop, jumped out of my car and ran over to the edge. The Porsche had landed on its back on a ledge about twenty feet down. I scrambled down the steep slope to get to it.

"I could see Patrice pinned inside. She wasn't moving. The frame was smashed and twisted around her. Somehow I got the passenger door open. I was just reaching inside to pull her out when the car lurched and plunged off the ledge, headed for the deep ravine below. The jagged metal on the passenger door caught me as it tumbled past, whipping me back against the rock.

"The next thing I knew, it was three days later and I was awakening in the hospital on the Indian reservation. I had a severe concussion and a wound that had opened me from neck to chest. My colleague had saved my life by dragging me back up to the road and then driving me to the hospital.

"When I asked about Patrice and Peter, she told me that Peter's Porsche had burst into flames when it landed at the bottom of the deep ravine. She told me there was no way either Patrice or Peter had survived. She also told me she hadn't reported the accident and that she wasn't going to."

"Why not?" Dr. Miller asked.

"Because she said she didn't believe the accident was my fault. She also knew that unless she prevented me from doing so, I would tell the police it was, and they would charge me with manslaughter. Even if I escaped jail time, I would be disbarred. She knew how much my work means to me.

"Dr. Miller, do not judge her harshly. My colleague is not a letter-of-the-law kind of attorney. She is ruled by her heart. And her heart told her nothing would be gained by reporting the accident. Peter and Patrice had assured us they had no family.

"When I realized my colleague had not reported Peter's and Patrice's deaths, in direct violation of the law, I also realized that were I to report it, I would get her in serious trouble. She had saved my life and then remained silent to protect me. To protect her I remained silent.

"However, Dr. Miller, had I known that Peter and Patrice had left a father, not even my concern for my friend would have kept me silent. You had the right to know the truth. And the truth is, I forced Peter into excessive speeds that made him lose control of his car and ended up killing both your foster children. If you call the authorities, I will accept whatever consequences that are due me. I will, however, keep silent about my friend's part. I alone am to blame."

Whitney understood now why Adam sought so diligently to control his anger. The one time he had let it control him had ended in tragedy. But now that she heard the circumstances, she couldn't blame him. She could only admire how his deep conviction to do the right thing was causing him to sacrifice his career.

Tears filled her eyes—tears of respect and love.

Miller let out a long sigh. "No, you're not to blame for their deaths."

"Everything I just told you is true, Dr. Miller."

"I believe you, Mr. Justice. And if I thought you responsible, believe me, my paternal anger would prohibit me from sparing your feelings. But you could not have caused Peter to lose control of his car and run off the road."

"How can you be so certain?"

"Because when Peter was studying in Europe, he made his living test-driving race cars. He was an expert behind the wheel. He thrived on the kind of speed and sharp turns you described. His reflexes and timing were superb."

"I didn't know. Still, under the duress of being chased—"

"Duress?" Miller interrupted. "I knew my foster son, Mr. Justice. He always took mountain roads at full speed. He didn't know how to drive slowly. When you beeped your horn and Peter turned around and saw you, he could have stopped and let Patrice simply convince you it was over. But the truth is, he was probably delighted with the idea of a chase."

"I don't understand."

"Peter was jealous of you. Patrice wasn't leaving you because she loved him. He was only getting her because they needed each other to escape Crowe-Cromwell's grasp. Peter probably looked on the opportunity of confronting you on that mountain road as a duel over Patrice. And he chose the weapon for which he was the master—driving. The fact that you were in sight of his car when it went over the cliff tells me he was still toying with you at that point. Had he wanted to, he could have left you in his dust at any time."

"Then why did his car go off that cliff?"

Miller sighed. "That I can't tell you. All I can say is that it wasn't driver error. Peter didn't make those kinds of errors. So there's no reason for me to be calling the authorities about you, Mr. Justice. Are you going to be calling the authorities about me?"

"For what, Dr. Miller?"

"For faking my death."

"Was there an insurance policy on your life?"

"No."

"Did you leave any debts unpaid?"

"No, I gave Peter the money, and he paid them."

"Since you didn't endanger anyone when you blew up your boat, nor defraud any creditors by your death, I don't see any problem, Dr. Miller. You can come out of hiding anytime. The statute of limitations for obstruction of justice—which is all the police could have charged you with—expired after two years."

"But what about Crowe-Cromwell?" Dr. Miller asked. "What if it was their man behind the wheel of that truck that ran me off the road nine years ago?"

As Whitney watched a very intense laser-blue light formed in the center of Adam's eyes. "Yes, let's talk about Crowe-Cromwell, Dr. Miller," he said. "I have a suggestion I think you might like."

"... AND THAT IS the basis of Crowe-Cromwell's debtor claim against the Patrice Feldon estate," Carver said as he finished his long explanation to Commissioner Snowe that afternoon in her chambers. "As you can see from the documents that lie before you, every portion is substantiated. The Emery Pharmaceutical stock clearly belongs to us."

As Whitney had listened again to Carver's version of the theft of Crowe-Cromwell's fertility drug, it had taken all her control to remain silent. And now that he had finished and Commissioner Snowe was looking over his documentation, Carver was staring at Whitney and Adam, his jaws open in an enormous predator's smile that reminded her of a python getting ready to swallow its prey.

Commissioner Snowe put down the papers she had been reading. "Mr. Justice, this documentation appears very impressive. Do you have any initial reactions to Crowe-Cromwell's claim?"

"Only to demand that Mr. Carver withdraw it immediately."

Carver snickered.

"What is all this about, Mr. Justice?" Snowe asked.

"This claim is fraudulent, Your Honor. It asserts that a fertility formula was stolen from Crowe-Cromwell. The truth is that the fertility formula was never stolen from the company by Patrice Feldon or anyone else, and Mr. Carver knows it."

"What I know is that your career is about to come to an end, Justice," Carver said. "Your Honor, Adam Justice married Patrice Feldon knowing full well what she had done. He was in on the whole thing."

"Gentlemen, please," Commissioner Snowe said. "Let's stick to one accusation at a time. Now, Mr. Justice, you just made a statement that the theft of Crowe-Cromwell's fertility formula never took place. Would you care to explain yourself?"

Adam slowly stood and faced the commissioner. "Nine years ago Mr. Carver was personally part of Crowe-Cromwell's conspiracy to keep a safe new fertility drug off the market by refusing to submit it to the FDA for approval. The reason for their refusal was to recoup their expenses and make a profit on an inferior drug, potentially harmful to women."

"That's a lie," Carver said, coming to his feet. Whitney noted with satisfaction that his python smile had disappeared and the bluster in his voice didn't hold near its normal pop-gun decibels. "You have no proof of any such thing!"

"But I do. The best proof there is. Your Honor, if you will give me a moment, I shall present it to you."

"Go ahead, Mr. Justice," Snowe said.

"This is preposterous," Carver protested.

Whitney watched as Adam stepped over to the door leading to the hallway, opened it and beckoned. A moment later a short, bald man, beaming from ear to ear, stepped inside.

"Surprised to see me, Carver?" he asked.

Carver's eyes bulged, then seemed to sink inside his head as his face blanched. His voice was a hoarse whisper. "No. It can't be. You're dead!"

"Your Honor," Adam said, "this is Dr. Lydon Miller, the developer of the new fertility process. You've heard Mr. Carver speak of him and his discovery this afternoon. Now, Dr. Miller would like to set the record straight by telling you how Crowe-Cromwell did everything they could to keep his discovery from the women who needed it."

"Is this allegation true?" Commissioner Snowe asked.

Whitney watched Carver swallowing over and over, as though something had gotten stuck in his throat. "It doesn't matter if he did develop it. It belonged to Crowe-Cromwell. It was Crowe-Cromwell's right to keep its discovery off the market."

"Right, Mr. Carver?" Adam said. "The entire governing board of directors of Crowe-Cromwell are medical doctors, each of whom has taken the Hippocratic oath. And the basic tenet of that oath is, first and foremost, to do no harm. That board of directors deliberately put out an inferior fertility drug that they knew could do harm, and they suppressed a superior one.

"And that is what Dr. Miller explained to the press thirty minutes ago, when he gave them copies of the memo from Crowe-Cromwell's board of directors telling him to squelch his discovery. It was at the same time that he handed them a copy of a memo you sent him, threatening his livelihood, his reputation and even his critically ill wife's life-support systems, if he told anyone about his discovery."

"You bastard—"

"And speaking of papers, Dykstra told me to tell you he won't be needing that envelope you promised him an hour before press time. He said his producer is very happy with the new story he's found."

"I'll get you for this, Justice."

"No, I'm getting you, Carver. I'm filing a billion-dollar, class-action lawsuit against Crowe-Cromwell on behalf of all the women who were deliberately given your inferior drug with its dangerous side effects, while a superior one existed. And when I win that lawsuit—and I will win it—Crowe-Cromwell will be bankrupt and you'll be lucky to get a job cleaning out johns. Now, you have ten seconds to withdraw your spurious debtor's claim and get out of here before I call the news reporters and let them know where they can find you."

Adam flipped out his cell phone and began to count aloud. "Nine...eight...seven..." Carver grabbed for the paperwork lying on Commissioner Snowe's desk, scooped it into his arms and literally ran out of her office.

As Adam flipped his cell phone closed, Whitney sent him a look of wonder. It seemed that Adam Justice could roar, after all.

"That was an...interesting face-off," Commissioner Snowe said, a faint smile on her lips. "Or possibly I should say 'massacre.' Dr. Miller, may I impose upon you to step outside now and give your complete statement to a court reporter? My clerk will arrange for one to accompany you to a quiet place."

Miller's round face beamed. "Yes, Your Honor."

He stepped over to the door. Before he opened it to let himself out, he turned to face Adam. "Thank you, Mr. Justice. You don't know what you've done for me."

As Whitney watched Adam's face, her heart leapt with joy at the real smile that circled his lips and came to rest in his eyes.

"It couldn't have been any more than what you've done for me today, Dr. Miller," he said.

"I look forward to reading the transcript of his statement," Commissioner Snowe said after Miller had left. "Well, now that Mr. Carver has officially withdrawn his debtor's claim, I can get to the next matter dealing with the Feldon estate."

"The next matter?" Whitney repeated, surprised.

Snowe buzzed her clerk. "Bring him in," she said into the intercom.

A moment later the door opened, and a slight-built, thirtyish man with a full head of light brown hair and a serious look in his similarly colored eyes strode into the office.

"Ms. West, Mr. Justice, I'd like to introduce Mr. Fabrice Feldon," Snowe said. "Mr. Feldon wants to know if he is our Patrice Feldon's brother. He's brought copies of his sister's birth certificate, his own and that of his parents, in hopes that we can tell him."

Snowe paused to hand copies of the aforesaid items to both Adam and Whitney, while Fabrice Feldon took a seat on the sofa. Whitney immediately flipped to the California birth certificate with the name Patrice Dulcinea Feldon and the birth date of August 2, 1964. She looked up at Fabrice Feldon with new interest.

"You'll forgive me, Ms. West, for not sending Mr. Feldon directly to you on this matter," Snowe said. "But as you have kept me so well informed as to the lack of bona fide blood relations to the deceased, and in light of the proofs Mr. Feldon brought with him, I decided to hear his story. Now I want you to hear it.

"Please begin," Snowe said, turning to Feldon.

Fabrice nodded and leaned forward. "I was born in the U.S., as was my sister. We moved to my mother's home—which is Paris—when I was two and my sister but a few months old."

Whitney noted the pleasant sound of a soft French accent in his voice.

"When I was fourteen, my family came to visit Washington State, where my father was born. We took a bus to the bed-and-breakfast inn where we would stay."

"An airport bus?" Whitney asked.

"Yes. It made many stops to let off passengers. My father talked with enthusiasm about his childhood. A pleasant man and his wife joined our conversation. She was holding her small baby. It was my sister's birthday and she chatted profusely—as was her way, with the bus driver's daughter. We were the only ones remaining on the bus when the terrible accident happened."

"Accident?" Whitney repeated encouragingly when Fabrice paused.

Fabrice gestured with his hands. "The bus ran into the back of a large truck carrying many long, heavy pipes. The pipes came crashing through the windshield like a thunderous mountain."

Fabrice paused again, whether from trying to blot out the appalling memory of what he had seen or to collect his thoughts, Whitney couldn't tell. The room was very quiet.

"I was knocked unconscious," he continued. "When I awoke, I could feel nothing, see nothing. I did not know where I was. Then I heard my sister moaning and moving beside me and I reached out for her. Pain swept through me. Then everything went dark.

"I awoke next in hospital with many broken bones. They told me my family had perished in the accident, and only I and the woman with the small baby had survived. Everyone else had been killed instantly by the devastating invasion of metal pipes into the bus. I told them about hearing my sister moan beside me. They told me I must have been hallucinating.

"My mother's sister brought me home to Paris when I was well enough to leave hospital. My home is still Paris, but I travel here frequently on business. It was a week ago that I read about this mysterious woman, Patrice Feldon. I asked my aunt to send me the birth documents you have before you. I would like to know if she was my sister."

"You don't believe the people in the hospital who told you your sister died?" Whitney asked.

"I can only tell you I did not imagine her moan."

"You said you couldn't see," Whitney said. "How did you know it was your sister's moan?"

"My father had bought her a long red silk scarf for her birthday, and my mother had sprinkled some of her perfume on it. I smelled that perfume as she lay beside me."

Whitney met Adam's gaze across Commissioner Snowe's desk. She knew they were thinking the same thing. Linda Carmichael had spoken of Patrice wearing a red scarf when she'd found her bruised and bloodied. Had Patrice gotten off the wrecked bus and wandered off in a daze?

"Where did this accident take place?" Whitney asked.

"It was north of Green Lake, near where my father was born."

"Your Honor, do you have a map of the city?" Adam asked.

Snowe retrieved one out of her desk drawer and handed it to him. Adam opened it and laid it in front of Fabrice.

"Mr. Feldon, can you point out an approximate location of the accident on this map?"

Fabrice studied the map for several quiet moments before placing his index finger down. "Somewhere in this area."

Whitney knew the area where Fabrice was pointing. Not ten blocks away was where the Rubins lived.

"Do you have a picture of your sister?" Whitney asked.

Fabrice's hand slipped into his pocket and retrieved his wallet. He took out an old picture and laid it on Commissioner Snowe's desk.

"This was taken by my aunt just before we left for America."

Both Adam and Whitney immediately crowded around to see the picture.

"Was the woman my sister?" Fabrice Feldon asked.

Chapter Sixteen

Adam sat back in his chair. "Mr. Feldon, your sister was not the Patrice Feldon who you have recently read about."

"You are certain of this?"

"Her facial features, her dark hair and eyes—nothing is the same."

"Then who was it I heard moaning beside me?"

"Perhaps the hospital authorities were right, Mr. Feldon," Commissioner Snowe said. "Perhaps it was your grief you were hearing."

"And then again, maybe it wasn't," Whitney said.

Adam could hear the rising excitement in her voice. "What is it, Whitney?"

Whitney turned to him. "Remember A.J.'s report on the accident? She said the newspapers reported three injured."

"Fabrice, Beatrice D'Amico and her baby, Danny," Adam confirmed.

"And five killed."

"The bus driver was one, Thomas D'Amico made two, Mrs. and Mr. Feldon made three and four, and Fabrice's sister made five," Adam said.

"What happened to the bus driver's daughter?"

Adam nodded in understanding as he turned back to Fabrice. "Mr. Feldon, might your friendly sister have told the bus driver's daughter her full name and the fact it was her birthday?"

"Yes. That would be like her."

"Might she also have let the other girl try on her new scarf?" Whitney asked.

"This would be like her, also. I understand what you are saying. You believe it was the bus driver's daughter who I heard moaning beside me?"

"Yes. And while you were passed out, I believe she got off the wrecked bus and wandered off," Adam said.

"It had to have happened that way," Whitney said. "Linda Carmichael said that when she asked Patrice what she was doing in front of the store window, she kept repeating, 'I wasn't supposed to be there.' The reason it didn't make sense to Linda was because Patrice didn't mean the store window. She meant she wasn't supposed to be riding in the bus with her father!"

Adam nodded. "It explains why the bus company had no record of her being there, and consequently no one ever knew she was missing."

He turned back to Fabrice. "What did the bus driver's daughter look like?" he asked.

Fabrice shook his head. "All I remember is she had very pretty hair—long and curly and golden."

"That's enough," Adam said, leaning back in his chair.

"So, MR. JUSTICE, Ms. West," Commissioner Snowe said after Fabrice Feldon had left. "We no longer even know the real name of the woman who has left this estate in our hands for disposition. And since you tell me the police couldn't identify the bus driver twenty years ago, because he carried a stolen ID, I very much doubt that we are ever going to be able to."

"Whoever the woman was who called herself Patrice Dulcinea Feldon," Whitney said, "it looks to me like she wished to forget the name she was born with and the family she was born into—probably with good reason. Maybe we should, too."

"Yes, I'm coming to that conclusion myself, Ms. West," Commissioner Snowe agreed. "As I see it, we've made the good-faith effort to find out who this woman was. Now let's make the good-faith effort to send her money where she wanted it to go."

"You're ruling in favor of the beneficiaries?" Adam asked.

"Your investigation has established why the Rubins and the Carmichaels were selected as recipients. Mr. Feldon's information about the bus accident explains the inclusion of Danny and his mother. I'm satisfied these bequests were made of the deceased's own free will and reflect her wishes."

"And my motion for a closed courtroom?" Whitney asked.

"It's too late, Ms. West. This matter has received too much attention."

"Your Honor," Whitney sad, "we don't know how many more Joes and Ginas and Melanies are out there. We owe those children a chance to be helped by the Rubins. If the records aren't sealed in this case, the Rubins will be exposed and shut down. Please. For the children."

"Ms. West, I am most distressed by these inevitable consequences, believe me. But, sealing the records after all this publicity will only attract more publicity to the case."

"It wouldn't if the press didn't hear about the probate having been settled and the records sealed," Whitney said.

Snowe looked at Whitney intently. "Are you suggesting we attempt to sneak this probate through?"

"Now's the time, Your Honor. The press has just been fed a very juicy story. They'll be focusing their prurient interests on Crowe-Cromwell's misdeeds for the next few weeks. None of them will be expecting a thirty-million dollar estate to have been settled so quickly."

Snowe's pale lips drew back into a small smile. "Ms. West, has anyone ever told you that you possess all the makings of a criminal mind?"

"Yes, Your Honor."

Snowe laughed, and for the first time Whitney saw some color splashing prettily beneath her pale cheeks.

"Mr. Justice, I'm about to succumb to a very strong impulse to accept Ms. West's unorthodox proposal. Is there no legal or ethical admonition you can offer to save me?"

Whitney looked over to see Adam smiling at her so fully that it squeezed her heart dry. "Your Honor, when it comes to saving oneself from succumbing to strong impulses regarding Ms. West, I am the last lawyer—or man—you should ever consult."

"ADAM, I CAN'T BELIEVE it's over. The Rubins and D'Amicos and Carmichaels are going to get the money, and it's all going to be done quietly, thanks to Commissioner Snowe," Whitney said as he drove her through the security gates to his home that evening.

"I'm so glad to discover," Whitney continued, "that Snowe's genuinely nice, as well as smart, under her staid exterior. Rather reminds me of someone else I've gotten to know recently."

She flashed him a mischievous smile, and he found himself smiling back.

It felt so good to smile again. She had done that for him. And so much more.

"Will Dr. Miller be safe from Crowe-Cromwell reprisals?" Whitney asked.

"Crowe-Cromwell would gain nothing by physically harming him now. He's gone public with the worst, turned over all the evidence, placed his sworn depositions on file. Besides, the spotlight is so focused on Dr. Miller and the company, that were anything to happen to him, they would be immediately suspected and they must know that. They're in enough trouble without adding a murder charge to the list."

"You don't think they'd do it anyway for revenge?"

"They're about profit—not revenge. Still, A.J. has placed a twenty-four-hour guard on Miller as a precaution. You don't have to worry, Whitney."

She smiled at him. "With you in charge, how could I worry?"

But the moment he pulled in front of his house, Adam watched Whitney's smile flee as she saw Sergeant Ryson and Detective Ferkel approach the car. With all the positive things that had happened today, he had forgotten this final business still hanging over his head.

"What is it you want, Sergeant?" Adam asked coolly as he circled around the Jaguar to open the door for Whitney.

"Inside, if you don't mind, Justice," Ryson said in his typical sour tone.

Adam led the way inside his house and closed the door behind them all. He turned to face Ryson. "Well?"

"The FBI's forensic report came back this afternoon, Justice. There's no use denying it. We know you were at that wreck of Peter Danner's car."

Adam knew Ryson was looking for some change in his expression. He made sure there was none. "And why would you think that, Sergeant?"

Ryson held up the thick golden chain with the cross dangling off its end. "Recognize this?"

"Patrice gave it to me on our first wedding anniversary," Adam said calmly.

"It was in the wreck. There are traces of blood on it. Not Danner's blood. Not your wife's."

"She was not my wife, Sergeant."

"It's your blood, isn't it, Justice? You were there, weren't you?"

Adam felt Whitney's hand grab his arm and knew she was afraid for him. But he was not afraid. A great weight had been lifted from his shoulders when he'd learned he was not responsible for Peter's and Patrice's deaths. He placed his hand reassuringly over hers.

"Have you determined how the accident happened?" Adam asked calmly.

The moment Adam saw the unhappy look descending on Ryson's face, he knew he was about to hear some good news.

"The rack-and-pinion gear failed," Ferkel said. "FBI lab sent back pictures. They say it was a manufacturing defect. When it sheared, Danner was unable to steer and lost control of the car."

Finally the truth after all these years.

Adam took the chain and cross out of Ryson's hand. "I appreciate your returning my property to me. I also want her picture back."

Ryson signaled to Ferkel, who produced the picture and handed it to Adam.

"You're damn lucky I couldn't match that scribbling on the back with a route to the car wreck," Ryson said.

Adam walked over to the door and held it open for the two detectives in a clear signal that it was time for them to leave.

"You were there, Justice," Ryson said as he filed past. "I know it."

"Goodbye, Sergeant. Detective."

As soon as Adam had closed the door behind them, he found Whitney throwing her arms around him and hugging him hard.

"Thank God that's over, Adam."

He hugged her tightly, loving the passionate exuberance of her response. Then, gently, he extricated her from his arms.

"I still have one last thing to do."

She followed him into the study and watched him light the match to the bottom of Patrice's picture. As the flame caught, he threw it into the fireplace.

"Why do I think burning her picture has less to do with a symbolic gesture than it does with getting rid of that map at the bottom of her note?" Whitney asked.

Adam smiled at her but said nothing.

"Octavia Osborne was your only partner at Justice Inc. seven years ago," Whitney said. "She drew that map, didn't she? She was the friend with you that day, the one who called the Native American chief who described a shortcut through his tribal lands. That map is the shortcut. That's why Ryson couldn't match it to a route on a regular map."

Adam wrapped his arms around Whitney as he watched the final ashes from Patrice's picture fly up the chimney.

"It's all in the past now, Whitney."

She turned in his arms to look up at his face. "Is it, Adam?"

He took a deep breath and slowly let it out. "You once asked me what emotion still tied me to Patrice. It was guilt,

Whitney—a mountain of it. I had given her everything I had, everything I was, and still she left me for Danner. I thought I had let her down as a husband. I thought I had been the cause of her death when Peter's car went off that cliff.''

"And now, Adam?"

"The guilt's gone, Whitney. I know the truth now."

"And what is the truth, Adam?"

"Their deaths were an accident. I did not fail Patrice as a husband. She failed me as a wife. At the heart of love is honesty and loyalty. There was no heart in Patrice's love."

"Has Patrice spoiled it for you, Adam?"

He pulled slightly away from her and looked at her with cool blue eyes. "Spoiled what?"

"Love and . . . marriage. I'll understand if you say yes."

He smiled. "And will you understand when I say no?"

The meaning in his answer—the sudden warmth in his eyes and voice—all swelled inside Whitney's heart.

"Now I have a question for you, Ms. West," he said in his most formal tone. "Why did you lie to me?"

His changing demeanor and accusation stunned her. "Lie to you? About what?"

"About having a tattoo. You have none. I made a very thorough search of that lovely body of yours."

"Oh, that," she said, laughing with relief. "It was one of those temporary, stick-on ones. It wore off ages ago."

"Are you telling me you deliberately deceived me into believing you had a tattoo in order to try to elicit information? Ms. West, you are a very unscrupulous and devious woman."

"Thank you, Mr. Justice."

"It wasn't a compliment."

She laughed. "I know. I love you, Adam, so much I can't ever remember when I didn't."

He hugged her to him possessively, as though he would never let her go.

"I think I fell in love with you the moment you started to jaywalk across that busy intersection and tried to get us both killed."

She laughed against his ear, then leaned back to look again at his face. The sincere blue of his eyes trapped the breath in her body, hushing it with joy. His deep, beautiful voice resonated in her soul.

"I love you, Whitney. You've brought color back into my black-and-white world—beautiful, vibrant hues of endless possibilities that I began to see the first moment I looked into the golden lights dancing in your eyes. I'm offering you everything I have, everything I am. Is it what you want?"

"Oh, yes, Adam," she said, tears of happiness stinging her eyes. "Just what I want."

He took her lips with his, and she felt the deep pledge of his love in his kiss . . . loyal and true . . . and good for a lifetime.

REBECCA

43 LIGHT STREET

YORK

FACE TO FACE

Bestselling author Rebecca York returns to "43 Light Street" for an original story of past secrets, deadly deceptions—and the most intimate betrayal.

She woke in a hospital—with amnesia…and with child. According to her rescuer, whose striking face is the last image she remembers, she's Justine Hollingsworth. But nothing about her life seems to fit, except for the baby inside her and Mike Lancer's arms around her. Consumed by forbidden passion and racked by nameless fear, she must discover if she is Justine…or the victim of some mind game. Her life—and her unborn child's—depends on it….

Don't miss *Face To Face*—Available in October, wherever Harlequin books are sold.

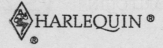

HARLEQUIN ®

®

43FTF

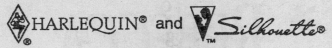

HARLEQUIN® and **Silhouette®**

are proud to present...

HERE COME THE GROOMS™

Four marriage-minded stories written by top
Harlequin and Silhouette authors!

Next month, you'll find:

The Bridal Price	by Barbara Boswell
Annie in the Morning	by Curtiss Ann Matlock
September Morning	by Diana Palmer
Outback Nights	by Emilie Richards

ADDED BONUS! In every edition of
Here Come the Grooms you'll find $5.00 worth
of coupons good for Harlequin and Silhouette
products.

On sale at your favorite Harlequin and Silhouette
retail outlet.

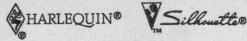

HARLEQUIN® **Silhouette®**

HCTG1096

1997
Reader's Engagement Book
A calendar of important dates
and anniversaries for readers to use!

Informative and entertaining—with notable
dates and trivia highlighted throughout the year.

Handy, convenient, pocketbook size to help you
keep track of your own personal important dates.

Added bonus—contains $5.00 worth of coupons
for upcoming Harlequin and Silhouette books.
This calendar more than pays for itself!

Available beginning in November at
your favorite retail outlet.

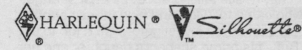

You are cordially invited to a

HOMETOWN REUNION

September 1996—August 1997

Bad boys, cowboys, feuding families, arson,
babies, mistaken identity, a mom on the run...
Where can you find romance and adventure?
Tyler, Wisconsin, that's where!

So join us in this not-so-sleepy little town and
experience the love, the laughter and the
tears of those who call it home.

WELCOME TO A
HOMETOWN REUNION

They're still talking about the last stranger
who came to Tyler, and now there's another.
He's an arson investigator with a job to do.
But...his prime suspect's daughter and her
kids make it increasingly hard for him
to do what he must.

The Reluctant Daddy **by Helen Conrad**

Available in October 1996
at your favorite retail outlet.

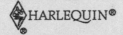

HARLEQUIN®

Weddings by DeWilde

Since the turn of the century the elegant and fashionable DeWilde stores have helped brides around the world turn the fantasy of their "Special Day" into reality. But now the store and three generations of family are torn apart by the separation of Grace and Jeffrey DeWilde. Family members face new challenges and loves in this fast-paced, glamorous, internationally set series. For weddings and romance, glamour and fun-filled entertainment, enter the world of DeWildes....

Watch for A STRANGER'S BABY
by Judith Arnold
Coming to you in October, 1996

Grace DeWilde's engaged niece, Mallory Powell, was pregnant by a man other than her fiancé. She could please her high-society family and provide the child with a father and a name, or she could listen to her heart, which was pushing her in another, more mysterious direction altogether.

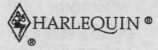

HARLEQUIN ®

Look us up on-line at: http://www.romance.net

WBD7

The collection of the year!
NEW YORK TIMES BESTSELLING AUTHORS

Linda Lael Miller
Wild About Harry

Janet Dailey
Sweet Promise

Elizabeth Lowell
Reckless Love

Penny Jordan
Love's Choices

and featuring
Nora Roberts
The Calhoun Women

This special trade-size edition features four of the wildly popular titles in the Calhoun miniseries together in one volume—a true collector's item!

Pick up these great authors and a chance to win a weekend for two in New York City at the Marriott Marquis Hotel on Broadway! We'll pay for your flight, your hotel—even a Broadway show!

Available in December at your favorite retail outlet.

Merry Christmas, Baby!

A romantic collection filled with the magic of Christmas and the joy of children.

SUSAN WIGGS, Karen Young and Bobby Hutchinson bring you Christmas wishes, weddings and romance, in a charming trio of stories that will warm up your holiday season.

MERRY CHRISTMAS, BABY! also contains Harlequin's special gift to you—a set of FREE GIFT TAGS included in every book.

Brighten up your holiday season with *MERRY CHRISTMAS, BABY!*

Available in November at your favorite retail store.

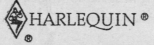

MCB

A brutal murder.
A notorious case.
Twelve people must decide
the fate of one man.

Jury Duty

an exciting courtroom drama by

Laura Van Wormer

Struggling novelist Libby Winslow has been chosen to sit on the jury
of a notorious murder trial dubbed the "Poor Little Rich Boy" case.
The man on trial, handsome, wealthy James Bennett Layton, Jr., has
been accused of killing a beautiful young model. As Libby and the
other jury members sift through the evidence trying to decide the fate
of this man, their own lives become jeopardized because someone
on the jury has his own agenda....

Find out what the verdict is this October at your favorite
retail outlet.